book 2 of the lakeside green coyotes

bank shot

josie mae

Dedicated to anyone who thinks their slump is going to last forever. It won't, even if it feels that way. Might as well dance in the meantime. ♡

Lakeside Green Coyotes Timeline

The Lakeside Green Coyotes books can be read in chronological order or as standalones (I try my best to make that possible, at least!). If you've read a book from this series before, welcome back to Lakeside Green! And if this is your first LSG book, I'm so excited to have you joining us.

Theo McCall and Maya Healy make appearances in *Bank Shot*—if you want to read more about them (bookworm & basketball captain; soft slow burn; navigating the complexities of dating a star athlete as someone who is new to college sports culture), their book is the first in the series, *Tip In.*

Author's Note

Kai's pronouns are she/they and are used interchangeably throughout the novel.

Summer

GJ

The one thing worth knowing about me was that I didn't underperform—not in bed and definitely not in basketball.

"Left! Left!" Nia shouted as she ran up the outdoor basketball court. It was a perfect Colorado summer—nothing like back home in Alabama, where the humidity was so heavy it felt like inhaling water. Here, it was dry. Sweat evaporated from our bare skin in the shade as quickly as it formed.

I passed the ball over to Nia, and she spun around toward Mags. All of us were on the Lakeside Green Coyotes basketball team, but when we played a pick-up game, it was every woman for herself.

After running up the court, I got myself into a spot for Nia to go for an assist. She bounced the ball my way, and I shot up an easy three. My stomach knotted when it bounced off the rim instead of going through the net. So much for easy.

The ball bounced hard on the pavement, forcing Mags to run after it before it could roll down the hill. The last time that happened, it ended up in the small creek at the bottom and completely killed the momentum—even if it was funny as hell.

"Your defense is shit, Moretti," I said, cracking a cocky smile as Mags came back with the ball. I wasn't about to let Mags know missing a three was enough to shake my confidence. It usually wasn't, but this summer had been different.

She rolled her eyes. "Yeah, and yours is so good. Too bad running your mouth can't be considered a form of exercise."

"I mean, I can name a few exercises that involve my mouth—"

"You guys are ridiculous," Nia said, always the most level-headed of the group. She'd never had time for the interpersonal mess, which was the exact opposite of how I liked to approach things. I didn't care if we shared a team name and locker room: Mags Moretti was consistently a pain in my ass.

Mags put the ball in play, and we kept talking our shit. I lived for this—the feeling of being on a court, fucking around with my teammates. I refused to take my foot off anyone's neck, way too motivated to win even in a casual pick-up game.

Gemma easily took the ball from Mags, the two of them working their way up the court. They communicated with each other silently, understanding where the other person was going to go without needing to say anything at all. That was what it meant to be teammates, even in a game that didn't mean anything. Communication, verbal and non-verbal, was key.

It helped that Gemma and Mags were essentially the same person. There was no use in separating the two of them—they always wanted to play on the same team for a pick-up game, always played their best when the other person was on the court.

I was skeptical of Gemma by association, but she was easier to be around than Mags, who seemed more interested in beefing with her teammates than working on her defensive footwork.

I stayed on Gemma while Nia rode Mags's ass. Nia was quiet off the court but assertive and quick on it; it benefited me that Gemma and Mags were obsessed with each other because I always ended up with Nia.

Gemma lined up her shot and fired close to the basket. It hit the rim and then just barely fell in, one of our weaker shooters. Mags didn't waste a single second running over to celebrate with her, while Nia and I brushed off the point and the game as a whole.

"Looks like it's another win for Team Gags," Mags said, flashing a quick middle finger in my direction in the midst of her celebration.

"I need some water, actually," I said playfully, stepping away from the court. As I walked away from my teammates, I forced myself to take a deep breath and push down the ridiculous feeling of disappointment brewing in me. It was just a dumb pick-up game and winning didn't really matter, but I'd needed a win. My shooting, even when I was just practicing by myself, had been terrible since our team roster announcement.

Mags rolled her eyes and then jogged past me to reach the bench first. "You're such a sore loser."

"Dude, you fucking reek," I said, ignoring her comment, and she flipped me off again.

Over at the bench, we dug out our bags from under the bench. The sun was *hot* out here—elevation and UV were high—so anything left to cook on the cement top was fair game.

Gemma laid out a towel on the bench and sat down. Her pale skin was flushed from the heat, her short brown hair pulled back into the world's smallest ponytail. Even though this wasn't a formal practice, all of us were wearing Lakeside Green University-themed items of clothing. Our basketball program was well-funded—or at least better funded than it had been—after a few consecutive years of making it to the March Madness Tournament, we had more t-shirts and shorts and random pairs of socks than the average person knew what to do with.

"I already miss this. Colorado winters are too long," Nia said, tilting her face up toward the sun. She'd gotten a new and much longer sew-in recently; it was pulled into a sleek ponytail that fell down her back. She reminded me so much of my sisters sometimes, how they were always the more feminine, more put-together versions of me. I never viewed it as a competition—mostly because I could never be bothered to wear the dresses they liked—but it stirred up feelings a therapist would probably ask about either way.

"Best time of year," I agreed. I'd always been a summer child—I grew up not far from the water, so it was impossible not to love it. My happiest memories from home involved my sisters and me in the southern heat. In the earliest summers of my life, my dad taught my sisters and me how to ride bikes and introduced me to basketball. My mom would try to throw a fit over how sweaty and sticky and dirty we'd get running around outside all day, but could never keep up the act when she heard us giggling.

I sucked down water as we all took a beat to be on our phones, figuring out what was next. I didn't have much to do—the only people who stayed on campus this time of year were people who were here to work or were taking summer classes. That was how the team always managed to find each other. Most of us didn't mind being home, but a lot of us didn't see a reason to go back during the summer. My sisters—Ada, Bev and Vivian—and I were all grown up now; I was the last one to graduate and the last one technically still under my parents' care. There wasn't anyone waiting for me at home with ice cream to watch the sunset anymore.

"Are you guys looking forward to the new transfer?" Gemma asked. It was an innocent enough question, but it made my stomach hurt just thinking about it. I'd been doing everything in my power to avoid it.

"Who is it again?" Nia asked.

"Anna Evans," Mags and I answered at the same time.

Nia nodded in thought, then her expression shifted when it clicked exactly who Anna Evans was. "Oh, shit," she said.

"Yeah, she's good. I remember playing against her last year," Gemma said. I unfortunately did, too—she was one of the few people who could meet us shot for shot. Her team hadn't won, but they were good enough that they'd shaken up the way we approached defense for the rest of the season.

"I can't believe we're at the point where people actually want to transfer here. I'm pretty sure our last transfer was literally Ellie, and she came from a school even smaller than ours," Nia said. "We're really becoming official."

"And she's actually coming here? Confirmed? Not another university in Colorado?" I asked, partially because I was also still surprised. I knew she was—the transfer portal was only open for so long, and announcements were a big deal. If I googled her, I was sure an article about her transferring to Lakeside Green would be the first thing to pop up.

"No, she's going to the other Lakeside Green University," Mags said, like I was the dumbest person in the world. "Yes, she's coming here."

"We don't need another starting point guard," I muttered. And it was true—we didn't. Everyone knew I was *the* Lakeside Green point guard now that Theo was gone. I didn't want Anna here, and I wasn't particularly thrilled when I saw the news. I was glad Lakeside Green was being taken seriously enough for players to transfer here because they thought they'd have a better chance at getting drafted or whatever, but that was the end of it. It didn't mean I actually really *wanted* those students to transfer.

"Feeling threatened?" Mags asked, because of course she heard me.

"No." I brushed the comment off. *Obviously* I didn't care that Anna was a point guard or that she'd definitely been one of the players to watch last season. I was *also* a point guard and had been one of the ones to watch last season. It didn't mean shit to me, no matter what my nights spent staring at the ceiling, ruminating over if I'd hold as a starting player with Anna in town, suggested.

No one—not even Mags—stated the obvious: Even if my coaches weren't looking to replace me, they were absolutely looking to fill the void left by my best friend, Theo McCall, when she graduated. She'd done a lot for the team and completely turned around the program in terms of bringing nationwide attention to us and bringing us to the championship

The only thing was that *I* was supposed to be the new Theo McCall. I'd been training for it, working directly *with* Theo, learning from the best. I was supposed to be the one who everyone said was carrying the team, the person who not only was just as good as Theo, but was able to bring the Lakeside Green Coyotes all the way to the finish and bring home a ring. Even Theo hadn't been able to do that.

My stomach knotted, but I pushed the feeling away. Anna was good, but she wasn't me. I had the benefit of already knowing the team and the rhythm we'd played with last year. She'd had less time on the court than I, started in fewer games than I, and played on a lower-ranked team. And she was coming from an Ivy League, which historically didn't have strong basketball programs, anyway.

I didn't have anything to worry about.

"Mags!"

All four of us looked up to see Mags's twin sister, Leah, had pulled up to the curb. She was sitting in her fancy ass car—their parents were fucking loaded in the way that made it hard for Mags and Leah to hide it—with her sunglasses on her face. Most students out here—myself included—didn't bother with keeping a car on campus because of the inconvenience, cost, and general lack of parking. But Mags and Leah were kept humble by only being allowed to have *one* Benz between the two of them.

Leah was a cheerleader, so we all knew her pretty well. She'd occasionally pop into the same parties my other teammates and I would go to, always flashing her perfect white smile and wearing clothes tight to her lean dancer's body.

Not that I noticed.

"Come on!" Leah said again, waving her arm to get Mags to hurry down to her. Mags rolled her eyes.

"What's up her ass?" Gemma asked.

"That girl she's seeing or whatever. I don't know. Not my business. All I know is getting yanked around has her on her bitchiest behavior."

"Tell her she can always call me if she needs a break from the fuckboys," I said, mostly because I knew it would piss Mags off. Leah was undeniably hot, and there weren't any explicit rules against us dating cheerleaders—or siblings of our team-mates—but I had enough common sense to know trying to date Mags's sister was a battle I wouldn't win. "Just give me a chance, Leah! I'll change your life!" I shouted down toward her car.

"Never in a million years," Mags said, warning in her voice. She turned to Gemma. "You coming?"

"Yeah." Gemma got up, throwing her tote bag over her shoulder, and followed Mags across the court, through the grass, and then down to the curb.

"You know how to reach me if you need me," I shouted again, my voice carrying easily down the way to her open car window.

Leah was too far for me to see her face in detail, but I thought, just maybe, I saw her lips perk up in a smile.

Summer

Leah

A million times a day, I told myself that I was better than a booty call. But a million and *one* times a day, I told myself that I wasn't. That was exactly how I'd ended up at Kai Henderson's door three times in one week.

This was my second summer at Lakeside Green University, and I'd quickly realized last year that summers out here didn't offer much more than ample time to fool around.

It made sense. Lakeside Green was a small town to begin with, and most of the commotion came from students. It was the opposite of a beach town—summers here were completely dead, and every other time of the year was packed full of students.

In the midst of all of them was Kai, a random student from one of my marketing classes. Before Kai, there had been Emerson—a girl who'd lived on my floor—which had gone about as well as things seemed to be going with Kai. And then there were what felt like a million other small things here and there.

One-off dates, dating app 'talking' stages that made me want to rip my hair out, the occasional cute girl from a party that fizzled out basically overnight.

I wasn't stupid. I knew when I was being toyed with. I was a good time to Kai—the hot, driven girl in her classes, the one who had been on student council and was a cheerleader and did things like volunteer. Maybe I even had a history of doing beauty pageants through my childhood into my late teens, not that I'd ever talked about that with my college friends.

To someone like Kai, who smoked a lot of weed and had misused more than a few pop psychology terms around me, I was an anomaly. I was something new.

Or maybe I was just a decent lay. Being a dancer for my entire life made me very flexible.

"Fuck," Kai said as I fell back into the mattress. She ran a hand through her short black hair, showing off heavily tattooed biceps. It'd never been a secret that I was more into the masculine type.

I took a moment to catch my breath, closing my eyes and relishing in how the afterglow would feel good for approximately two more minutes until Kai said something that would bring me back to reality. Despite being ridiculously hot, Kai had a way of ruining the mood in hardly any time at all.

"You finish?" Kai asked, readjusting on the bed so she could grab her vape.

There it was.

"Yeah," I said, my automatic response whenever anyone asked me that question in bed. The reality was that my orgasms with partners never felt even half as good as the orgasms I achieved when I was on my own. If anything, I wasn't entirely sure I'd ever actually orgasmed with a partner before. But that didn't really feel like the number one priority when I seemed to be addicted to dating the worst kinds of people.

It wasn't to say anything was wrong with Kai. She was nice enough, funny enough, cool enough. She was undeniably hot in that unwashed, disheveled kind of way. And she was in a band on campus that frequently played gigs at Stephen's, the local dive bar—and by *the* I meant *the only*. She just wasn't the kind of person there would ever be a future with, not that something like that ever affected my decision on who to sleep with. If anything, I wanted them more because there was no future.

Sometimes, I didn't understand how I'd ended up here—in this small town, on this campus, bed hopping between people who were always just *good enough* because pickings were so slim. It was a fine school in terms of academic ranking, and the network I was building was okay, but Colorado hadn't been my dream. Cedar Creek, the largest city in the county, definitely wasn't large enough for me.

But my parents wanted me and my sister to stick together for college, which included me going wherever my sister decided to go for basketball. Story of my fucking life.

I rolled over and traced my hand over Kai's chest. When she pulled me toward her, so kindly blowing the smoke from her vape in the opposite direction of my face after being asked many times not to do that, I almost felt happy.

It was hard being someone who logically knew I deserved better, while also not actively seeking it. Kai was a warm body and company. She was also, unfortunately, really good at giving me just enough to keep wanting to come back. That was the *thing* about me—I craved acceptance. I wanted to feel hot, wanted to feel desired. I wanted to leave before being left.

But I never left. I was never the one who ended things.

Instead, I was turned into a pathetic boomerang—getting tossed away, only to come right back. It was a cycle I was hooked on and kept returning to, just with different people.

"You want a hit?" Kai asked, offering me her vape.

"No, thank you," I said. "So, when's your next show?"

"Oh, I don't know," she responded, drawing the words out. "I'll let you know, though."

"Yeah, cool," I responded, as if I wasn't bursting at the seams to get her to tell me more. I wanted her to invite me to something, take me somewhere. We'd matched on a dating app the last week of classes and had been fooling around for weeks now, with nothing to show for it other than going out for drinks a few times.

I knew what that meant. Logically, I was there. I could take a hint. I was prepared for the inevitable—*it's casual, it was never supposed to mean anything, you're nice, but I don't want that.*

But denial was one hell of a drug.

We lay there a few more beats, my head on her chest. I didn't like that the human body craved warmth and connection. It would make my life so much easier if I could just swear off dating forever and not be bothered with any of it anymore.

But the reality was that I'd rather take less than the bare minimum than be completely alone. No 4.0 GPA or merit-based scholarship or recognition from the university president could dig me out of this personal hell of my own creation.

There was at least a small part of me that was convinced that this was how it was for everyone. That no marriage, no relationship, was actually truly happy. It wasn't like my parents were happy; they were two people who were only still married because they immersed themselves entirely in work. They probably saw each other less than Mags and I saw them, and we lived in a different state from them now.

My mind flashed back to GJ, who'd taken up a home in my memory ever since I'd overheard her conversation with my sister a few days ago. *Tell her she can always call me if she needs a break from the fuckboys. Just give me a chance, Leah! I'll change your life.*

I was skeptical. Beyond the fact that GJ was possibly one of the worst players of them all—I'd heard more than a few stories—I was hard pressed to believe anyone could actually change my life. At this point, I was certain that anyone who was going to change my life was doing it in a way that was harmful to my mental well-being.

But still, there was something about her that made me wonder how good it'd feel to be in her arms, how fun going on a date with her would be. At the very least, I was confident the sex with her had to be better than a lot of the sex I'd been having.

Maybe fantasizing about someone I'd heard positive reviews from other girls about wasn't what I needed, but it was sure as hell better than facing my current reality.

Kai replaced her vape with her phone. "I gotta meet up with the band in a little bit, but this was fun."

"Right," I said, knowing my cue. We'd never made it to the point of a sleepover—we'd never really made it to the point of much. Kai seemed hellbent on offering me as little as she possibly could.

And despite knowing that, I seemed to be physically incapable of telling her to fuck off and to never contact me again. If anything, all it made me want to do was dig in my heels, curl up into bed with her a little longer, and continue answering her texts embarrassingly quickly.

After taking a beat—as if I were waiting to see if Kai would change her mind and tell me to stay, probably because I kind of was—I got up and turned around in bed to pull on my clothes. I got dressed with my back turned to her. I didn't have to be turned toward her to know that she wasn't looking at me, doing her best for a peek at my naked body; I could hear the sound of a video playing on her phone.

God, dating was the fucking worst.

After getting dressed, I grabbed my purse from the floor next to Kai's bong and a stack of tattered pre-owned paperbacks I would bet a million dollars she'd never read—and ran my fingers through my hair.

She looked up at me, still having not even budged from bed. "I'll text you."

"Okay," I responded, mostly because I didn't know what else there was to say. Kai would text me, and I'd go running to her because this was the option I had. Maybe something better would come along, or maybe I just wasn't destined to have real romance in my life. It wasn't really my business and didn't feel particularly up to me; I was leaving that one to fate.

I left Kai's room to the sound of her watching another video, not even bothering to interrupt to say goodbye.

As I walked home alone, I did the math on how much longer it would be until the end of summer, and how many more days I had until graduation.

Chapter One

GJ

For the first time since I was a freshman, it felt like the first day of school all over again.

Every year that I'd been going to Lakeside Green University, the women's basketball coaching staff hosted a beginning-of-the-season banquet to celebrate the closing of preseason and our exhibition games and the start of the regular season. It kicked off what would be a schedule of playing and traveling straight through from the end of November to, hopefully, early April if we made it to the Finals. It also gave us a good excuse to get a few more truly wild nights out of the way before we were expected to behave for the rest of the season.

This year wasn't any different, other than the fact that Theo wasn't going to be there.

And as much as I prided myself on my independence and confidence, I'd grown up with siblings. Reunions and family gatherings always sucked without them. Basketball requirements outside of games—no matter how much I loved my team—felt the same way. There had to be at least one person there I could crack jokes with in the back of the room when it all became a little too stiff.

Theo and I had never bothered to become a trio, which was an oversight on my part. Now that I was facing an event where I knew everyone but wasn't siblings-close with everyone, I didn't exactly know what was waiting for me.

I walked up to the front of the same restaurant we'd been going to since my first Lakeside Green banquet. That was one thing about a small college town—it was the same few places, the same routine. I didn't mind it most of the time, but after spending all summer feeling sour toward my small campus and the upcoming season, the tradition felt stale.

Inside, the restaurant was decorated the same exact way it always was—dim lighting, warm wood accents throughout, cozy western adjacent decor. It was the kind of restaurant I would never eat at on my own dime with my friends, but I'd bring my family when they came to town to visit.

A hostess looked up. I flashed her a practiced smile when I caught her eyes flicking up and down, checking me out. I didn't blame her—my linen pants and coordinated button-down shirt fit my lean frame well. "Party?"

"I'm with the Coyotes," I said, pointing to the back room reserved for events.

She pushed her hair behind her ear, standing up a little straighter. "Basketball player?" she asked, looking up at me through her lashes. "GJ, right?"

"I am," I said. Being a women's basketball player here carried weight now since Theo put us on the map. Girls had always liked that I was an athlete and that I was tall, but it'd never been easier for me to get laid than in recent months.

"You had a great season last year. Shame about the tournament," she said. It was true—we'd had a stellar season last year. We hadn't gone all the way, but we'd done better than any other team in the history of the Lakeside Green University basketball program—both men's and women's. There was a lot of talk about whether we'd be able to surpass—or even maintain—our record from last year without Theo. I was confident we could do it, even when it seemed like a lot of fans and commentators weren't.

"It happens," I said, even though I spent most nights playing through what we could've done differently to have won last season's final game.

"GJ!" Gemma called and I looked up to see Gemma, Nia, and Mags practically stacked on top of each other, waving to get my attention. The restaurant was far too nice for a bunch of college students to be shouting at each other across tables, but I was immune to being embarrassed by them.

I looked back at the hostess. "What time do you get off?"

Her cheeks went pink and she looked back at me with surprise. "A few hours, if all goes well."

"There's a party at The 151 tonight. You should swing by." The 151 was one of the big party houses on campus; everyone knew about it and pretty much everyone went at least once during their time at Lakeside Green. It'd been passed down for years, often inherited by siblings or close friends. It was an honor to be one of the girls living there, and typically a lot of pressure. They ended up hosting most of the hottest women on campus and a lot of the female athletes—meaning it was also somewhat of the lesbian hotspot on campus, which I appreciated.

The 151 was one of the things I'd missed most over the summer—there was no use trying to throw ragers when no one was in town—and I was grateful to be back in the swing of things. The first week of classes had been a breath of fresh air after feeling like I was trapped between my studio apartment and the gym for the last few months.

Her lips turned up in a smile. "Okay."

I offered her one last glance before brushing past the hostess stand and heading to the back of the restaurant where my teammates were waiting for me.

The back room was mostly full—I was one of the last people to arrive, which was ideal. There were no more than twenty people back here; our full roster was thirteen players and then the coaching staff had also received invitations. We were all scattered around the room into our various social groups within the team, picking off the charcuterie board before sitting down. Coach Darlene had always made it clear that this was meant to be a celebration of us as a team more than a stuffy, formal get-together, but I felt a little like I was wearing my Sunday best and being forced to mingle with the grown-ups.

Nia, Mags, and Gemma chatted around me, adding me to the circle, while I pulled out my phone. The regular WNBA season wrapped up last month in September, and the Cedar Creek Blizzards—Theo's team—had been knocked out of the playoffs in the first round. But Theo didn't need basketball to fill her schedule; she had about eight thousand different brand deals and was constantly roped into one thing or another. She also had a hard time saying no to any charity event invites or anything she could do for Cedar Creek. The city had totally fallen in love with her, even after they didn't make it as far into the playoffs as everyone was hoping.

But, despite all of that, it was also still the offseason. During the summer and into early fall, she was considered basically unreachable—other than FaceTiming me from Ohio for my birthday—but that wasn't the case anymore.

It didn't mean I knew where she was, though. No missed text notifications, no response to my earlier text about going to the last banquet of my Lakeside Green career.

I put my phone away, annoyed by my own jilted lover act. Theo was enjoying her time off—I was pretty sure she'd mentioned she and her girlfriend, Maya, were going on a weekend vacation as soon as the season ended and they could find time between Maya's graduate school classes. But it'd been weeks since I'd last heard from Theo, so I didn't actually know if that happened.

"Okay, let's settle in our seats," Coach Darlene said, waving us over to the table. "Family dinner." She looked older off the court than she did when she was on it, the wrinkles around her eyes more prominent. That was how it was for all of us—we were different people on the court, to a certain extent. Larger than life. Superstars. Budding professional athletes. Off the court, we were just students who had to show up to our 8 a.m. lectures.

As we headed over to the table, I spotted Anna with her dark, slicked-back hair and cat-like eyes. I looked away immediately, scowling.

"She's our teammate," Nia reminded me gently. I'd never been subtle.

"She came in our senior year. She's not one of us, even if she's on the roster." I kept my voice intentionally low; I didn't mind stirring up some shit, but this wasn't the place to do it. Even I had enough sense to know what I could get away with saying and what I couldn't.

"And that attitude has nothing to do with her getting time on the court during the preseason?" Nia asked. I hated that she was perceptive and would try to pry my feelings out of me. Theo and I had mostly just fucked around, teasing each other more like brothers than anything else. Nia actually tuned into how we were all doing. It was impossible to hide anything from her.

"No," I said, even though a memory of Anna setting up a play on the court I never in a million years could've seen through was on replay in my head. She'd come in like she owned the place—there was no required easing in, no rust in her shooting. She fit in easily, too, and played to our rhythm, which was the most frustrating part of all. It was like she'd always been one of us.

I'd never been the kind of asshole who set boundaries in a team. I'd pick fights, but in the same way siblings picked fights. I was never the type to isolate or force out or pretend there was some type of hazing you had to go through to become a Coyote. I'd accepted my other teammates without question.

But I wasn't warming up to Anna. Not even a little bit.

Coach Darlene stood up from her seat at the table, tucked in between our assistant coaches. I'd always appreciated that she was so down to earth. My high school coach had been intense, like how most coaches with a lot of state titles tended to be. He'd taken his team to the championship ten times over his career—including twice while coaching me—which meant that people usually overlooked him yelling and breaking clipboards.

Darlene was the opposite. She'd never coached anyone to the finals, never really had a coaching career of note until Theo came around. It was nice to have someone who felt like someone's mom in charge, but sometimes I missed the thrill of a coach who would threaten to leave us behind during away games if we pissed him off.

"I hope you're all excited about the start of the season," Coach Darlene said, which was about how she usually started her speeches at these things. The team hooped and hollered in response. "You've been working hard during your exhibition games and during practice. I know I've been tough on you going into this season, but there have been some pretty significant adjustments we've had to make. Thank you for being patient and working through them with me."

Nia, Gemma, and I exchanged knowing looks. Somehow, *significant adjustments* still felt like an understatement. We'd had to completely rebuild the team without Theo. Most of the starting line-up was still the same, but our functions on the court were different. We had to depend on each other to fill the void where Theo used to be, which had turned out to be more difficult than we'd realized. We all *knew* Theo was good, but it definitely rattled us to see just how much our playing changed without her.

Fortunately, we were gaining our footing; it just hadn't been easy. My preseason was always rough, so I'd been prepared for that, but I hadn't been prepared for it to be so difficult to glue our starting line-up back together.

I chose to ignore that most of it was credited to Anna rather than someone who was actually one of us.

We were one week away. One week from the start of my last season ever as a college basketball player, one week away from asserting myself as a first-round draft pick. One week from having to prove that I was just as good, if not better, than the new girl, and that no one could replace me.

Easy enough.

"As we know, this will be the last season some of you play with us," Coach Darlene continued. She glanced over my way. "CJ, our captain this year, included."

My teammates and coaches cheered again. Captain had been one of the top things I'd wanted to accomplish this year. If there was anyone who could handle taking over the reins from Theo, it was me. I was relieved that my coaches believed in me as much as I believed in myself, and even more relieved that they didn't think some fresh blood was going to be a worthwhile replacement.

Captain to me had always meant that I was going to have the best season of my life, which would lead to me getting drafted, which I'd then turn into a massively successful career. It was the first big stepping stone to kicking off my dream career. There wasn't any other option—I wanted to play basketball for the rest of my life like most people wanted to breathe.

But all of that fire I'd felt over the years, the times I'd confidently told Theo I was ready to be captain, had begun to slip away over the summer. New feelings were settling in that I'd never experienced before: doubt and uncertainty.

But I wasn't about to let anyone know that.

"Any inspiring words from our team leader?" Coach Darlene asked.

My mind went completely blank. It was a new thing I'd been struggling with over the summer—never finding the right words, never knowing what to say. It was like someone had put a curse on me. All of the years of people telling me to shut the fuck up, both on the court and off, had caught up with me.

"Let's kick some ass," I said, the best I could come up with. I raised my glass as laughter filled the room. Everyone else raised their glasses, too, a mix of amusement and tolerance in their faces.

As I looked around the room, it was hard to believe this my last Lakeside Green pre-season dinner. I'd spent all summer trying to wrap my head around the major changes to come, but it didn't feel possible. The end of the season felt so far away compared to now; it might as well have been a lifetime until March.

"Always so eloquent, GJ," Coach Darlene said with a small chuckle. But I could hear the tone underneath her words—the small, imperceptible to everyone else reminder that we would never have the bond that she had with Theo.

After Coach Darlene closed out her mini-speech with her usual words of encouragement, we ordered our entrees and non-alcoholic drinks.

"I think East Hill will be a good one," Mags said and then stuffed a piece of cheese from what was left of our appetizer platter into her mouth. "They have that sophomore on the rise."

"Ellie, she's from your hometown, right?" Gemma asked.

Ellie looked up at us, blinking her wide blue eyes. Despite being on track to be a consistent starter next season, she always looked like a deer in the headlights whenever any of us acknowledged her. "Yeah, thereabouts."

Ellie was from a small town in Texas, a few hours out from any of the major metro areas. We were both technically the most culturally Southern of our teammates, but her home was an entirely different beast. She grew up with cowboys and ranches; I was from a suburb just outside of Mobile.

We usually didn't have much to say to each other; I didn't think I'd ever even heard her curse. But Theo had always liked her, and we both talked about her being a solid addition to the team. It was hard to know if she'd go pro because she was so quiet and unsure of herself, but she had the focus of someone who could pull it off. It was just a matter of whether her athletic abilities could get her there.

"She was good?" Nia asked.

Ellie nodded, her face as red as her hair, like it always was whenever we spoke to her. I didn't know if that was a team-specific thing—even though Ellie was a junior, she still came across like the baby of us—or if she was just perpetually embarrassed by being acknowledged. "She's been good," she said. "She was part of my AAU team one year before she moved. She's quick."

"Interesting." Gemma chewed on the words, probably already thinking through her defensive strategy.

"We'll get Ellie on her," Mags said, the corners of her mouth turned up.

Ellie was a consistent and level shooter, nearly by-the-book perfect, but she was *really* good on defense. Most people at a college level didn't have the strength she did, and most basketball players in general didn't have the build she did. She was 6'2", which was still considered tall for a women's college player, and had a broad, solid build. She *looked* strong, something most of us didn't have working in our favor.

"I don't know about that," Ellie responded shyly.

"You have a good eye on the court," Anna offered, seemingly out of nowhere. I didn't know she'd even been listening in on the conversation. Her expression was as flat and unexpressive as it always was off the court. "Mags is right about putting you on her. I think you'll be an unexpected weapon to keep her out of the paint."

Ellie kind of looked like she appreciated it, but also looked like she might throw up. Gemma offered a supportive smile in Ellie's direction. "If we can beat Point Brook, we can definitely handle East Hill."

I set my jaw as my teammates nodded in agreement. None of us wanted to state the obvious—we'd beat Point Brook last season. We hadn't played them yet this season. And things had a way of changing.

My stomach knotted the way it had all summer. It was a new, uncomfortable feeling that was usually accompanied by about a million little voices saying variations of *you're an idiot if you think you'll play well this season.*

I tapped my fingers against my thigh, overwhelmed by the urge to get the fuck out of here.

I leaned over to Nia, dropping my voice. "We're going to The 151 after this, right?"

Nia smirked. "Duh."

Chapter Two

Leah

I leaned into the mirror, taking a closer look at my makeup. I'd done it the same way I always did—my lips coated with a thin layer of lip gloss, my mascara dragging my lashes up about a mile high. Even for a party, I didn't like to do nighttime looks. I kept things light and fresh—usually with my mother's voice in my ear, saying, *Are you sure that's the right shade of blush?*

"You look fine," my best friend, Soph, said from behind me. I could see her through the mirror; she was sprawled out on my bed, feet kicked up behind her.

"You haven't even looked up at me," I said. I pushed my dirty blonde hair behind my ears, sighing. I had a knot in my chest that was so tight I could hardly breathe. I would say that I didn't know why I was so nervous, but I knew exactly why.

"I don't have to look up at you to know." She readjusted on the bed, propping herself up. "Any word on if Kai will be there?"

She said *Kai* with the flat tone of someone who felt compelled to ask but didn't really want the answer. I knew for a fact she was sick of hearing about her, sick of hearing about her and me. It'd gotten so bad that she went from thinly veiled *you're sure you want to see them again?* comments to turning my inability to just let the brief summer fling go into a drinking game. She'd gotten five shots deep one night before she nearly put a gag on me to stop me from asking *Do you think I should just text them?* again.

It would all be a much-appreciated gesture of love in about three months, but while I was in the throes of it, I didn't really want to hear it from her—even though I knew someone had to keep me in check.

"I don't know," I responded simply, because it was true. I didn't know. After a summer fling that was mostly made up of sex—still with no orgasm—and underwhelming departures in the middle of the night, Kai had completely ghosted me. Initially, I'd chalked it up to being busy during the first week of school. But then another week passed. And another.

And now I was here, deep into October and scared to go to a party because she might be there and I might have to navigate whatever would be waiting for me.

"This will be a good chance to maybe find someone new," she said. "Lots of things happen at The 151."

"And not all of them good," I reminded her. "I still haven't forgiven you for giving me a Buzzball that one time." I sighed. "My gut is telling me she'll be there."

"What makes you think that? Our campus is small, but it's not *that* small. You're not going to be, like, on top of each other. You haven't even run into her yet."

That was true—in addition to being ghosted, Kai had been nowhere to be seen. I hadn't run into her in any of the spots students frequented, academic buildings or otherwise. The only proof of life I had was that she occasionally posted on Instagram—usually perfectly curated photo dumps of the intentional-but-pretending-it-wasn't variety—and her band was still playing gigs in the area.

"That's what makes me think it's coming," I said. "And The 151 is, like, *the* lesbian hangout. I don't want to have to avoid it all year, but I also..." I shrugged defeatedly.

"You guys fooled around for, like, two months *very* casually." Soph put her whole body and spirit into the *very*, which was reasonable because it seemed like it still hadn't completely sunk in for me yet. "It's not like she left you at the altar. I know it'll be weird, and it'll suck to run into her, but it won't be the end of the world. People do it literally all the time, and with people who were actual exes of a serious, *exclusive* relationship."

"I know," I lied. I'd tried to explain it to Soph before, but she never understood. She was the ultra-confident one of the two of us, always out flirting and meeting people and flashing her bright smile. We met through cheerleading, but that was where most of our similarities ended—other than a strong, unwavering dedication to each other and our friendship.

I didn't know why I couldn't just let everything with Kai go. I'd tried to think it over logically, tried to give myself the ick a thousand times, and still couldn't dig myself out of the hole I'd willingly dug myself.

The only saving grace—and I truly meant the only—was that I hadn't texted her at any point after she ignored the last text I sent. I stood firm, waiting for her to follow up, wanting her to be the one who had to ask for my attention again. Even if I couldn't be cool and under control internally, I was absolutely going to give that impression externally.

"We're also, like you said, going to *the* lesbian hangout," Soph said. "Even if Kai shows up, she definitely won't be the only option there."

"You can keep encouraging me to go back into the dating scene, but—"

"Someone has to remind you that you're hot shit."

I flicked off the light in my en-suite bathroom and threw myself down on my bed next to Soph. "I know I'm hot shit."

"You're definitely not giving that you feel that way." She turned to look at me, propping herself up on one elbow. "Which is fine, but you also have about a million new people you can meet tonight. Or a million old people who, after a drink or two, suddenly become a new object of fixation."

"I don't know if there will be anyone worth paying attention to."

"Hello? Nab an athlete? There are very few problems muscles can't solve."

"You know my sister would never in a million years let that happen," I said. Mags being on the basketball team meant that everyone on the team was completely off limits. It'd always been that way, with every team she'd ever played on. No matter how cute or nice a teammate was, they were always a teammate first.

Even if they had incredible arms, which I knew GJ did. Not that I was specifically thinking about GJ during this very generalized, very broad conversation about hooking up with athletes. Not at all.

"It doesn't have to be someone on the basketball team." I'd never been so grateful that Soph and I hadn't yet developed the ability to literally hear each other's thoughts; there was no way she'd ever approve of GJ. "Plus, if you can't handle potentially running into Kai at a house party, you would *definitely* not be able to handle running into a fling multiple times a week for the rest of the season. You have softball, field hockey, swim team—"

"I get it." I laughed, playfully smacking her arm. I sat up fully and looked her in the eyes. "It's going to be okay, right? You can't actually die from, like, embarrassment?""I promise you, seeing the campus fuckgirl at a party will not kill you," Soph said, putting her hand to her heart. "Swear."

"Okay," I said, taking a deep breath. It didn't do anything to calm my nerves; the only solution was liquid courage. "Let's do it."

The best time to arrive at The 151 was just after 10 p.m., which was exactly when Soph and I arrived. We were able to walk to the house and combatted the chill settling over northern Colorado with copious amounts of alcohol and light coats we'd hide in our usual spot.

By the time we walked through the front door, my muscles had relaxed, and I no longer felt like I was at risk of throwing up any second from nerves. It became a tiny bit easier for me to consider hearing Soph out and finally let go of the grip I'd allowed Kai to have on me, at least for the night.

Music blasted through the entire house, bass making the walls and floors vibrate. I could feel it in my chest, a much-needed sensation after being wound up so tight.

I took a swig from my water bottle—Soph and I knew better than to go for the lukewarm beer offered here—and looked around for familiar faces. The house was packed full as usual. People were hanging out on couches, making out against walls, flirting during games of flip cup. House parties in Lakeside Green were wild and almost always the preferred spot to be; on a campus this small, there were only a few places to go out and get a drink, and they were too controlled for my liking. This was the closest we could get to a dingy, underground club.

"Leah! Soph!"

Soph dragged me over toward a group of our friends. Some of them were cheerleaders, and some of them were friends of cheerleaders. A handful were of the *randomly assigned room-*

mates variety instead of the initial common interest variety. It was a mixed bag on how long or how well I knew everyone.

The group had gone through major transformations since our freshman year. There'd been fallouts, replaced best friends, new additions, even some heartbreaks between members of the group. Most of the girls in the group were not the ones I'd expected to stay in touch with. But I could see the current group of us, the six or so who shared a group chat and stayed in touch even after the party was over, making it past graduation.

"How are you, Madame President?" Reese, one of my friends who wasn't a cheerleader, asked. She threw an arm over my shoulders, her blonde curls falling into my face in the process. "Change the world yet?"

"President no longer. And I don't know about changing the world." I'd been elected student body president of Lakeside Green last year and didn't run again this year. It was impressive to accomplish as a junior theoretically, but it'd also been a role that essentially meant nothing other than boosting my resume. University administrators only allowed me to accomplish so much, which had taken away any vigor I'd gone into the position with. But I was a textbook overachiever, always looking for a new goal to fixate on, so I did it and spent the entire time wondering why I was doing it. It was a predictable pattern that I should've seen coming.

"You could've been our Elle Woods." Reese sighed playfully.

"I'm sure my parents would love that," I said, even though it was hard to imagine them truly *loving* anything I did.

"Yeah, well, fuck our parents. We can figure this shit out on our own," Reese said, knocking her cup against mine in a mock cheers.

Reese and I had gotten close last year after she'd made a joke about her mom that sounded scarily similar to some of my own experiences. Despite growing up differently, we understood each other better than most people I'd met at Lakeside Green.

Unlike me, Reese was born and raised in a small, rural town in Colorado. She'd gone here because they were able to offer her a full-ride scholarship. It was a double win—she'd graduate debt-free, and she could stay close enough to home to help out with her dad, who couldn't work after getting permanently disabled during a shift. Her mom, like mine, was a piece of work who only ever said the wrong thing.

Seemingly from a completely different planet, I'd grown up just outside of San Diego. Both of my parents were working professionals who cared too much about appeasing their HOA and country club friends to give a genuine fuck about my sister or me. They made it clear they preferred Mags over me, but that definitely had to do with her having drive and direction over our personalities, something I'd always struggled with. I was objectively nicer and easier to be around than Mags, but she was at least born to be a basketball player; I'd spent my entire life throwing things at the wall to see what would stick. So far, nothing had.

"Well, now that you're not busy running the school on your own, you have time to come to one of my classes." She smirked, and my eyes widened.

"Wait, you got the job?" I squealed, and Reese nodded, absolutely radiating joy. "Oh my god, Reese! That's amazing! Congratulations!"

"Thank you, thank you. Only took several years and *really* learning how to smile without hurting my cheeks, but it's been *so* worth it."

Even though Reese wasn't a cheerleader, she still understood us as a lifelong dancer. A lot of us in our friend group had come up in dance, cheer, or both, and bonded over the very specific experiences that came with that. Mostly, it was a lot of feeling weird about our bodies and the pressures that tended to stereotypically come from the kinds of parents who encouraged competitive dance.

Reese had been taking classes through the Lakeside Green student gym for years and had finally worked up the nerve to apply to be one of their teachers. It was a highly coveted job for a niche population, and she'd been stressing over it for months.

"Are you teaching contemporary?"

Reese nodded. "Of course. I always get what I want."

I snorted. "I'm so proud of you."

"You still haven't answered my question—are you coming to one of my classes? Or should I say, since you *are* coming to one of my classes because I demand it—which one do you want to come to?"

"Oh, I don't know." I drew out the words. "You know, this time of year, it's busy—"

And it was true—the cheerleaders were brought out for every women's basketball, men's basketball, and football game. But that also wasn't saying a lot when it came to Lakeside Green. Other than women's basketball, our programs were historically really bad for D1 and were typically not funded well because of that. The school budget included cheerleading, but we didn't travel, and we were more of a club than an actual powerhouse cheering squad seen at the bigger schools. The hope was that it would change eventually, but it wasn't going to happen while I was a student here.

"I literally don't want to hear it from you. You're basically superwoman and have more hours in the day than anyone I've ever met." Reese nudged me. "It'll be fun, I promise."

I sighed a little bit. "You know how it is. I haven't danced in a long time—"

"Right, and dance is stressful, and you can't do it casually, and you haven't properly danced since high school and blah-blah-blah."

"Alright, alright," I said, laughing. "You're not technically wrong, but I don't like feeling so exposed."

"We've all been there. I had to remember why I wanted to do it in the first place and allow myself to enjoy it again. The hardest part is remembering that you did it because you loved it."

"Or because my mom told me I had to and would be so mad at me if I'd told her I didn't want to go."

"No, that's other people. *You* specifically loved dance. You talk about it like it's the one who got away."

I rolled my eyes at her good-naturedly. Reese was right about a lot of things—I didn't join the dance team or even take casual dance classes because I didn't know how to do it in a normal way. It was too stressful, too hard, too weird. There was so much pressure to make sure I was doing it right. I found it hard to even just dance when I was alone; I was too aware of what I was doing to just let go.

But the one thing Reese didn't get right was my love for dance. I'd always *liked* it, and the physical activity felt good, but if I really loved dance, I would've kept doing it in college rather than opting for cheer.

Cheering felt like a perfect middle-ground—it kept me busy, it introduced me to amazing friends, it looked good on a re-sume, and the Lakeside Green cheer program didn't cheer com-petitively. I could've theoretically quit at any point—especially when it became obvious my parents weren't impressed and the whole reason I'd pursued it was for their approval—but I had no interest in leaving.

"*Anyway*." I brushed off her comment. "Have you run into Ainsley yet?"

"Yeah, nice job with changing the subject." Reese snorted. "But no. And she better hope we don't run into each other. I don't want to see her here. This is *my* spot."

"I still can't believe you guys broke up," I said. That was another thing Reese and I had bonded over—we'd both recently gone through some kind of heartbreak, albeit mine much more minor. There was nothing that could turn a casual friendship into a suddenly very close one like processing our singlehood in real-time together. "I thought you were going to be together forever."

Reese shrugged. "Wasn't meant to be. Stay away from the athletes, especially the volleyball players."

"Noted."

She brought her drink to her lips and I looked around the room to see who else I recognized—and if anyone was worth attempting to take home. I knew a lot of the faces in passing because I'd seen them around, but I wasn't confident with everyone's names. Maybe that was a good thing and exactly what I needed, but it was hard to know. My heart wasn't in it either way.

My sister and her teammates then walked through the door, loud and rowdy as usual. They'd had their start-of-the-season banquet earlier in the evening, and all of them were still dressed from it. I wouldn't be surprised if they'd left the dinner, stayed together to sneak a few swigs from a flask, and then wandered over this way.

The same deeply agitated feeling that I experienced every time Mags was in the general vicinity washed over me. We'd just gotten into an argument earlier today because she was insistent that I was loading the dishwasher the wrong way. It was just the cherry on top that during our FaceTime with our parents last week, they'd spent the entire time talking to and about Mags, like I wasn't even there. And Mags, as usual, didn't even realize.

Fortunately, she and I tended to ignore each other at these things whenever we saw each other. It was mostly to avoid the bickering that seemed to follow us everywhere, including to our shared apartment.

Then, out of the corner of my eye, I saw her.

My heart fell to my feet, my heart rate shooting up. "*Fuck,*" I whispered.

"What?" Reese asked, looking around to see what I'd just spotted.

"Kai is here," I said, averting my eyes so Kai wouldn't know I was looking over at her. But there was no question it was her. I knew that hair, those tattoos, the sleepy look to her eyes. I kept stealing glances back into the corner where she'd positioned herself, sitting on the edge of the couch with her arm wrapped around the waist of some other girl. There were friends circled around them, all of them the cool artist type with tattoos and moody expressions and vapes in their hands.

Everything about it was so not me. I *was* an Elle Woods—I was pink and bubbly and spent too much money on my hair and nails. I could try my best to cosplay as the type who preferred dive bars and drank cheap beer and wanted to get high and listen to Pink Floyd, but it wasn't me. I knew it. Kai definitely knew it, even if she'd never said it out loud. But still, I felt this desire to prove myself to her and her friends. I wanted to be accepted, prove myself as the chill girl I'd never been able to be.

"Oh, shit," Reese said sympathetically, looking over that way. Reese and I were close, but we weren't as close as Soph and me. Soph was the friend who picked up the pieces and told me to get my shit together; Reese was the friend who offered a listening ear and told me that it was okay to be obsessed with someone who couldn't be bothered to give me the time of day, even when it wasn't.

I ducked my head, probably bringing more attention to myself than if I'd just stayed in place. "Fuck," I whispered again. I'd prepared myself emotionally for this exact moment for weeks, but nothing compared to the real thing—the realization that someone else had been picked over me, the crushing weight of seeing someone who was so painfully, annoyingly hot that I knew I'd never have. None of the feelings swirling in me were heartbreak, but I was sick to my stomach all the same.

Reese pushed me toward the packed kitchen, taking me out of Kai's line of view. I didn't know if that was for my benefit, so I'd stop staring, or Kai's benefit, to save them before I did something stupid. I was too embarrassed to ask.

We settled in an empty spot against a wall. People moved around us, unbothered by my obvious freakout. This was about par for the course at The 151; everyone cried, and everyone threw up.

"Okay, so, you're handling this better than I expected," Reese said.

"*Am I?*" I asked through heavy breaths. "My palms are sweaty."

Reese waved it off. "That's okay."

Soph pushed through the crowd of bodies dancing and talking like her *best friend in distress* alarm had just gone off. "What happened?" she asked.

"Kai is here," I said, keeping my voice low. I wasn't sure Soph would even be able to hear me over the music, but I wasn't going to get myself into something by saying it any louder. The last thing I needed was for word to spread that I was obviously unwell, and it was because of Kai. The only thing more embarrassing than my hurt feelings getting around the party was that Soph had been right about Kai—pretty much every other gay girl here had also been done dirty by her. I wasn't the only one. I should've known better, but I never did.

"Oh, shit." Soph turned her head, looking around. "What do you want to do? Head home? Or it's early enough that we can probably still go to the bar."

I considered the comfort of leaving. I wouldn't spend the entire night aware of Kai in the other room, tuned into the fact that she was here and acting like nothing had happened between us. I also wouldn't have to spend the entire time I was here pretending I wasn't distracted by how Kai was *definitely* going to take her date home.

I fought off a sigh. At least I knew the sex would be mediocre.

"No, I have to stay," I insisted. As much as it sucked to be here, it was just as embarrassing to leave so suddenly with my tail between my legs. If Kai hadn't already seen me, she would definitely see me leaving shortly after she'd arrived. It wasn't particularly subtle.

"Are you sure?" Soph asked. "Really sure?"

"We can sneak you out back," Reese offered.

I considered it, thinking over the options in front of me. My gut was telling me to leave, but the prideful part of me was telling me to stay and stick it out.

I bit my lip, and as I brought my eyes back up to look at my friends, I landed on GJ instead.

She was standing across the room with a few friends—my sister nowhere to be seen—looking as hot as she always did. The creamsicle-orange linen she was wearing contrasted beautifully with her dark skin. Her smile was bright and easy, her confidence radiating so far off of her that I could feel it all the way over here. And her arms...

GJ's words from this summer echoed in my ear. *You know how to reach me if you need me.*

I briefly considered the consequences, just tipsy enough to think they couldn't possibly be *that* bad. Mags was always clear on the rules, and I knew she'd hate it if I went after one of her teammates. But my entire family had rules for me and never seemed particularly grateful I'd spent my entire life doing everything I could to follow them. It couldn't hurt to break one of them just once.

And, I mean—she'd have to find out about me and GJ in order for it to become an issue.

Things suddenly clicked into place for me. It was a universal truth—going home with someone was the best way to prove to an ex that you weren't still hung up on them.

GJ was right that I knew how to reach her. And I was starting to realize that, just maybe, I needed her after all.

Chapter Three
GJ

Leah was not the girl I was expecting to approach me at a party, but I wasn't complaining.

"Can I borrow GJ for a second?" she asked my friends, never short on confidence. Leah was the kind of girl who was so blunt with her communication that it was hard to bullshit her. I didn't know her that well, but she was a Moretti, and that was all I needed to know.

She was also so blunt that it was hard to tell her no, so it wasn't surprising that my friends didn't put up much of a fight.

"Yeah, I mean...sure," Tamia, one of my few friends who wasn't on the basketball team, said and shrugged good-naturedly. She glanced over at me to make sure things were cool, and when I nodded, she headed off.

"I'll catch you guys in a few," I said as they walked off. I turned toward Leah, immediately intrigued. "How can I help you, Leah Moretti?"

She stepped closer to me, tilting her head up toward me. She was somewhere around 5'10" so there wasn't much of a height difference between us. Her dark blonde hair fell down in shiny, perfectly maintained waves over her back and shoulders. She used to bleach it, but I liked that she'd decided to stop last year. There was a nice warmth to her natural color. "Did you come here with anyone?"

My eyebrows raised of their own volition. It wasn't exactly hot to be surprised when a girl was flirting, but Leah was catching me off guard. I was rarely approached so directly, and it was never this early in the night. But it made sense. She was the former student body president, the winner of various big-name scholarships, and was celebrated on campus all the time for one thing or another. She didn't have time to waste.

And I wasn't interested in wasting hers. If she wasn't going to play coy, I didn't have to either.

"I didn't," I said, because it was technically true. I'd invited the hostess from the restaurant, but I hadn't seen her yet, and we'd never exchanged numbers. I wasn't exactly waiting on her.

"Do you want to leave with someone?"

My lips turned up in a smile. "Isn't your sister going to be pissed?"

"I don't really give a fuck about Mags right now, to be honest."

Fuck, she was so *sexy*.

I'd always acknowledged that she was good-looking—everyone knew it. The Moretti genetics were categorically absurd. Their parents were tall and rich, and Leah and Mags were athletically stacked and smart—if not just so incredibly driven that it didn't matter whether they were smart or not, like Mags. They were the kind of rich where it took time to piece it together because it was all so casual to them. Mags would say things like *My neighbor taught me how to throw a football* and later, it'd be revealed that the neighbor happened to be Russell Wilson.

Mags was always considered the hot one of the Coyotes, probably because she was blonde and tall and built muscle like a supermodel instead of a regular person. But with her sister standing in front of me, it was obvious that Leah was, without a doubt, the hotter of the two sisters. Mags was lucky they didn't both play basketball because Leah would've been the easy fan favorite.

"I have to say, I'm flattered by the sudden interest," I said.

Leah bit her lip like she had something to confess.

"Are you about to tell me that Mags sent you here to test me? Are you a mole to see if I'd be willing to sleep with her sister despite warning us all you're off-limits?" I teased. "You can tell her that I would if offered, whether she approves or not."

Leah laughed. "No, oh my god. Nothing like that. I promise." Earnest giggles bubbled out of her in a way that surprised but charmed me. I'd never experienced this side of her directly, but I'd seen it in her at parties with her friends. She always had a way of catching my eye. She was expressive and social, talking freely with her hands and laughing.

I didn't keep my distance because of Mags specifically—I wasn't afraid of her—but mostly because it was a line that I didn't want to cross without knowing Leah was mutually interested in crossing it. I wasn't going to cause a problem for no reason.

But I *would* willingly cause a problem for a good reason. And the opportunity to have sex with Leah definitely fell under that category.

"What is it?" I asked. "Is it my new shirt? You can be honest. I had a feeling when I ordered this that women would flock to me."

Leah laughed again with her perfect, incredible laugh. I'd been hearing it for years in passing at parties, but it sounded even better when it was directed at me. "No. I mean, *yes*, the shirt is great. But honestly, someone I was seeing is here with someone else, and I'm..." she waved her hands instead of finishing her sentence.

"Right," I said, catching on immediately. "You want to make them jealous."

"Is that petty and stupid?" she asked.

"Not even a little bit," I answered honestly. "If it is, it doesn't matter to me. I'd do the same thing."

She scoffed, rolling her eyes with a smile. "As if you've ever been serious enough with anyone to have to be petty."

I laughed. "Fair enough." It was true—no one had ever made enough of an impact to be upset when we were no longer a thing. Everything was always casual with me. I didn't really want to involve feelings, didn't have an interest in getting to know anyone that seriously. College wasn't meant for something like that.

"But it's okay if you don't want to be, like, a revenge fuck. I won't be offended," she said. I knew she meant it, too. One thing Theo and I had connected on was our love for women who radiated confidence. It was nice to be matched in that way, since both of us were so cocky.

Hearing the confirmation from Leah so plainly that she wanted to have sex was a high like nothing else. I could listen to her say *revenge fuck* all day on repeat, shamelessly. I was open to anything Leah wanted to do—we could've left the party together and left it at that, just giving everyone here enough to talk about, without actually following through.

But she was serious. She really wanted to move on from her ex, and she wanted to do that by having sex with me. And I wasn't about to say no to something like that.

A rush of desire flooded through me at the thought. I imagined my fingers in Leah's hair, her brown eyes squeezed tight as she moaned out my name. Her sleeveless black top was tight to her body, and her jeans fell perfectly on the curve of her hips. I liked how they looked on her, but wouldn't hate getting her out of them, either.

"I don't care what reason you give me if it means I get to have sex with you," I said.

Leah's eyes flashed, her cheeks pink. Even though we'd been flirting the entire time, the way we'd been discussing sex was so practical, like a business deal. But the air between us had changed in an instant. Leah might've been attracted enough to me to initially offer, but the look in her eye suggested she was *really* thinking about it now.

"I can walk you home," I offered, because I was suddenly now *very* eager to get out of here.

She nodded, and we cut through the crowd, careful to maintain distance. We had a weird line we had to toe—she wanted to show off to her ex and make sure they knew she was still getting laid, but her sister would be pissed at us if she knew we were alone together. My team knew me well enough to know what my talking one-on-one with another woman at a party meant.

"I'm walking her back," I said when I saw Leah's friends staring at us. I could see from their expressions that they had no idea what to make of the two of us together.

"Okay," Soph, who I knew from the cheer squad, said. She squeezed Leah's arm and then looked back at me with a warning in her eyes. "Let me know if you need anything. We'll come get you if you need it." She turned her attention back to me. "On your absolute best behavior."

"Yes, ma'am," I said with a mock salute. "Always."

"Thanks, Mom," Leah said with a partial eye roll.

We continued through the crowd. I placed my hand on Leah's lower back to guide her through, keeping an eye out for Mags. I was less worried about the rest of the players on the team—everyone tended to mind their own business. And I wasn't sure any of the Coyotes, other than Gemma, really *liked* Mags enough to intentionally go out of their way to give updates on her sister.

I also kept an eye out for whoever it was that Leah had been seeing. I didn't have a name or face, so anyone at the party could've been them. I almost asked her, mostly because I wanted an opportunity to stare down the competition. But I didn't want to risk making her uncomfortable by pushing it too far.

"I'm going to walk her home," I repeated, this time to my friends. They expressed much less concern than Leah's friends, mostly just waving before we went on our way. All of them knew better than to ask questions. Mags was nowhere to be seen, which was a relief. She was probably off somewhere with Gemma.

Outside, the cold air felt good on my skin. It'd been about a thousand degrees inside The 151 like it always was.

"Where's your apartment?" I asked as we headed down the driveway. The bass from inside was so loud I could still hear it from out here. Despite the suburban appearance of the neighborhood, the rest of the houses were also lit up and bustling with students. Lakeside Green had expanded pretty dramatically over the years, the family-owned homes turning into rentals as more and more students enrolled with each passing semester.

It wasn't just the housing that had been taken over by students. Pretty much all of the restaurants and bars were dedicated to us for a minimum three-mile radius. It didn't sound like much until I was actually standing on campus, when it felt like we were floating in a weird island away from all other civilization. I spent all day, every day, surrounded by college students and professors. I couldn't remember the last time I'd seen a child out in the wild here, outside of the occasional baby brought to a game.

"About that," Leah said. She crossed her arms over her chest and shivered, and I wished I had a heavier coat to offer her.

My lips turned up in a smile. "Another secret? You live with an ex or something?"

"Not an ex. My sister," she said. "I think an alarm would go off if you stepped within even ten feet of the front door."

I nodded. "I totally forgot about that."

"But...your place?" Leah offered.

I ran through a mental image of my somewhat pathetic bachelor pad studio near the main campus. I'd moved into one of the new-build apartment complexes after deciding I didn't want to live with any of my other friends on campus. I liked my non-basketball friends, but my schedule was particular and intense to a degree that it made it hard to cohabitate peacefully with non-athletes, and Theo was confidently the only person I could handle living with and playing basketball with. I didn't feel weird about giving up our old house to some other student athletes on campus—it felt like the right time—but it did feel weird moving from there to being on my own.

Maybe calling it pathetic wasn't fair—it was just depressing compared to where I'd been living. It was a nice apartment and clean enough to bring someone back to, nothing to be embarrassed about. A few clothes on the ground never hurt anybody.

I shook my thoughts away. What the fuck was wrong with me? I'd never been the kind of person who was weird about inviting girls over. I'd only ever been ego-first, so certain that a girl would only care about sleeping with me that I never thought twice about it.

"Yeah, that works," I said, doing the best impression of myself from last year that I could muster. "I'll lead the way."

Chapter Four

Leah

"Cute," I said as GJ opened the front door and flicked on the light in her entryway.

Her apartment was not what I imagined. Her clothes were always impeccable—it was obvious where her NIL money went—but she didn't have a reputation for being particularly neat or orderly. The running joke amongst the people who knew the team was that GJ was never in class, never knew what was going on when she wasn't on the court. But she was always there for a good time and fiercely loyal teammate when it mattered, which I found way more charming than someone who only had a 4.0 to offer.

Her apartment, however, was more aligned with her clothes than her personality. It was carefully organized, all of the furniture coordinated. Her bed was even made; not so tightly that it was like she was expecting company, but just enough to show that she liked to do it for herself.

I nearly let out a sigh of relief. This was—admittedly—a much-needed change of pace from the apartments I'd gotten used to seeing during my escapades. I didn't think Kai even owned a vacuum.

"That's a nice way of saying that it's small," GJ said as she stepped into the room. It *was* small. Everything was laid out in a box—her kitchen lined one wall, her bed lined another wall, and the bathroom was to my right. She had a small balcony through a sliding door directly across from me. There wasn't much to explore beyond the surface, no square footage I couldn't see from here.

"No, I mean it. I really like it." A tiny part of me envied the freedom of having space to herself. I had no idea what that felt like. "It's really well-decorated, actually. Like, it looks expensive in here."

"My sisters. I gave them a budget, and they did what they had to do." GJ waved her hand at the space around us, like she barely even noticed. "It's never been my strong suit. Theo and I had a nasty old couch at our place."

There wasn't an ounce of sheepishness in her voice. The confidence was sexy. Even as the alcohol I had consumed going to the party exited my body, I didn't have any regrets about being here.

Mags flashed into my mind briefly, along with all of the years she'd told me that teammates were off limits. For a beat, I considered turning back around just to avoid the meltdown she would have if she found out.

But I was already here. And this was the kind of thing—GJ was the kind of person—where things only ever happened once. Or at least, only happened over the course of one night. I'd heard enough stories about GJ's stamina to know that if we did have sex, it'd be dirty, but it definitely wouldn't be over quickly.

Mags didn't have to know. I could get this out of my system, remind myself that I was hot and cool and didn't need Kai, and that would be it.

We were standing close to each other in the doorframe, body heat radiating off of us. There was barely an inch between us. The air was heavy with the familiar anticipation and knowing that we probably were going to have sex tonight—we just needed one of us to initiate.

But I also didn't mind taking my time—there was something nice about being able to be here with her, pretending that this might be something more than just a one-night stand. I hadn't had anyone new on my radar since Kai, either romantically or sexually. This was exactly what I needed.

I wandered into the room, easing some of the tension between us. The bed nearby was a reminder of what we'd both come here for. I kept waiting for my liquid courage to dissipate, but instead, I felt increasingly confident in my decision. Just being here made me feel better. The way GJ was looking at me, the way I'd taken control of the situation. I'd needed this; my *ego* needed this.

GJ followed behind me, meeting me in her living room, which was just a couch and a massive TV. I'd kicked off my heels at her front door, so our height difference of a few inches was more noticeable than before.

"Do you do this often?" GJ asked, sending a flutter through my body.

"What? Sleep with my sister's teammates?"

GJ's full lips turned up in a smile. "Sleep with anyone."

"Don't worry, I know exactly what this is," I said, my eyes trailing down to GJ's lips.

GJ closed the gap between us, our chests nearly touching. She put her hands delicately on each side of my face, her thumb tracing my jaw. By the time she leaned in and kissed me, my nerves had turned into excitement and relief.

For the first time ever, I was going to have sex without the anticipation of what would come next. I wasn't going to worry if she liked me, if she'd call. Finally getting out of my head made fooling around so much more enjoyable.

Her lips were soft, and I could feel her carefully gauging what I wanted. She kissed me slowly, testing the waters. It didn't take her long to match my style of kissing. It wasn't too wet or too aggressive or too gentle; it was just right. It was obvious GJ was an expert at fooling around with someone new.

Even though I'd come here for sex, I let myself get swept away for a moment in how good it felt to kiss GJ. It was *fun* the way we'd become hungrier as we learned what the other person liked. Our kisses went from cautious to full-on making out with a sense of urgency and need. GJ's hands trailed down my body, moving to my waist, where she pulled me in closer. I opened my mouth for her, and we were off to the races, desperation swelling in me as I got increasingly turned on.

I reached for GJ's shirt, unbuttoning the loose material. GJ shook it off and let it fall to the ground, and then pulled my shirt over my head. We stepped back toward the bed as GJ's mouth traveled from my lips to my neck. The wetness pooling between my legs told me everything I needed to know.

She guided me back toward the bed, and we eased onto it together, careful about putting her hands on my waist to soften my landing. She hovered over me—me fully on my back, her standing at the edge of the bed.

Her lips traveled from my mouth to my jawline to my neck, trailing in a slow, careful, and thoughtful way I'd never gotten from anyone else before. Not even the people who I'd been dating treated me so gently.

I pulled her toward me and kissed the soft skin of her neck before bringing my lips to hers again. The action was pointed—hot, hard, fast. She took the cue like I hoped she would, no longer acting like she had to be soft with me just because it was our first time together.

She dragged her mouth to my nipples, putting pressure on them with her tongue and fingers. A rush of pleasure coursed through me, and I wiggled impatiently.

"Breathe," GJ said, surprising me. She hovered so close to my skin that I could feel her breath on my chest. "Let me take my time with you."

The urge to protest swelled in me, reality coming right back to me in a tidal wave I didn't want. "You don't have to."

GJ kissed the soft skin of my stomach. "I want to, especially if this might be the only time I'll be able to have you."

I couldn't even think of an appropriate response, probably because the logical part of my brain was reminding me of how stupid it was to argue against something like that. I had someone—and not just any someone, but someone effortlessly sexy and cool and confident—telling me that she wanted to give me a good time. If anything, she was *insisting* on me having a good time.

I didn't know what kind of alternate dream reality I'd accidentally stumbled upon, but this was definitely a new experience for me. All of it was—from picking her up at the party to willingly deciding to go against my sister's wishes and flirting with her teammate to coming home with that same teammate. And now, someone who would be nothing more than a one-night stand was offering me more enthusiasm than people I'd slept with for months ever had.

It was hard to process all of it through the haze of foreplay and how badly I wanted GJ. All I knew was that I was done talking, done thinking. I wanted to relish in my escape from reality.

"Do you want me to keep going?" GJ asked.

I nodded. Surprisingly, none of my hesitation came from the risk of going home with her. It was already too late to turn back; the line had already been crossed. With her hands and lips on my skin, it was impossible for me to walk away, even when I knew this was probably a bad idea. Even if we stopped now, I would've still fooled around with my sister's teammate—I might as well try for an orgasm at this point.

The only thing that was giving me pause was that GJ was nice to me, something I was going to have to unpack at a later date when I wasn't mostly naked in front of her.

"I want to hear you say it," GJ said, brushing a piece of hair from my face. The softness and desire in her expression were laid out so plainly for me; I had to avert my eyes to avoid blushing.

"Yes," I breathed. "I want you."

"Good girl."

Being called a good girl wasn't new to me. I'd tried out a lot of different things over the time I'd been having sex, asking my partners to call me things, patiently wading through the waters of whether I liked the new nickname they wanted to give me in bed. I wasn't afraid to try something, especially if I knew it would help maintain my partner's attention for just a little bit longer.

But no one had ever said it to me in the way GJ had, with the same steadiness, the same certainty. It sounded so natural coming from her lips that I was certain she'd probably said it a thousand times before to a thousand different people.

Fortunately—or maybe unfortunately—my insecurity was reserved for partners where feelings were involved. All of the women who'd come, literally, before me in GJ's bed before weren't my business. If anything, I was grateful for their service.

GJ reached for my waist, and I lifted my hips to make it easier for her to slide my pants off. She was gentle about it, her fingers gently brushing against my skin as she trailed down my thighs and then calves.

I readjusted on the bed so GJ could join me on top of the sheets. She stripped down to her briefs and joined me, finding the spot between my legs. Her weight against me shot through my core; every cell in my body begged for us to move faster, for her to touch the only part of my body she hadn't touched yet.

She slipped her hands between her torso and my thong, finding my clit through the fabric. Her movements were gentle and intentional, and wetness pooled where she touched. Even though I hadn't thought about GJ in a particularly explicit way before tonight, I was responding to her like she was the only person I'd ever wanted. My desire for her was uncharted territory, stronger and more intense than any other partner had managed to bring out in me.

I really thought I might explode if she wasn't inside of me soon. I ever-so-gently bucked my hips against her fingers, encouraging her to take the next step.

"You want something?" GJ asked with a confident smile on her lips. My heart fluttered at the sight of her—her locs falling over her face, her deep brown eyes carefully taking in every movement I made. Even though I could tell she was learning my body, she didn't look at me like she was studying for a test; she looked at me like she was amazed by what my body could do, amazed by how I looked undressed in front of her.

I couldn't pretend to have patience even if I wanted to. "*Please.*"

GJ moved my panties to the side. When her fingers touched my bare slit, my body felt like it was on fire with need. My nerves were at their most sensitive; every brush, every movement, was almost overwhelming.

She surprised me by slowly easing her fingers inside of me, initially trying one and then quickly including a second when she realized it could fit. "Is this what you've been so impatient for?"

I could tell from her tone that she already knew the answer to that question. I could only softly moan in response, my brain emptied out from how good her hands felt.

GJ moved her fingers in and out of me, taking her time. Despite the urgency I'd gone into this with, I didn't mind matching GJ's pace. Maybe she was onto something with taking our time.

Sex was hot when it was quick, but it turned out it was also *really* hot dragged out like this. If anything, it felt even better.

After figuring out what was working on me—not that GJ had to try very hard; I liked everything she was doing with her hands, from the curve of her fingers to how she'd started increasing her speed—we settled into a rhythm. Our bodies moved together, my back arching toward her.

"Oh, *GJ*," I moaned, feeling more like an adult film star than I ever had in my life during sex. I didn't even feel particularly sexy, like I was putting on a show for her—the moans and pleading and whimpering were coming from deep within me, from a place I didn't recognize. I'd never seen this side of myself before, never gotten so lost in the sex I was having before.

I gripped the sheets as GJ thrusted her fingers into me, filling me completely. My eyes squeezed shut, a feeling fluttering through me that was familiar but not like this—not with a partner.

"*Oh*," I cried out, so breathless I couldn't believe I was actually able to get the word out. My orgasm spread through my entire body like a wave. It was new and different having someone there with me to witness it, but I was so caught up in all of it that there wasn't a moment to be embarrassed.

As the feeling crashed, I was left as nothing more than a puddle. My entire body felt light and ultra-sensitive, GJ's bed suddenly the safest and coziest spot in the world. I inhaled slowly, my eyes closed.

GJ left kisses on my bare shoulders and neck and joined me on the bed.

"*Wow*." I exhaled, mostly to myself, before I could think about the words leaving my lips.

GJ smirked. "Happy to be of service."

"What, not going to ask me if I finished?" I joked. I was almost relieved that those hadn't been the first words out of her mouth; I couldn't remember the last time I'd had sex where someone hadn't had to ask if I'd had a good time.

"I don't have to ask." She responded with so much certainty that I knew the words were true. She fell down onto the pillows next to me. "Is it okay if I touch you?"

"You can do whatever you want to me," I said and then blushed. I didn't mean to be so frank with her. Even if there weren't feelings involved, I still wanted to come across as *cool*. And it was hard to imagine that the effortlessly sexy cool girl would act like that—so suddenly desperate, so unwound—with a one-night stand. The cool girl probably would've left by now, her mission complete.

I flashed back to the girl Kai had brought to the party, wondering if she was a true cool girl, and my stomach swooped. My therapist would be disappointed in my inability to name how I was feeling, but it also felt too complex to be summed up by just one word. Disappointed? Betrayed? It wasn't like Kai had done anything explicitly wrong. Ghosting was mean, but it wasn't like she hadn't been dropping obvious hints as long as we'd been fooling around.

GJ's eyes danced over my face. "Where'd you go just now?"

"You're more attentive than I thought you'd be."

"All I'm hearing is that you've thought about how I'd be in bed."

A laugh escaped me that turned into giggling. My orgasm had made me giddy, and it was annoyingly difficult to hide. "No, I just mean...I've seen you with Mags. And I've heard the stories. I guess I didn't imagine you'd be so adept at reading faces. Or that you'd care enough to ask."

"I mean, I try my best."

We laid there for a second in silence—my cue. GJ didn't have to say it for me to know that she was coming up with an excuse to get me to leave.

I sat up and was about to push myself off the bed when I felt a hand on my wrist. "Where are you going?"

I turned to look at GJ over my shoulder. "I'm not about to overstay my welcome."

"You're not overstaying anything," GJ said. Her voice dropped lower, her eyes tracing my naked body. "Come here."

I looked at her like I was waiting to see if she was fucking with me. I hovered just by the edge of the bed, not getting in.

"If you don't want to stay, that's fine, too. But I'm happy to have you here as long as you want."

My eyes traced her lean muscles, the easy way she was laid out in bed. She still had a sports bra on, her abs tight even though I was pretty sure she wasn't even flexing right now.

I would be a fucking idiot to leave.

I got right back into bed, GJ's arms wrapping around me as she kissed me again.

The next morning, Soph stared at me from across the dining hall table with a curious expression on her face. I'd been eating my french toast, mostly oblivious, until it became too difficult to ignore her eyes on me.

"Yes?" I asked after swallowing my bite of food.

"You're humming."

My eyebrows furrowed. "I'm what?"

"You're humming," she said and then pointed a perfectly manicured finger to the ceiling, "to the dining hall radio."

"Oh." I considered her words and then shrugged. "I didn't realize."

Soph leaned closer to me from across the table, putting her weight on her arms. "Are you okay? What happened to you?"

I put my fork down, laughing. "What do you mean?"

"Dude, the last time I saw you, you were literally having a meltdown over Kai."

"Can you not?" I said, dipping my head and looking around as if somehow word was going to get back to Kai from here.

"It's a bunch of freshmen here, it's fine. No one knows who she is," Soph said, waving her hand. It was true—the dining halls here tended to be mostly first-year students. We only came because dining hall passes were cheaper than getting hungover brunch every weekend from nearby restaurants. We only trusted this place for breakfast food and dessert, but both were admittedly pretty good. "And, anyway, my point still stands. You were not doing well. You literally had to leave early…" I could practically see the wheels turning behind Soph's eyes. "You didn't."

"What?" I asked, mostly playing dumb. I knew where this was going. Soph was smart enough to put together the pieces.

"GJ walked you home, and I know that look on your face. That's a post-sex glow," she said. When I tried to protest, Soph put up her hand to stop me. "You can't argue your way out of this one. You might be able to lie to your sister, but you definitely can't lie to me." She gave me a look like I was her PR client and she was about to have to spin one hell of a story. "*Leah*. You can't tell me you thought this was a good idea. Have you told Mags?"

I thought back to earlier this morning when I walked back into the apartment. Mags had been drinking a protein shake and was about to start her five a.m. workout; I was obviously doing a walk of shame with my smudged eyeliner and messy hair. As soon as she saw me, she made a half-joking, half-snide comment about how I'd been out late. I was worried she knew I'd gone back with GJ, but all she'd said after that was how she didn't want to hear about whatever mess I'd gotten myself into now.

It was fair enough of her—she'd earnestly tried for the first few years of college to pick up the pieces after bad dates and heartbreak, but most people tended to get tired after the one-hundredth *I really thought this one was different.*

"I definitely wouldn't be here right now if I'd told Mags," I said, imagining the hours-long battle we'd probably end up in. I didn't like to fight, but Mags had a way of bringing it out of me. The only person more stubborn than her was me when I didn't want to lose an argument. "And I'm not planning on telling her because it was a one-time thing and that's it."

"Oh, really?"

"Yes, really," I insisted. "It's GJ. Nothing serious is going to happen between the two of us."

"Because you don't want it to become anything serious or because it can never be anything serious?"

"Both!"

"Leah." Soph looked at me skeptically.

"I can do casual. I can handle a one-night stand."

"I love you, but your track record strongly indicates otherwise," she said. "You couldn't even handle being in the same room as Kai last night. I mean, shit, you couldn't even handle being in the same *house.*"

"That's different. Need I remind you, Kai ghosted me. I wasn't given any indication around expectations. If anything, she'd kind of made it sound like she wanted something with me based on the times she'd made casual references to us going somewhere or doing something. GJ and I, however, actually discussed expectations, and we're on the same page. Things are clear. Everything is fine."

That genuinely was true—after going for the world record in most orgasms achieved in one night—a welcome change of pace from my previous experiences—I'd eventually insisted on heading home. As I was combing my fingers through my sex hair and pulling my clothes back on, we'd given each other a look that was the equivalent of a *thank you for your service.*

When I told Soph this, she put her head in her hands. "So you didn't actually talk about it."

"Emotionally, I'm there. We basically did talk about it. I told her I knew what it was. She knew from the very beginning that I was there to make someone jealous. I just wanted one easy night to get Kai out of my system. We didn't even exchange numbers or anything."

"As if you're not going to see her at games. Or at The 151."

"And we can just act like nothing happened between us. It's *fine.* Really. You can trust me," I insisted. "The only person here you have to worry about is me, and I am verbally saying to you that it's fine. I do not have feelings for GJ."

Soph was quiet, clearly thinking over what to say next. She took a sip of her iced coffee—from the coffee shop down the street; the coffee here was terrible—and looked at me. "Well, was it good?"

I fought off a shy smile. "It was *really* good. The reviews are true."

"And did she at least help you get over Kai?"

Last night—and into this morning—it really seemed like it had worked. The sex with GJ was so good that I couldn't even chalk it up to beginner's luck or a happy accident or me purely wishing it into existence. She was just that good in bed.

But sex, of course, couldn't be enough. It could never be that easy.

I sighed. "No," I said, defeated. "It did not."

Chapter Five

GJ

My chest rose and fell with hard breaths as the shouts around me faded into white noise. There were players who were good with noise and used to it, who loved the hum of a crowd. I usually loved it—ate it up, in fact, and demanded as much praise as I could get. But today, I wished everyone could be quiet, just for a moment.

I dribbled the ball at the free throw line, taking a second to level out my breathing. My hands were sweaty for reasons unrelated to the fact that I was in the midst of intense physical activity. Getting nervous on the court wasn't new to me, but getting nervous to this degree was.

Our first game of the season was a home game, and we had a dedicated fanbase, so they fortunately did quiet down—as was tradition—so I could focus on my free throws. But it didn't feel like enough. Even with an arena of people intentionally trying to help me get my head in the game, I couldn't get there.

Everything was taking me out of it. The lights were too bright, and the sound of my breathing was too loud, and if I heard *one* more sneaker squeak on the waxy floor, I was going to lose it.

I didn't know what was wrong with me.

I closed my eyes for a beat, traced my hands over the comforting texture of the basketball I was dribbling. I'd been doing this since I was a kid—I *knew* basketball. I knew how to shoot, and my shooting percentage was better than average, even amongst the best college basketball players in the nation. I was smart on the court and quick on my feet. There was a reason I was here and a reason I was the captain of this team.

I poised my hands to finally launch the ball, letting my muscles relax. There were certain shots in basketball that were universally acknowledged as embarrassing to miss. There was the wide-open dunk. The airball. And then there was a missed free throw. No one was guarding me. I was in close, direct range of the basketball hoop. It should be effortless.

But as the ball left my fingertips, I knew it wasn't making it.

The entire arena held its breath as the ball arched through the air and bounced off the rim.

"That's alright, Mitchell," Nia said from beside me. She clapped a hand against mine as I waited for the ball to be given back to me to try again.

Despite Nia's attempt at comforting me, the crushing weight in my chest told me everything I needed to know. It was over. The game—at least for me—was a wash.

I knew what most people, especially my family, were going to say. It was the first game of the season. There was a lot of pressure following the run that Theo had brought us on last year. Our fanbase hadn't just doubled or tripled, it'd expanded across the entire United States.

And beyond a growing fanbase, we also had the millions of people who were waiting for us to crash and burn. People who couldn't wait to prove that they had been right the entire time that Theo was the only reason we were ever good enough to make the cut.

But my season wasn't going to have just one bad game. I knew that already.

I tossed the ball up again, trying to tell myself that I didn't care, that I'd done this a million times. I did everything I could to keep my muscles loose, to remind myself it was only one point. I even tried to tap into the feeling of what it was like shooting for fun, just hanging out in the park, and playing with my teammates.

But again, the ball bounced off the rim. The only way it could've been worse was if I'd missed the rim completely.

Crushing disappointment sat on my chest, making it hard to breathe. I knew people missed free throws all the time; I wasn't the first and I wouldn't be the last. Two of my other teammates had missed at least one free throw earlier in the game. But it felt different. I'd needed this—the easy win, the reminder that the sport I loved loved me back.

There wasn't time to linger on things like that right now. I wasn't shooting the last points of the game; we still had five minutes to gain a lead, five minutes to shut the other team out, and close the gap.

But entire games, entire finals, had been determined by only one point. Everyone knew how much something like a free throw could mean when it came to the closing minutes.

"You're alright," Nia said as we got back into position to resume play.

Her words still didn't help. I knew what was coming. And sure enough: as we moved into the next play, I was benched.

Things like that happened—even to Theo, even to me when I was at the top of my game—but it hurt more than usual right now. Getting pulled because we had a strong lead, or I wasn't the player that was needed against a certain team at that moment, was fine.

But getting pulled during a shooting slump was a personal nightmare. It was like getting scolded by the teacher in front of the class. I wasn't just hearing my coach's voice in my ear about being disappointed in me; I was hearing the voices of all of the people watching, all of the fans saying the same exact things that I would be saying if I were watching the game instead of playing.

I would say it was easier on the other side of the screen, where the pressure wasn't on, and anyone could say things like *I never would've made that mistake*, but right now, the voices definitely had a point. I should've made those. Just like I should've made every other shot I'd tried tonight. But instead, I was closing out the season opener shooting 1-11. I fucking *sucked*.

Rubbing salt in the wound, the person replacing me—of course—had to be Anna. I'd done the best I could to keep my one-sided beef to myself so Coach Darlene wouldn't get pissed, but right then, all I could imagine was that she knew how much I hated Anna and was punishing me for playing like shit.

As Anna ran out and took my place on the court, I stared at Coach Darlene's back, wishing I knew what she was thinking. I'd always responded better to coaches who were unforgiving. My family was a mess of blunt communicators and big personalities, so it was easier on me to get my feelings hurt for a second and work through it, rather than wondering.

My teammates erupting into cheers pulled me out of my thoughts. I glanced up to see that the score was even. Without me on the court, we weren't just doing better—we were on track to *win*.

I spotted Leah and the cheerleaders at the edge of the court, waving their pom poms. They were all seated, legs crossed on the wooden floor. She had the perfect cheerleader smile plastered on her face, the perfect cheerleader posture.

I thought back to her in my apartment. In my bed.

I hadn't thought about sleeping with Leah much before the other night, but now that we'd done it, she'd find her way back into my mind without warning. Sex with her was a line that couldn't be uncrossed—and apparently also a memory that couldn't be erased.

I'd lie and say that I didn't know why, of all the girls I could get hooked on, it was her, but I knew exactly the reason.

I'd known the Moretti twins for as long as I'd been at Lakeside Green University and I'd never considered either of them to be particularly undone or casual people. They carried a specific kind of intensity that came with having parents constantly riding their asses. Leah *could* have fun. I'd seen her at parties before, and obviously, she wasn't afraid of casual sex. But seeing her, of all people—the girl with the perfect, practiced smile and perfect hair and perfect clothes—unravel and lose herself in me was magic. It was a high that I wasn't confident I could replicate with anyone else.

But I acknowledged what we had for what it was—one extremely memorable night with a girl who completely surprised me. Never to happen again.

The clock ticked down with the Coyotes holding a steady lead. Things were looking really good for us, and Anna was undeniably a massive part of that—not that I would ever say that out loud to anyone.

When the final buzzer sounded out, and we officially won, everyone jumped up from their seats to celebrate. I mustered up as much enthusiasm as I could, but the moment felt different than it had previously. I didn't feel connected to the team, and it didn't feel like a win I was allowed to celebrate. My smiling and cheering didn't feel authentic. I just hoped no one else noticed.

I attempted to shake it off, scared by my own feelings. There'd never been a single moment in my life when I'd felt withdrawn when it came to basketball. Even if I only played two minutes the entire game, I was always excited about a win or devastated by a loss because basketball was a team sport.

"This is our season, baby," Mags shouted, jumping up and down.

"Welcome to the Coyotes, Anna," Gemma said with a massive smile, and the rest of the team cheered. I clapped my hands, less enthusiastic than I probably should be as captain.

Our school fight song played out over the speakers, and the crowd roared out lyrics. I'd always looked forward to the fight song and the excitement of the crowd after a win, but I mostly just want to go home rather than relish it.

Whatever the fuck was wrong with me, I desperately needed to sleep off. I couldn't go into my last season as a Coyote in this headspace. This was how a shooting slump started, and I couldn't afford to go into one when getting drafted was on the line. The WNBA was too competitive for me to afford slipping even a little bit.

I glanced over at Leah again. She and Soph were leaning toward each other, singing their hearts out. The joy in her face was obvious—her smile wide, the brunette highlights of her ponytail catching in the overhead lighting. An intense desire to be around that kind of glowing, radiant happiness sucker punched me in the chest. I could still hear her easy laughter, the warm tone of her voice, from the party in my ear.

I'd used a million different excuses to text girls before; I'd never been above a booty call, a lame *this made me think of you* text. It was easy to pretend to be vulnerable or do something sweet when nothing was on the line, and I wasn't afraid of getting rejected. But reaching out to Leah felt different. She felt different.

I grimaced to myself, icked out by my own feelings. I was drawn to her *happiness*? What the fuck was I on?

I shook the feeling off. I'd never been given such an obvious sign before that I needed to text one of the many random girls in my phone tonight and see if they were busy. Whatever weird pull I was feeling toward Leah needed to be extinguished and quickly.

I followed the rest of the team back to the tunnel, shaking out my jersey where sweat had pooled around my sports bra. I'd never been so happy to get off a basketball court, and it was leaving me feeling deflated more than anything else, even though we'd won. But there was no other option than to put on a brave face and smile through it—there was a postgame panel and a party after the game. As if it wasn't annoying enough that I had a rough start, Anna would be there for all of it. The panels, the parties. She was somehow always everywhere.

I'd never, in all of my years of basketball, felt this way about another player on my team. I'll shamelessly hate players from other teams, but it'd never been one of us. I didn't know where to put all of the feelings I was experiencing.

"GJ!"

I looked up at the seats at the edge of the tunnel where fans would gather for autographs. The weight on my chest lightened. There were still people here for me. Even if I sucked this game, people still wanted to see me play.

But that feeling quickly turned into a completely different one.

"Holy *shit*, dude!" I said, my jaw dropped. She was wearing a baseball cap as low down on her face as she possibly could, but I would know Theo anywhere. It also helped that Maya was standing right next to her, her usual bright smile plastered on her face. "What the fuck is up, guys? I had no idea you were coming. I'm surprised they didn't have you blasting all over the Jumbotron."

She leaned over the metal barrier between us and we slapped our hands together in greeting. "We kept to the back so people wouldn't see us. This game isn't about me." Theo held her hand out, and I slapped mine against it.

"Are you sticking around in town?"

"Long enough for us to catch up," Theo said. "Pizza?"

"*Hell* yeah," I said. For the first time in what had to have been months, the knot in my chest loosened just the tiniest bit. "I'll see you guys in a minute."

Lakeside Green University could feel a little bit like an island. We had very few restaurants, even fewer bars, and no easy public transit out of the area. But fortunately, Theo and Maya had driven a car out here from Cedar Creek, so I was free of the campus for the night.

I slid right into the middle of the back and then leaned into the gap between the driver and passenger seats. "I feel like I'm being driven around by mom and dad," I said. "Your new car is *sick*, dude."

"Thanks," Theo responded, about as enthusiastic and talkative as she always was. She messed around with the car temperature and radio as Maya turned to look at me.

My phone vibrated, my family group chat has been going nonstop since the game. I had three older sisters—Ada, Bev, and Vivian—who could not give less a fuck about basketball, but they loved an excuse to blow up our phones. I'd never met chattier people in my life.

Dad

Coyotes looked good tonight, solid game.

Vivian

Isaiah wants to know who this new girl on the team is. He's not happy about the amount of time you spent on the bench.

Bev

Look at you, knowing what the bench is

Vivian

I'm quoting directly from him, don't ask me what any of this means

GJ

Vivian, what did you think of my shooting percentage from the paint?

Vivian

You better be nice to me or you're not getting shit for Christmas and that's a promise

Also Isaiah said that it wasn't great but your career shooting percentage is still one of the best in LSGU history

GJ

Damn right

Ada

What if we all took fifteen minutes of phone-down time? I think we all need a screen break.

Vivian

I just miss you guys

GJ

When are you guys able to make it for a game?

Vivian

We're hoping we can make it out to one soon, the girls have been asking about you

Ada

When I feel like I can be out of office without it leading to my entire office shutting down, I'll lyk

Bev

I want to make it out to one before I finally pop

Vivian

Another baby!!! Get ready to not feel human for the next few years of your life. Enjoy getting to watch GJ play while you can

Dad

Your mom and I will let you know when we can make it, GJ.

I smiled at my phone, an ache in my chest at how much I missed my family. I'd never considered myself particularly sentimental about them, but something about having a string of bad luck made me want to be a kid at my parents' house again.

I looked out the car window, hoping at least some of my family members could make it to a few games this season. It was tough now that there were babies and husbands and Very Important Jobs, and playing basically across the country from them didn't help, but my family did a good job of being there for me when they could.

Maya turned back to look at me, pulling my attention away.

"Are you excited for your last season *ever* as a Coyote?" Maya asked.

I shrugged. Despite the warmth my family group chat brought, it wasn't enough to completely fix my mood. "You know how it is."

Theo snorted from the front seat. "What does that even mean?"

I spread my legs out over the back seat, taking up as much space as I could. "Just looking forward to playing ball."

I ignored the look that Theo and Maya exchanged. Since practices started for this season, it felt like I'd been seeing the same look between people. It was like every single person around me had thoughts and feelings about me that they didn't want to share with me—Coach Darlene especially. I'd never been so appreciative of having a faceless family group chat; it was so much easier to pretend that I was fine there.

I was an instigator by nature, but I also wasn't interested in hearing whatever it was that Theo and Maya were thinking about me right now. "Where we heading to?"

"There's a new pizza place a little bit out of town. As much as I want to walk down memory lane, I'm not in the mood to be gawked at."

"You are so annoyingly modest. Personally, if I had one of the biggest rookie years in women's basketball history, I would be shouting it from the rooftops, but that's just me."

Theo brushed the comment off, and Maya turned back to look at me with a teasing, knowing expression. Theo and I had always been on opposite ends of how we felt about the attention that came with playing women's basketball at this level. Even though I knew I shouldn't, I loved googling the team—and my name—to see what people were saying. Theo would probably sooner throw her phone into the ocean than ever willingly look at comments being made about her online, good or bad.

The drive wasn't long, but it felt like we might as well be heading into an entirely different city. It was weird to leave for something other than a game. I'd done more long-distance traveling during my time as a Coyote than I'd gone to some places ten minutes down the road.

Theo pulled carefully into a spot and parked. Unsurprisingly, being able to pretend that we were just normal people going out for a normal dinner lasted for about three seconds.

"Theo! Holy shit!" one of the waiters called out from inside the restaurant, just past the hosting stand. Even though his hand had been poised to start writing in his notepad, he instead bent his neck and held his arms in front of his body like he was bowing to royalty. "Welcome back, dude!"

"Oh, thanks." She brushed it off easily, a smile on her face—always polite but never particularly warm.

"*And* GJ," the guy continued when he spotted me. "This is so fucking cool."

I tried to stop my brain from immediately reading that as me being an afterthought, but it was hard. There was an obvious difference in enthusiasm—and it made sense, considering where Theo was in her career. She'd made it. She was *the* women's athlete of the moment. Her jerseys were everywhere, she had her own shoe design—everyone wanted to work with her. I was just a college athlete on the rise who might get drafted, but also might not. I wouldn't be the first who'd been hot shit in college and then was forgotten by fans as soon as I didn't get picked up to play professionally.

As I looked around the restaurant at the people not-so-casually snapping photos, I experienced what I knew was jealousy. I'd become increasingly acquainted with the feeling as Anna continued to make herself more and more at home with my team, but I'd never felt it toward Theo before, so it felt new all over again. And being jealous of my closest friend instead of someone who was just any other teammate made it feel infinitely more pathetic.

It wasn't that people liked her, it was that she could be so nonchalant about it. She was just *good*. I knew how hard she worked, and there was no denying that she deserved the attention and respect. But she made all of it look so easy. She loved her fans, but she didn't like attention. And she always talked about how, at the end of the day, she was just someone who knew how to move a ball around a court really well. She never pretended to be saving lives.

Watching her smile and pose for photos like she'd done a million times before made me realize how badly I wanted it to feel that easy for me. I wanted to be that indisputably good and be so confident in my skills that I could brush off attention instead of starving for it.

Maya took on her usual role of offering to take photos as Theo moved from person to person.

"GJ! Get over here," one of them, a woman who looked like she was about my mom's age, said. She waved me over to her and her family, the daughter wearing a Lakeside Green Women's Basketball shirt.

I hesitated for a second, like I wasn't sure she'd actually called me over. But when she looked me in the eye and waved, my lips turned up in a smile. I walked over, posing with everyone.

That part—getting roped into photos with Theo—felt like old times. As Theo gained more and more attention, the rest of us—other than Mags, who already had her own social media following—benefited significantly. It helped that Theo always made sure we rose with her. It was never about her; it was always about the entire team. Any opportunities she could include us in or swing our way, she did.

I posed on the right side of the family while Theo posed on the left. We crouched slightly, towering over the family of four, and smiled. For just a moment, it felt just like last year. Theo and I were on the same team again, and I was still someone people were rooting for.

It felt really fucking good.

But it was over just as quickly as it began.

"Thank you so much," the mom said as she gestured for her family to follow her out the door. Maya handed the woman's phone back to her and waved goodbye; the dad took a second to shake Theo's hand before leaving.

"That was sweet," Maya said and reached for Theo's hand.

"Yeah," Theo said. As much as I knew she tried her best to have normal nights out, she hadn't had one in years—especially not within a fifty-mile radius of Lakeside Green. But she was too nice to ever be upset about it, always gracious and humble. One of us had to be.

"It's sweet of them to include you in the photo," I joked. Even now, as I was feeling the worst I'd ever felt about my basketball skills, I'd never gotten insecure about how many people liked Theo. I could admit to wanting to be good at basketball and was jealous that I was probably about to end up in a slump that Theo had never experienced. But there was no use in competing with her when it came to characteristics I knew I'd never have and didn't want. I had no business even trying to be the level-headed, big sister type.

"Maybe one day I'll get to sign an autograph," Theo said, not missing a beat. I cackled with laughter.

We walked up to the hostess stand, where we were then quickly brought to our seats. It was busy, a hum of conversation and pop music throughout the retro-inspired restaurant.

The hostess, a teenager with braces and a long black braid down her back, laid out three menus for us. "Your server will be right with you," she said. She glanced over at Theo and then did a double-take, like she was certain she was supposed to know Theo or had met her before.

I smiled a little bit as she walked away, and then redirected to focusing on food. I was unsurprisingly starving—the most I'd had since the game was a power bar. I flipped open the flimsy laminated menu as Theo and Maya did the same.

Maya twisted her lips as she reviewed the menu. She was so used to going out with Theo at this point that she didn't seem phased by all of the attention our table was still receiving. I felt a little bit like I was under a microscope, but I could play it cool. "I don't know what I want," she said.

"The pepperoni is really good. And a classic," Theo responded, the air between them so easy. It seemed like it'd been like that since the first day they'd met. It was weird to think that I'd been there for their first conversation, there to see the way Theo's expression changed when she saw Maya for the first time. Maya brought out an entirely new Theo that none of us had ever seen before.

Sometimes I wondered if the same thing was in store for me, but I was skeptical. I'd already met and had sex with so many different women, and none of them had changed me. I'd never had any of the feelings everyone says happen—no butterflies, no waiting by the phone. It didn't seem like it was in the cards for me to be in love like that. And I was okay with that, but I sometimes wondered what it would feel like to get to experience that, just once.

For just a split second, Leah's face popped up in my mind, but I brushed it away. She was just the last person I'd slept with—it didn't mean anything.

We ordered a round of drinks and our food, and I waited to see if Theo and Maya were going to interrogate me or not.

"The rest of the team is going to be jealous I got you to myself tonight," I said, partially to quell my nerves. The longer we spent together, the harder it was for me to keep up any kind of act that I was fine. There was no way Theo wasn't going to notice I was feeling off, and absolutely no way she'd let it slide. It wasn't a question of if, but when, she would say something.

"I'll see them for other games this season. I just wanted to catch up with you first." Theo leaned back in her chair. "It's been forever."

"Yeah, I know. I can't believe you're not only a pro baller now, but you're officially done with your rookie season." I shook my head. "Doesn't even feel real."

"It's right around the corner for you, too."

It was a valiant attempt at making me feel better, but it was going to take more than that to get rid of the knot that'd been in my stomach since over the summer. It was like something had switched off in my brain, and I hadn't been able to flip it back. I didn't know if it was Anna or the looming possibility of getting drafted or the end of my career as a Coyote, but I hadn't felt like myself in months.

I smiled good-naturedly. I'd never been one to make self-deprecating jokes, so it was easier to just smile and nod, even though there was a voice in the back of my head that said *I'm not so sure about that.*

The rest of our meal was spent—fortunately—on casual chatter and hearing the ins and outs of the professional basketball world. Theo told me the gossip on players who were absolutely secretly dating, players with shitty attitudes, and behind-the-scenes drama between teammates. Maya chimed in occasionally to add in details that Theo forgot.

I almost thought I was home free, our pizza platters and glasses empty, without a single probing question. I was really thinking I wouldn't have to talk about anything substantial when Maya's phone suddenly lit up on the table. "Oh, Iris is calling. I'll give you guys a second to hang out and catch up," she said.

Shit.

I should've known better than to think Theo would ever drop me off on campus without grilling me.

When Maya stood up from the table and headed out the front door, I turned back to Theo. "Did they coordinate that so we'd have time to catch up alone?"

Theo laughed. "Yeah, they did. She texted Iris a few minutes ago to give her a call."

I smiled. I'd known the single version of Theo longer than I'd known the version of her in a relationship, but this felt like the most organic version of her. She was so happy and looked so comfortable. It didn't feel fake at all, either, like they felt like they had to put on a show of being a happy couple. It was obvious that she and Maya genuinely respected and loved each other

Even though I'd always been of the opinion that dating and committing to someone—especially in college and heading into the pros—was a mistake, Theo was making me realize it worked with the right people. It was just weird to see the person I'd bonded with over our intense schedules and ambition being too big for a relationship actually settle down.

"So," Theo said, her palms out and ready like a mob boss waiting on an offer. "What the fuck is up, dude? Tell me everything."

"It's good." I avoided eye contact with her, staring at the silver napkin dispenser to my right instead of looking at her. "Basketball, girls, senior year."

"Yeah, I bet," Theo responded flatly. I knew what Theo sounded like when she was annoyed—it wasn't common, but it happened, usually related to people being too invested in her personal life—and it didn't sound like that. But I knew she wanted more out of me.

I fiddled with the empty straw wrapper I'd left on the table. I could see Theo eyeing it, desperate to throw it away, but she was doing a good job of resisting. "I don't know. Things are alright, I guess."

Theo's expression switched from unamused to concerned in half a second. "What the fuck is wrong with you?"

"What do you mean?" My tone was unintentionally defensive, and I immediately regretted it, but I didn't know how to stop it. The feeling in my chest was a solid wall, too strong to break through and impossible to climb. I wanted to just say it—admit to someone else that things were hard and they'd never been hard before and I didn't know what to do with that—but I hadn't said it out loud yet.

It was difficult, if not impossible, to say it, even to Theo. I'd never had a reason to bullshit her before—college had been generally good to me. I was living the fucking life. I really did have girls and basketball and parties and a future. Now, I wasn't so sure, and it was scary to have to admit that.

Except for girls. Some things I knew would never change.

Theo looked reasonably offended that I would even attempt to lie to her. "Dude, you've been *so* weird."

"It's, you know." I half-heartedly shrugged.

She nearly rolled her eyes. "You're treating me like I'm your mom who won't stop nagging you." She dropped her voice low, imitating the guys from the men's team we used to play pick-up games with. "*School was fine. Yeah. Cool. Can I go to my room now?*"

"I—" I scoff, waving my hand. The words were sitting on the tip of my tongue, desperate to come out.

"Not to pretend to know what I'm talking about, but I'm pretty sure the first step to feeling better is almost always just talking about it."

"Now you really sound like my mom."

Theo laughed. "Loretta is a really nice woman, don't make her out to be pushy."

I half-smiled, too distracted to find anything truly funny right now. My leg bounced under the table. I was never this nervous, ever. Even my parents said that I came out of the womb with confidence and undeniable charisma.

My stomach knotted. For the first time ever in my life, I was legitimately speechless. I didn't have the right words, and I was too scared to say the words that were coming to mind.

"I think I'm experiencing anxiety," I admitted, finally, the words coming out in one big rush.

She scoffed as if she'd been waiting for me to catch on. "You *think*? You sound like a man experiencing emotions for the first time."

"Like you've ever experienced anxiety in your life."

"I was an only child raised in a small town who did most of her socializing at basketball camps. I have *definitely* been anxious before."

"Yeah, but anxious about *playing*?" I asked.

There it was. I'd never been to therapy before, but I could only imagine that this was the feeling people got when they had a major revelation. Theo and I stared at each other for a second, neither of us following up. I wasn't sure I wanted to elaborate on my question; that felt like a can of worms I didn't want to open. It was too close to the truth, too vulnerable.

"Not yet, but that doesn't mean I'm immune," Theo finally said. "I'm worried I'm not good at basketball anymore," I finally blurted out.

So much for not wanting to go there.

It felt horrible to say out loud for a second, and then almost immediately, I felt better. Finally, the thought that I'd been keeping to myself and buried away as deeply as I could force it, was out. It wasn't my secret anymore. The nervousness that had burrowed deep into my stomach didn't go away completely, but it got a little less deep, and that was something.

Theo dabbed at her mouth with a napkin, clearly thinking. "It sounds like you could use a distraction to get you out of your head."

Despite the simplicity of her statement, it did—annoyingly—make me feel better. I appreciated that she knew me well enough to realize I didn't want sympathy or to hear *that I was a great basketball player*; I just needed someone to listen to what I was saying. I couldn't keep thinking it over and over and over again, staring at the ceiling and feeling like my future was slipping through my fingers.

"I don't know, man. I don't know what I need," I said. It was the most honest I'd been in what felt like months. "Actually, that's a lie. What I need is to stop being a fucking idiot on the court."

"It sounds counterintuitive, but I really think the easy solution to that is not thinking about basketball. Get out of the game a little bit. Remember that there's more to life than being good at a sport, and it's not the end of the world if you're not the best of the best. Taking off some of the pressure doesn't automatically mean you're going to suck. It'll probably make you better."

"I mean, I *guess*. But the whole thing in basketball is to literally shoot through it."

"Yeah, shoot through it when you're *playing*. But when you're not playing, you can't get yourself all knotted up. There's nothing to shoot through right at this very moment." Theo leaned onto the table, her weight on her elbows. "Look, you're naturally an excellent basketball player. You're a solid shooter, a solid playmaker. You're fast. Your overall records in college have been phenomenal so far—"

"Except for this pre-season. And tonight's game."

"Everyone goes through a slump. Literally. It's, like, impossible to play a sport without having a period of time where you're convinced you're the worst player who's ever been let onto a court."

"Oh, yeah? You went through a slump?"

Theo shrugged. "Just because I haven't doesn't mean I won't. And it's not like I haven't *lost* a game before. We literally lost during the championship last year." When Theo could tell I still wasn't convinced, she sighed. "I'm sure eventually it'll all catch up. I went into the big leagues riding high—I'd closed out an incredible college career, and I was the first round pick.

I basically went straight from playing with you to playing pro with no time to think about what a major change that was. The adjustment was hard, but I had the energy and motivation for it. That doesn't mean it'll always be there, though. The yips can come for anyone."

"That's depressing as fuck, man."

"It's just how things go. This game is half skill, half mental. You don't want to assume the worst will happen, but you want to prepare for it. Pretty much all of the greats, if not literally all of the greats, have had their off-seasons."

"But right before the draft? Being able to get this far and not keeping it together at the finish line is so *fucking* ridiculous," I said, shaking my head. Plain annoyance had slipped into my tone. I was anxious, but I was also, more than anything, pissed at myself. All of this felt entirely unavoidable. Sophomore year—even junior year—GJ would've never let this happen.

"This season *just* started. You're allowed to need a second to get your sea legs—especially because there's a huge amount of pressure on you. You're the captain of a team that has a reputation now. It sucks to lose, but coming off a winning season is arguably even harder than a losing one. People actually expect stuff of us—of *you*—that they haven't before. And you're at the forefront of that now."

"I'm not even. Anna has been taking over as the hotshot of the team."

"Anna is Anna. She plays well, but she plays differently from you. You both have your own strengths and weaknesses—that's literally the whole point of being on a team together. You're supposed to balance each other out. You know better than anyone that it's not about having the best individual team members on paper; it's about team chemistry."

Just thinking about the team made my stomach swirl. I'd always liked them, but this year it just felt *different*. I knew I was a bigger personality than Theo and a different kind of captain, and no one played like her; I just hadn't realized how obvious those differences would become when she left.

"Have you been talking to Dr. Liecht?"

"Yeah, you know me. Have her on speed dial."

"Maybe you should call her and set up a meeting," Theo suggested.

I was overwhelmed by the sudden urge to crawl out of my skin. Theo and I didn't talk about feelings. We talked about basketball, about girls, about what was next for us in our careers. But the team therapist was never included in those categories, and I'd assumed she probably never would be. "Did you ever talk to her?" I asked, the best deflection tactic I could think of. I already knew the answer.

Theo paused for a beat. "Okay, no, I didn't, but—"

"Exactly!"

"Yeah, whatever." Theo's lips turned up in an amused smile. "Just hear me out on this. I didn't, *but* I definitely should have.

We went from a no-name team at a no-name school to one of the most talked-about women's programs in the nation. I was about to graduate from college and hopefully go into the world of professional sports. You're about to do the same, but with the added pressure of knowing how far we made it last season. It's a lot to take on. *And* I might not have done it in college, but I do it now. The Blizzards signed me up for therapy to help with the transition. It *is* helpful, I promise."

I tossed my napkin onto my empty plate. I wasn't sure if encouragement from someone going to mandated therapy was what I needed. "Yeah, okay."

"What, you're anti-therapy? Can't handle talking about your feelings?" she asked, teasing me. "So big and tough on the court, but feeling shy now?"

I laughed. "Shut up. I'm not *not* anti-therapy, I'm just...anti-therapy for me. I don't want to get into all of that. And I already know what's wrong."

"A shooting slump is usually psychological." Her voice was a playful sing-song, but I could hear the intent behind it. She really meant it; she really wanted me to go.

"I'll consider," I said, which we both knew meant I was not going to talk to Dr. Leicht. I leaned back into my chair, ready for this conversation to be over. I was glad to have Theo back around, but I also wasn't prepared for this to be such a soul-bearing conversation.

Fortunately, Theo dropped it. "More importantly, are you going to be carrying on the tradition of finding love in your senior year? I wouldn't mind setting a precedent on that one."

I threw back my head, laughing so hard it got the attention of the table next to us. "Did you forget who you were talking to?"

Theo chuckled. "I'm just saying. Maybe it wouldn't be a bad thing. A hot girl cheering you on from the stands is a great motivator."

Leah, on the sidelines, literally cheering for me—or technically the whole team, but whatever—popped into my mind. I shook it away, unsure of what to make of it. Thinking about her once was annoying, but twice was uncalled for. Flashbacks to women were reserved for exclusively sex-based memories; I'd never given a fuck about them going to my games before.

It had to be because she was a cheerleader. That was it, the only reason. Just word association.

"Oh, trust me—I know. I have plenty of hot girls cheering me on already," I said, and Theo just rolled her eyes. "But no, absolutely nothing serious. *Never* anything serious."

"Don't speak too soon. Things have a way of catching up."

"Yeah, *right*. And anyway, I didn't meet a girl at some house party before the season started and develop a crush on her," I teased because that's exactly what happened with her and Maya. As the words came out of my mouth, Leah's face popped into my mind *again* and immediately stole my momentum. I brushed it off quickly, but I should've known better than to assume Theo would let that slide.

She sat up straight. "What just happened?" she asked and leaned toward me. "Did you meet someone?"

She looked just as surprised by my hesitation as I felt. "No," I said. And then I repeated the word more confidently, certain that it wasn't true. "No. Definitely not."

"Oh, yeah?" Theo asked, amused.

"No, it's..." I paused, thinking about how much I'd liked having Leah around. That entire night with her had been really good in a way that was new to me. I'd had all different types of hook-ups, flirted with all different types of women. There were times it went better than others, times when it wasn't obvious if the girl would be able to keep up with me and my personality or not. More often than not, they were nice or funny or a good time, but they weren't necessarily memorable.

Leah, however—for whatever reason—seemed to be.

Theo widened her eyes at how long it was taking me to answer what had always been a simple question for me. "I can't lie, I think I'm a little...scared?" Theo offered, half-joking. "Like, who are you and what have you done with the GJ I know? I wasn't expecting this to actually be a conversation. You've literally *never* hesitated before."

"I don't know what's wrong with me," I admitted, a little caught off guard. "Weird lapse in judgment. I'm chalking this up to a side-effect of absolutely sucking at basketball right now."

Theo snorted. "Can I ask who it is? Is it someone you hooked up with before?"

"No, she's…new," I said. It felt so strange to actually be talking about a girl; I hardly even recognized myself. I'd never felt even the tiniest bit interested in leaning into a crush or attempting to develop one. I didn't even know if I was really physically capable of having a crush in the way everyone talked about in movies. And being publicly down bad for a girl went against my whole *cool and casual* athlete thing, so I'd never worried about it.

"I don't even know what follow-up questions to ask you. You've never made it this far with anyone."

I laughed, but it came out more like a nervous chuckle. "Shut up."

"But seriously—who is it? Have we met? I'm assuming it's a girl who passes through The 151. Or did you snatch up a transfer student?" Theo's eyes widened. "Is it *Anna*?"

"Oh, absolutely the fuck not," I said, but that was the extent of my confidence.

I weighed my options. I could make someone up, say that it was just some girl Theo never crossed paths with. Or I could be honest with the *only* person I'd be able to be honest with about this.

"I'm only saying this because I'm hoping saying it out loud will make it stop," I said. "But do you remember Leah?"

Theo thought it over. Her eyes stayed locked on a spot on the wall across the restaurant. I could see it on her face when the lightbulb went off. "Mags's sister? No fucking way, dude—"

"Listen, *listen*—I know it was stupid."

"*Stupid?* That was, like, the single worst decision you could've made."

"I mean, she's hot and cool—"

"Yeah, and you've said yourself there are a lot of hot girls. You wanted to go after not only a cheerleader but your teammate's sister? And the one teammate who would literally kill you if she ever found out?"

"You act like no one on the Coyotes wants me anywhere near their sister."

"Fair point, but I mean, seriously, dude. That's..."

"She *is* a distraction."

"So this has happened multiple times?"

My mind flashed back to our night together. I could only assume a second round would be just as good as the first. "No, just the once."

"But you want it to happen again," Theo said, and when I didn't immediately answer, Theo groaned. "Oh my god. I graduate and leave you to your own devices, and *this* is what happens?"

"You can't really be that surprised. I have feelings! I'm not afraid of love! I just didn't think anyone here would offer what I want."

Her brows shot to her hairline. "Now you're talking about *love*? What happened to you?"

"Enough." I laughed.

"Sorry, it's just...definitely throwing me for a loop. I expected just about anyone else first. I think the only thing that could've been more surprising was someone on the team."

I grimaced. "I'm good off that. That feels borderline incestuous."

"Speaking of, are Mags and Gemma hooking up yet?"

I nearly slammed my hands onto the table in surprise. "What the *fuck* do you mean by that?"

Theo shook her head, immediately backtracking. "I'm not getting into it, I'm just curious."

"No, you're not getting out of this one. You can't just drop a bomb like that and then pretend it didn't happen."

Theo groaned, rolling her neck. "It's stupid. It's something Maya pointed out one time, and it's been kind of a running joke between us. I shouldn't have said anything."

"Your secret is safe with me, but I will be looking for signs of any fooling around." I thought through every Mags and Gemma interaction I'd ever witnessed. Everyone already knew they were basically the final bosses of codependency, so that wasn't anything new. They never dated other people. There weren't even really rumors about them hooking up with other people. It made a *lot* of sense. "Dude, Maya really might be onto something with that. I feel like a fucking idiot for not seeing it before. I didn't even realize Gemma was gay, but now that it's being said…"

"I doubt it's actually a thing. I'm sure some people thought we were in love, too," Theo joked.

"What's with the past tense? We literally are, dude. I'm in my masc for masc era. I've been harboring secret feelings for you for years, just waiting for the chance—"

Theo playfully tossed her crumpled up napkin at me. "Shut the fuck up. I'm so sick of you."

"Former teammates and roommates by chance, lovers by choice."

"Happy pride to us."

I threw back the rest of my drink. "How much longer is Maya giving us?"

"Until I text her again to tell her she can come back." I didn't have to ask to know that was entirely Maya's idea. Theo tapped her fingers on the table, thinking. "I'm sorry I haven't been able to be around much, by the way. It's a big year for you, and I knew that, I just got caught up in my own shit."

"You're the hot new thing in a professional women's sports league. I wouldn't expect you to be around like that."

"Yeah, I know. But still. I can't just abandon you because I'm busy. It's stupid."

I would never say it out loud to her, but it felt good to hear it. The pressure of the season was a lot, and it was hard to navigate it alone. This was my first year without Theo, and not only was she not on the team, but she was basically nowhere to be found. But I couldn't hold that against her—she had a life and was busy, too.

"I really miss you guys," I said, my throat tight. All of my feelings were betraying me at once. I'd never been the sentimental type—even when my sisters all moved out one by one to go off to college, I'd teased them about how glad I was they were leaving. I let myself cry once when they left and then kept it pushing.

It all felt so different now. I'd just been a kid then. But developing these grown-up relationships, these specific bonds that I learned to depend on only to have them disappear, made everything hurt. Theo went from being there every day to hardly being around at all. And even if it wasn't her choice, it was a big transition. I had no idea how I was going to handle this season without her.

"I know." Theo clapped a supportive hand to my back. "I've missed you, too, dude."

Despite her best efforts, hearing that didn't make me feel much better.

Chapter Six

Leah

I sipped on my iced coffee, taking in what would inevitably be the only moment of peace I'd have for the next few hours. On the sidewalk below me, students were rolling out in packs for day parties around campus. I was jealous; normally, that wasn't my scene—I preferred being drunk when the sun was down—but today, I would've done anything to be down there with them.

"What time do we have to leave to get there on time?" Mags asked, and I turned to look at her. She smoothed down her shirt, her always agreeable hair falling in an easy blowout. We both used to dye our hair, but I'd ended up giving up because, while Mags never seemed to have damaged hair despite bleaching the fuck out of it, I'd completely fried mine. After months of not bleaching and using a *lot* of hair masks, it finally felt healthy again. It'd been a big transition to go back to my natural shade, but I'd grown to like it, even though it'd been borne of necessity.

I turned back to the window, already annoyed, and she'd only been in the room for about thirty seconds. "10:22, like I said twenty minutes ago," I mumbled. This was about what I expected from Mags. She never knew where we were, what was going on. She was used to people giving her a structured schedule. Ever since we were little, it was always *Get on the bus to go here, Get in the car so we can drive to practice, Get dressed because we're going out to dinner tonight*. College was the first time either of us had any amount of control over our routines and schedules, but even then, D1 basketball didn't allow for much flexibility. Mags was still able to skirt around being an independent adult in a lot of ways, all of which were infuriating.

"I'm excited to see Mom and Dad. First trip down senior year." I could hear her rifling through her things, picking up her keys. It'd only taken her this long to remember that she needed them when she left the house. The number of times I'd had to run across campus to let her into our dorm over the years wasn't small. "Big deal."

"Yeah."

My tone conveyed possibly negative enthusiasm, but Mags was unaffected, as usual. She poured herself a cup of coffee and moved onto her phone. It was like she'd hear the words other people—or maybe it was just me—were saying, but wouldn't process anything else. She was physically incapable of reading the room.

I took two giant gulps to finish off my coffee and then put my mug in the dishwasher. Mags kept her eyes glued to her phone. Being this close to her confirmed my suspicion that she wasn't wearing makeup. My chest tightened with familiar annoyance and the same raging jealousy I'd experienced around her since we were children. There was the basketball star who could dress however she wanted, do whatever she wanted. And then there was me, the one who wasn't and the one who couldn't. Nobody at the county club gave a fuck how Mags looked, but they apparently gave a fuck about me. If I couldn't have high aspirations for my parents to brag about, I needed to at least be pretty.

"We should head out, we're going to be late," Mags said, glancing up at the clock on our microwave. It was 10:22 a.m., exactly the time I'd said we'd needed to leave. Even though she might as well have been agreeing with me, she had a way of making it sound like every idea was hers first.

"Okay," I said and headed to the front door for my shoes and purse, not even bothering to wait for her.

Every time my parents came to town, they stayed at the same hotel and ate at the same restaurants. They'd become honorary regulars, memorable between campus celebrity Mags going everywhere with us and all four of us towering over most people that we met.

"There they are," Mom said when she saw us walking toward her on the sidewalk. She was dressed impeccably as usual, in a dress that I recognized from a Southern California-based boutique we both loved, which fit perfectly on her body. She treated pilates like her full-time job, and it showed in how lean and firm her arms were. Her blonde hair—hers wasn't natural, either, but she'd been dying it so long it might as well be—looked freshly blown out from a salon; it wouldn't surprise me if she'd gotten it done somewhere locally this morning. When she leaned in to hug me, she gave me two polite taps on the back like I was an acquaintance she barely remembered the name of. She did the same thing to Mags, but I still couldn't help but feel like there was a little less love behind the hug I received.

"The campus is beautiful this time of year," Dad remarked. He looked just as expensive as Mom did, his dress pants and made-to-look-casual dress shirt tailored to him. His warm, dark blonde hair had gone fully gray when Mags and I were in middle school, but he'd always pulled it off well. Rather than aging him, it added a cool, relaxed, California-appropriate air.

"The leaves turned beautifully," Mom acknowledged with a curt nod. The intentional physical distance between my parents was noticeable. Mags and I exchanged a silent look. No matter how agitating I found Mags, my parents' dynamic was one thing we were always able to connect on.

"Hard to believe this is our last fall at Lakeside Green," Dad continued. My parents were experts at talking around each other, neither of them directly responding to each other, but also not completely ignoring each other. It was practically an art form. "Maybe our last fall in Colorado, too."

"Definitely our last fall in Colorado. I'm not playing for Cedar Creek," Mags said. The fact that she didn't want to play for Cedar Creek because Theo was there was such a given for our family that she didn't even need to say it out loud. She'd never been good at being a team player and would throw anyone under the bus for her own benefit, but Theo in particular really brought it out of her. Mags would never say it out loud to anyone—and probably hadn't even admitted to herself—how jealous she was of Theo and her career.

"Should we head inside?" I asked. The sooner we started our meal, the sooner it would be over, and that was what I was banking on right now.

Dad glanced at his watch. It was a new one from the last time I saw them. My ballpark guess was that it was about as much as one of my semesters here. "It is that time," he said and nodded.

The four of us walked inside. "Four under Moretti," Dad said in greeting to the hostess. The restaurant was busy, mostly with families. Even though Lakeside Green University wasn't exactly a small campus, I was always surprised by the number of parents I saw on a random weekend. People seemed to really love it here—they loved the peace and quiet, the cute main street, the tailgating, the views of the mountains. I didn't get it at all; I never had.

"Right this way," the hostess said. My sister was deep in a conversation with my mom about the first game of the season, and I spent the walk over trying to figure out if the hostess was in my psych class last year.

Our table was near a window, which was perfect because it gave me ample opportunity to zone out and people-watch. Meals with my family were an obligation, and usually just gave Mags the opportunity to brag about herself in person. I used to try to compete, but that stopped in my senior year of high school when I realized my parents truly only saw me as an extension of my sister. They made it clear when I was told I'd be going to Lakeside Green, no questions asked. Wherever she went, I'd go too—purely out of convenience.

Mags and I sat next to each other while my parents sat on the other side of the table. For as long as I'd been cognizant, their preference was to sit where they couldn't look at each other.

"I can't believe this is really your last year here. And the last season of you playing college basketball," Mom said, a hand to her heart. She pressed her lips together, doing a really good job of doing the *my baby is all grown up* face despite not being able to move it much due to Botox.

"I know." Mags let out a breath. "I'm looking forward to a change of pace, though. You know this was never my first pick of schools."

"I know. But look at you—and the legacy you're leaving behind. It's so wonderful."

"If I just hadn't gotten injured in high school," Mags lamented, and I nearly groaned, already bored with this story. I'd heard it too many times to possibly want to rehash it. It was all so classic—*star basketball player in consideration at some of the biggest basketball schools in the country gets hurt. She's good enough to be considered, but not good enough that they think they'll recover fully and be worth the risk. She does recover, but only one school has an offer left for her. Will she be able to go pro?*

Gag me.

I genuinely felt bad about her knee the first one-hundred times I heard about it, at least. But when the moral of her sob story began essentially boiling down to *everyone should feel bad because I'm not playing for a school like Point Brook* instead of *I'm just so lucky I'm able to play again at all*, I started tuning it out. Mags had never known how to keep herself humble for long.

"Maybe I could've ended up at a school I would've chosen for myself," I mumbled.

"What was that?" Mom asked, looking over at me. It was a genuine question—the restaurant was loud enough that we had to raise our voices above our normal volume to be heard.

"The specials look good," I said to her, gesturing to the menu.

Mom's expression told me she couldn't give less of a fuck. "I haven't looked."

I looked out over the restaurant for our waitress, hoping we could get out of here quickly. My parents liked to complain about the service no matter what, but my preference was that their complaints would be about how fast the service was today and how they felt like they were being kicked out of the restaurant. It'd mercifully happened before, and I wasn't above wanting it to happen again.

Eventually, our waitress arrived. I sat up straight in my seat, silently communicating to her how badly I needed her to come through for me right now.

"Hi, can I get you anything to drink?" she asked, her voice cheery. She looked out over us and paused. "What a beautiful family—special occasion?"

"Just celebrating another great game." Dad looked across the table, his eyes shining with pride. "She's on the women's basketball team."

The waitress pressed a strategic hand to her chest, her expression softening. She looked around the table, making eye contact with each of us. When her eyes met mine, I offered her a smile that I hoped made it look like I wasn't in physical pain. "Oh, that's wonderful."

I nodded along with the rest of my family, my parents thrilled with the praise. For a brief moment, my parents leaned toward each other. The only thing they could agree on—and the only thing that seemed to bring them together—was how much they love being praised for being the figureheads of a happy family.

"Can I get you guys started on anything?" the waitress asked, turning her head to look at me first for my order.

"Just water for me—"

Mom cut in before I could finish my order. "Let's do mimosas for the table." She turned to look at Mags, the only person who ever mattered. "It won't be an issue with your training schedule, right?"

"Oh, I don't know," I interrupted. As much as alcohol could make a brunch go by faster, it could also very, *very* quickly turn it into the kind of tense, uncomfortable meal that would make fans of the *Real Housewives* franchise happy. Mags and I haven't been of legal drinking age for a very long time, but we'd been of it long enough to recognize a pattern.

Or at least, I recognized it. Mags was probably oblivious as always.

"I insist. And we're paying for it," Mom said with a good-natured laugh, as if things would ever be any different. She didn't look at me, her smile directed at the waitress.

"Coming right up. I'll get waters for the table, as well," the waitress said, glancing over at me with a smile.

As she walked away, I focused my attention back on the menu and tuned out the small talk that was eventually just going to turn into the Mags Show. I was proud of my sister—genuinely—but every single conversation coming back to her basketball career was a little excessive.

After deciding what I wanted to order, I looked out the window at everyone wandering down Main Street. There were groups of girls out in their cutest fall attire, soaking up the warm sun. They carried boxes of food with them, having just wrapped up their brunches, giggly and tipsy. It made me miss my friends, desperate to be out somewhere with them instead of here.

It also, weirdly, made me think about GJ. Things with her had been so *fun*. I couldn't remember the last time I'd flirted with someone and actually laughed and had a good time. And the sex had been unbelievable, which was just an added bonus.

I'd stayed true to my word that things were casual, not once approaching her or going through her social media pages for clues about other girls she might be fooling around with. I was kind of impressed by my own self-control. It turned out it *was* true that I was capable of being cool so long as I knew what to expect.

But still, there were times before I fell asleep where I thought about her gentle voice and gentle hands and the way I felt so confident around her. I felt like the best version of myself. And maybe that was a one-time thing, but maybe it wasn't. I wasn't sure I wanted to take on the risk of finding out.

The drinks came out, and I sipped on my mimosa, my attention going between GJ and the conversation my parents were having with Mags.

When the waitress finally came over to get our food orders, I'd never been so relieved to see anyone. Depending on how long it took for the food to get out, I knew there wouldn't be much longer until we'd be able to leave. My parents never minded meeting us somewhere, but they were predictable in that they never stayed for more than a basketball game and a meal. As much as we disagreed, it was a relief that they never overstayed and never expected us to host them.

"Leah, what are your plans for after graduation? You've hardly given us updates," Mom asked, my name pulling my attention back toward the conversation. I blinked and realized I'd been staring at my still mostly full glass, completely zoned out.

"What?" I asked, coming back to reality. I had no idea what the segue had been to loop me into the conversation.

"Post-graduation plans. Have you put much thought into it?" Mom was an expert at mean girl speak, her tone just light enough that someone not used to it might not realize she was quietly being bitchy.

I inhaled, mulling over how I even wanted to start answering her question. Thinking about life after college made me want to break out in hives. It wasn't because I loved Lakeside Green, or even really college, for that matter—it was just impossible to imagine what my adult life was going to look like. School was easy and structured: join clubs, attend class, make friends, party. I knew exactly where to be and when. I knew who was going to be at a given party, knew that they would be reliably on campus and usually available, barring periods of being too obsessed with the crush of the moment to hang, or swamped with classwork.

Adulthood wasn't like that. Adulthood was people moving away, getting jobs, and finding partners to build long-term lives with. I couldn't predict a single thing that was going to happen next. I had to basically rebuild my entire life.

As much as I was itching to get out of Lakeside Green so I could be in a city of any kind, I was scared to leave, and I knew it.

"I'm not sure yet," I admitted.

Dad looked like he didn't know what to do with that information. It didn't help that he seemed to have come out of the womb knowing he wanted to work in fucking *wealth management* of all things. Or at least, that might as well have been the case with how he told the stories. I'd heard a couple of variations over the years when my parents got embarrassed about me not having any explicit goals. *Well, I always knew what I wanted to be. And Mags did, too. What about you?* "Anything standing out from your classes? Surely there's something of interest."

I kept my answer as noncommittal as possible. "There are a few options."

"I've always said you would do exceptionally well in law school," Mom offered. "You wouldn't be able to apply for next year, but there's time to prepare for the cycle after. Have you looked at those LSAT prep books I bought you?"

My lips turned up in a polite, closed-mouth smile. I respected my mom's various attempts at tempting me to follow in her footsteps, but law school felt like a last-ditch effort—the thing I would turn to when I really didn't know what else to do.

"I'll figure it out. There's still time."

"There isn't much. You're a few weeks away from Thanksgiving break and then the end of the first semester of your senior year. You can't wait forever," Dad offered. It was the exact opposite of what I needed him to say.

My chest tightened. "I'll be okay. Even Mags won't know where she's going until, like, April."

"That's different. That's the draft. I already know *what* I'm doing, I just don't know where," Mags said, entirely unhelpful as usual. It was obvious where she'd gotten that trait from.

It was so tempting to break character for just a second and say, *Can you please just have my back for once?* But I'd never been someone to cause a public scene. Or a scene in general, really. I'd mastered the art of leaving a conversation with some dignity, knowing from my country club-trained parents how to shut something down in a subtle way that never sounded rude.

"I'm considering options. A background in marketing can be applied pretty universally, so I'm fortunate."

"That's also code for a major that will never actually get you a job anywhere. Hopefully, some of the connections you've made out here will be able to get you in somewhere. Maybe that internship you had last year," Dad offered.

I thought back to the summer internship I'd held. I'd worked on some enrollment campaigns and encouraged students to apply to the school. Most of the work had felt empty because it was hard to sell a school that I didn't even want to attend. It wasn't a bad job. I was grateful my coworkers were amazing, and the work wasn't overwhelming; it just wasn't necessarily what I wanted to do forever.

The waitress returned along with another waitress to place our food on the table. We all smiled politely, and I tried my best not to show that I was about three seconds away from starting to cry.

"I can always talk to some people at whatever team I end up going to, too." Mags picked up her fork and knife to start eating like she didn't just say something straight out of my nightmares.

Mom's eyes widened with obvious excitement. Yet again, her favorite daughter was there to save the day. What else could possibly be expected? "That would be wonderful! You two could continue living with each other. It'll get you by for at least a few years and help you learn some new skills. Maybe do some LSAT prep in the meantime."

My fake smile pulled even tighter across my teeth. That would be what would happen—I'd end up taking a job with Mags' team, move wherever she went. And of course, my parents would love it. Yet again, Mags to the rescue. Yet again, the star of the family. Always looking out for me.

I tried to think of the most diplomatic, inoffensive answer I could muster. Inside, I was nearly bubbling over with rage. "I don't know. I might want to do something else."

"It's not like you have anything else going on," Mom said simply. The dig felt like someone thrusting a knife into my chest.

"I'm not even sure what you're doing here that's been beneficial for your future."

"I was the student body president," I argued, trying my best not to get defensive but failing miserably. The worst part of all was that my parents didn't even mean anything to be offensive—they were just making plainly stated observations. They had no idea how much their comments hurt me.

"For one school year," Dad said. "You opted out of doing it again this year. It's becoming a pattern, Leah. You show a lack of commitment."

It was so hard to resist asking them, *And why do you think it is that I keep changing up my extracurriculars? Could it be my unsupportive parents?* "I've been a cheerleader the entire time I've been at LSGU."

"With no aspirations or avenues to do it professionally, as far as we know." Mom waved a perfectly manicured hand. "Not like cheerleading is even a feasible pathway. It's a part-time job most of the time, even for professional sports teams. I'm glad it's been fun for you, and you've stuck to it, but it's not a career."

I swallowed down the rest of my mimosa, trying to think of how I could politely ask, *What the fuck is your problem?* as I stared out the window. Meanwhile, my parents had already gone off on a tangent about how thrilled they'd be to see us continue to live together and be employed by the same team.

I looked over at Mags for help, but as usual, I was expecting too much of her. She didn't even look like she felt bad or realized how shitty this all was.

My family began digging into their food, still chatting. It was a full conversation involving me, but it was like I wasn't even there.

"You only want us in the same place so that you'll feel like you don't have to take care of us," I finally spat out.

My parents both blinked at me. Even Mags looked taken aback.

"Pardon?" Mom asked.

I nearly brushed it off, but then I realized that this was just going to continue on. Mags essentially offering for me to continue following her and having my life hinge on her career was going to continue to come up. She'd opened a can of worms I'd have to deal with until at least graduation, if not until I landed my first job offer. And even then, I'd keep hearing things like *You know, you could always work for your sister's team.*

"I don't want to go everywhere Mags goes. We're not children," I said firmly. The liquid courage coursing through me was working overtime, but it didn't stop my shaking hands. I put my fork down, no longer interested in my eggs benedict. "I can find a job outside of her team and outside of her. And it's not like Mags can even promise she'll be on a team. It's not for her to decide."

Mags frowned, immediately on the defensive. "Hey, I'm more than capable of going pro."

"And we love taking care of you guys and seeing you. It just makes us feel better knowing that you two are in the same place, especially when you're so far from home," Dad said, immediately going into customer service mode. He was talking to me like I was one of his clients. "That's all."

I would've maybe believed it if my parents had been around at all while we were growing up. But the most involved they ever were in our lives while we lived with them was setting extremely structured schedules for us, and occasionally going to Mags's basketball games. They made it so there wasn't time to see them.

I went quiet, the energy to pick a fight expelled from my body. They had a way of making me feel so guilty for ever trying to stand up to myself, it was almost impressive.

"Eat your food," Mom said, nodding from across the table at my plate that was still almost full.

I looked at it and then shook my head. "I'm not hungry," I mumbled.

My mom didn't bother to fight with me on it—she just moved on, going back into a conversation with Mags.

I pulled out my phone, not even caring that I was breaking our strict no phones at the table rule, and texted Soph.

Leah

Are you out right now?

She started typing back a response almost immediately.

Soph

Of course I am. Walk to my location, we'll be here for a few more hours.

Leah

Perfect. Save me a drink.

Or twelve.

Soph

Rough brunch with the parents?

Leah

You have no idea. I'll see you soon.

Chapter Seven

GJ

I'd always hated being told what to do, but it was hard not to listen to Theo when she recommended something. Regardless of whether Theo was the one offering the advice or not, I knew I had to follow it. Even I wasn't too proud to do that—it'd just taken me some time to get there. And a few really shitty games. The Coyotes were holding on as one of the few undefeated teams, but I'd had consistently bad stats.

Admittedly, I was only out here doing this because it was a last resort. I was tired of still playing like garbage. But that was neither here nor there.

I dribbled the ball, the texture familiar under my fingertips. Playing felt like home; it always had, but it was tinged with something else now. I used to love an excuse to get out here and play a pickup game, but now, all I felt was a sense of dread.

I was the only person at the outdoor court. It made sense—it was early in the morning, and I was a decent walk off campus, tucked deep into a surrounding neighborhood. None of the families were awake yet, too early for even the buses to be doing pickup. Theo and I had found this place together and would come up with every possible excuse to get out here when we could. It was like we physically couldn't get enough time on a court. It'd always felt good to let loose—practice and games were intentionally structured and high-pressure. Playing out here felt like taking a deep breath comparatively.

Or at least, it used to. I hadn't been out here since the summer, when I would play with the other Coyotes who were still on campus.

I shivered as cold fall air blew over me. That was a bad sign—it meant that I hadn't been playing for long enough to start sweating.

The sun was comforting, and the sky was a bright cloudless blue, but even so, November in Colorado always hit like a kick to the chest. I was used to the cold at this point, but I preferred the heat. I'd always liked humidity, unforgiving sun. Part of the reason I gravitated toward basketball growing up was that it was an escape from how miserable and gray winter could be.

I took a deep breath. *Focus.*

My fingers were numb, and my cheeks stung as I looked up at the metal rim in front of me.

Maybe this was a waste of time. I knew why I was out here, but I didn't know why I was bothering with actually doing it. I could just wait until practice later or get all of my nervous energy out during weight training.

But no—the issue was *playing*. And running from it was only going to make it worse. I didn't need Dr. Leicht to know that was true.

I bounced the ball against the blacktop, my breath a visible puff of moisture in front of me.

I hadn't told any of the girls on the team I'd be out here this morning. Normally, we all liked to play together, even if it was just a one-on-one. But as much as I wanted to think this was stupid, Theo was right that I needed to get out of my head. And the easiest way of doing that was forcing myself to be alone with the game that I loved, even though I'd just spent weeks intentionally avoiding it. I didn't like it, but I knew I had to do it.

Don't think about it. Shoot the ball in three...two...one.

I tossed the ball up in an easy jump shot. It arched beautifully through the air and slipped through the rim effortlessly, exactly like it was supposed to. Exactly like I'd been training to do for the majority of my life.

It felt good, but it didn't shake the feeling that had settled in my stomach. Shooting out here all by myself was infinitely easier than shooting during a game. I had people trying to block my shot, the roar of a crowd, the pressure of having to think and move quickly. But even so, I found it hard to forgive myself for not making shots when I had the chance.

I chased the ball and shot it from where I was standing, not allowing myself the time to position myself or think about what I was doing. It was the closest I could get to imitating real game-play while I was alone. I had to give instinct an opportunity to take over.

I did it again and again and again, intentionally shooting in ways that would force me to run for the ball.

After taking a beat to rip my sweatshirt over my head and toss it to the side, I grabbed the ball from under my foot and bounced it a few more times. The only thing I liked about Colorado winters specifically was how the sun felt almost like summer sun—warm, comforting, familiar.

I tossed the ball up again, watching as it bounced on the rim and then went in. I kept going, making all of the shots smoothly and, most vitally, without being stuck in my fucking head.

It didn't make sense to me why game day had to feel different than just playing out here alone. I understood the basic psychology of it—there was pressure during a game, an audience, and other people intentionally doing everything they could to stop me. But that didn't mean it *had* to feel different. My brain was betraying me by making me feel that way.

As I practiced my shooting, I ran through the most recent game in my head. I'd always been shit when it came to school—mostly because I'd never given much of a fuck whether I had an A or a C as long as I passed—but my brain power kicked into overdrive when it came to basketball. I remembered every breath, every step. I knew where everyone was on the court at any point and could recall the game back with scary accuracy even weeks later.

To me, it was what it meant to be the point guard. I was the playmaker—my entire job was knowing how to move the ball down the court. In order to do that, I couldn't miss a single detail. All it took was me missing one person to give up a turnover and points in the process.

But remembering everything included remembering every single mistake. And while I could be a dick when I wanted to be when another player on my team did something stupid, I mostly fixated on my own missteps.

I ran through my own moves, trying to rewrite history in my own way. Now with the ability to think about things in retrospect, I played smarter. I didn't give balls up because I knew where the player guarding me was moving, and I didn't misstep and send a ball to someone too heavily guarded to catch it.

In this version of the game, Coach Darlene didn't take me out. In this one, Anna barely had a chance to play at all because I was doing so well.

After playing through a sped-up version of the game, I took a breather to drink some water and check my phone. The knot in my chest had loosened and, annoyingly, I did actually feel better. I pulled up my text chain with Theo and shot her a quick text.

To my surprise, Theo responded almost immediately. Since Theo didn't know how to take a day off, I must've caught her in between the things she had on her calendar for the day.

My cheeks went hot with embarrassment at remembering what I'd disclosed to Theo. Since I'd only had about half a beer at the point I told her about Leah, I had to chalk it up to sheer stupidity. I was just glad only Theo knew; if there was anyone who was impressively tight-lipped, it was her.

But anyone at all knowing felt so...vulnerable. Leah and I had hooked up *once*. I barely knew anything about her. It'd just been one fun, ridiculous night of flirting and having sex and then going our separate ways. And on top of that, there'd been time between us hooking up now. I'd gone to away games and seen her cheering on the sidelines, neither of us giving each other a look even in passing. But part of me knew that it meant something that I'd noticed us not noticing each other.

It was all so annoying. Weeks had passed, and I was not only still consistently playing like shit, but I couldn't seem to shake this one random girl.

It was like the more time passed between us, the more I found myself thinking about her. It'd just been one stupid night. But it'd gotten completely blown up in my head to be something special.

I couldn't believe I'd suddenly been turned into the kind of person who had a ridiculous crush with barely anything at all to work with. There were girls out there who'd been shooting their shot with me for *years* and had never gotten anything in return. And now, suddenly, *I* was the one with feelings? It didn't make any sense.

I rolled out my shoulders. It had to be connected to playing like shit somehow. It made sense—I was in a shooting slump for the first time ever in my life, and now I was down bad for some girl. Probably for validation or some shit. I was sure any therapist would back me up on that.

I was about to put my phone down when it vibrated again. Expecting it to be Theo, I went to my messages immediately. But my heart went into double time when I quickly realized that it was, in fact, not Theo texting me but instead a social media DM notification.

It was like she'd known I'd been thinking about her. After a few weeks of not talking to each other and not even looking at each other at games, Leah was suddenly messaging me out of the blue.

Leah

This is embarrassing but we never ex-changed numbers so this is the best I can come up with

I'm bored at a party and I want you to come get me

And then she sent a follow-up with her phone number. I smiled to myself at the messages. It was impossible to ignore that she seemed to have the same exact brand of bluntness that her sister did; it was just much more bearable, if not just extremely cute.

I copied her phone number over and texted her.

She didn't take her time responding.

I bit back a smile. She really had put me under some kind of spell. I didn't even recognize myself. Smiling at my phone because of a text message? I felt like Theo.

My phone vibrated again with Leah's location.

It wasn't difficult to find where Leah was. Once I was back on campus, I realized I knew the exact house she was partying at because I'd been there before. It was a huge honor to be considered one of the best houses on campus—an honor that came with some exclusivity—and it wasn't at all surprising that Leah and her friends would've been invited in.

It also helped that pretty much everyone on campus was headed to this same exact place. I followed along the sea of students dressed in various levels of winter-appropriate wear. Most people were depending on an alcohol blanket for warmth, which I appreciated. I stuck out as very clearly having just come from a workout.

When my Find My Friends circle was nearly on top of Leah's, and it was obvious she was in the backyard of the house I was standing in front of, I pressed the call button on my phone.

Leah answered after two rings. "Hello?" she raised her voice over the music that was pounding from the house.

"I'm here, out front," I said.

"Perfect." She hung up without warning.

She didn't give me enough time to get nervous about seeing her again or think about how stupid this might be. A minute later, she wandered out of the house and walked down the front yard to see me. The green maxi dress she was wearing fit her perfectly, but it didn't exactly seem like typical day drinking wear. We looked ridiculous together—the girl who was too dressed up for the setting, and the girl wearing basketball shorts. "Thank you for coming to my rescue." She took in my outfit. "Practice?"

"Just some shooting in the park."

Leah nodded with appreciation, her eyes tracing my exposed arms and the basketball against my hip. I'd worked up enough of a sweat walking over here that I wasn't cold yet. "Hot."

I smirked. "You look nice." And she did—if anything, she looked ridiculously beautiful. Her nose and cheeks were flushed pink, either from the cold or from drinking. The green of her dress brought up little bits of green in her brown eyes. The way the afternoon sun was catching her made her practically glow.

Leah looked down at her dress like she'd forgotten what she was wearing. "Oh, thanks. Brunch with the family."

"That's one way to kick off some day drinking."

"Also great inspiration to keep drinking into the late afternoon." She giggled to herself.

"Are you drunk?" I asked, laughing. The answer was obvious, but I had to tease her at least a little bit.

"Not anymore," Leah said and then thought it over. "I don't think I am. Maybe I still am."

I smiled. She was doing a decent job of playing sober, but the alcohol would definitely wear off in a few hours, and she'd realize she'd been drunk the entire time. I knew Leah was bold, but messaging me to retrieve her from a party was a big move. "Right."

"Can we go back to your place?" Leah asked.

I blinked at her. "Uh, yeah. If you want," I said. "I still need to shower since I wasn't planning on seeing anyone after being out."

"Just save it for after," she teased.

Even though the meaning behind her words was clear, and it sent a wave of desire through me, I knew we weren't going to get into any of that. I'd take her back to my place since she'd asked, but with the intention of getting her something to eat, some water, and probably some Ibuprofen since her hangover was going to be a bitch.

"You're sure you don't want to go home?" I asked. "Not that I don't love the company, I just want to check."

"I definitely do not want to go home. I don't want to be anywhere near my home or my family right now." Her tone was as serious as I'd ever heard it. Clearly, it had not been a good brunch.

I nodded, knowing this wasn't the time to ask follow-up questions. With a half-salute, I said, "Rodger that."

We walked in silence, Leah doing a poor job of walking in a straight line and bumping into me occasionally. I put an arm around her shoulders instinctively, doing what I could to keep her warm and keep her from accidentally stumbling into the street. She leaned into me, wrapping her arms around my waist. It felt so scarily organic that I didn't even recognize myself.

But I wasn't about to be the one who stopped us.

I kept Leah as close to me as she wanted to be throughout the walk back, the silence comfortable. I could tell she was deep in thought, but it felt intrusive to ask questions when it was obvious she wasn't ready to talk. She was drunk and most likely had gotten drunk because she was upset; she'd tell me if she wanted to tell me.

I keyed us into my apartment complex and opted for the elevator this time, noting that Leah's feet might not hurt in her heels now because of the alcohol, but definitely would later.

Despite this not being our first time going up to my apartment together, my heart was beating in my chest like it was. Seeing her during the day was *intimate*. I didn't do things like this. I'd made it a personal mission not to do things like this. I didn't date, I didn't pick up girls from parties, and I didn't plan on letting them crash in my bed. If she'd been anyone else, I probably would've found a polite but passive way to remind her we weren't dating and our time was strictly reserved for booty call hours.

But over and over again, Leah had ways of feeling different to me. Maybe it was just me being under the spell of undoubtedly the most confident, self-assured, beautiful woman I'd ever met in my life. Or maybe it was just her, that indescribable thing that people spent their lives trying to capture in movies and music.

After taking the elevator up to my floor and walking the hall, I pushed my apartment door open and gestured for Leah to lead the way. As she walked inside, I actually felt a little sweaty with nerves.

I rolled my eyes at myself. For the first time since Theo graduated, I was grateful she wasn't on campus because there was no way she was going to let this go—and also no way I was going to be able to pretend to be normal about it.

"It's so quiet here, it's so nice," Leah said. She kicked off her shoes and carefully placed them near my front door. I did my best to ignore how her dress fit against her ass as she bent down to move them.

"Honestly, it's kind of weird. I grew up with sisters who love to talk, and I lived with teammates last year. I don't think I've adjusted."

She walked deeper into the apartment and leaned against my kitchen counter. "I have the opposite thing. My house was always so...quiet growing up, but it was nice. The trouble always started when people started talking, so I love the quiet. But Mags can't shut up to save her life. And then Gemma is, like, literally always over."

"Are they a thing?" I asked as I kicked off my own shoes.

Leah's head shot up. "What?"

Unlike Theo, I'd never felt weird about gossiping or po-tentially airing people out. Especially when it came to Mags. She'd always done a good job of keeping her sexuality just vague enough that anyone could theoretically pine after her. My gay-dar had gone fucking nuts from the moment we met, so it wasn't so much a question of if Mags liked women—it was if she knew, and which women she liked.

"They're always together." I knew better than to rope Theo and Maya into this—no one needed to know they were the ones who started the theory. "I'm just curious. A little secret teammate action or whatever."

"As far as I know, they're not, but that would be hilarious. And it would make sense. They are obsessed with each other," Leah said. It wasn't serious enough to inquire about, but I did think it was interesting that Leah didn't seem to have much at all to contribute about Mags's dating life. It was kind of an impressive feat considering they were roommates and also sisters. I'd known probably way more than I should've about my sisters as they dated through high school and college.

I couldn't help but feel a little smug about how it suggested Mags probably didn't actually get laid as much as people seemed to believe online. Despite her reputation as being the hot influencer on the team and all of the rumors about how girls must literally chase her down on campus, she didn't seem to partake really at all. Even if Mags seemed to believe she was superior to all of us, at least I had game.

Leah sat down at the edge of my bed, leaning her weight back onto her hands. My eyes trailed her body, every cell in my body remembering in extensive detail the last time we'd been alone together here.

But no matter how much she wanted to, we couldn't. Not right now.

"Water?" I asked.

Leah's gaze wandered shamelessly over me, not looking anywhere near my face. "Sure."

I got her a cup of water and then grabbed the ibuprofen from the cabinet nearby. I brought the two things over to her, dropping the pills in her hand.

She looked up with surprise. "What are these?'

"An attempt at saving you from a nasty hangover."

Leah was quiet for a long beat—so long that it was starting to make me kind of nervous. "You don't have to take them, I just thought I'd offer."

"No, this was just..." Her expression softened, her eyes fixed on her palm. "This was really nice. Thank you."

I smiled, amused. "It's just some basic drug store meds. I'd consider that kind of the bare minimum."

"I get a lot of whatever would be less than the bare minimum," Leah admitted. She looked so plain-faced, so *sad* as she said it that I couldn't tell if it was a drunken confession she'd forget she said, or if it was just an honest acknowledgment.

Either way, it made my chest ache for her. Not from pity, but from knowing that she deserved better than that. It didn't require knowing her that well or for that long to see that.

Leah threw the pills back and then swallowed them down with water. The strap of her dress fell down her shoulder, and I reached out to move it back up, my fingers grazing over her skin. My mouth went dry, my hands still and steady—no matter how nervous I was, my hands never shook; if anything, I'd gotten used to performing well under pressure—but my heart rate skyrocketed.

Leah gazed up at me through her lashes. Her hazel eyes were warm, soft. I didn't know how long I was staring at her, but it felt simultaneously embarrassingly long and far too short.

"I'm going to shower," I said, because if I didn't leave the room, I'd probably explode from how badly I wanted her. "Do you want a shirt or anything? Sweatshirt? Might be more comfortable than your dress."

"You just want to see me in your shirt," Leah teased.

My lips lifted in a smile. "Maybe I have an ulterior motive."

"I'd love a shirt, thank you," she said softly.

I turned to my closet and pulled out a shirt from my overflowing and eternally expanding collection of Lakeside Green Coyotes merch. We got new shirts constantly, the school taking full advantage of any special event.

I pulled out whatever shirt was on top and handed it off to her. When she reached for the straps of her dress to drop it to the floor, I quickly turned around to give her privacy.

Leah giggled. "It's nothing you haven't seen before. You can look."

"I didn't want to make an assumption."

"When it comes to you, the answer will always be a yes."

Despite Leah's permission, I still didn't turn around. I kept my eyes locked on the wall in front of me, focusing on counting down from one-hundred instead of thinking about the perfect curves of Leah's body, the softness of her skin.

Or the fact that we were here, together and alone in my apartment.

It occurred to me then that I hadn't invited anyone else over in the time since Leah and I had hooked up. This was admittedly one of my longer drought periods for calling someone over, and I hadn't even noticed. My phone buzzed with options periodically, but I'd gotten in the habit of just brushing them off.

I cleared my throat. "I have makeup wipes, too, actually," I said, still not looking at Leah, and turned left to head into the bathroom.

"Oh, for all of the makeup that you wear?" Leah teased, her voice muffled by the wall.

My skin went hot. "It's..."

"It's okay, I get it," she said. "I also know exactly what this is. Your reputation goes pretty deep."

Her tone is teasing, but the slightest bit of shame still cuts through me. I'd never been worried before about my perception or the talk of the town. I *knew* what my reputation was—I'd heard earfuls of it from the girls themselves. And their friends. And my teammates. But realizing that Leah probably knew a lot of that made me feel exposed and nervous, desperate to explain myself to her.

I found a travel makeup wipe loose and still in its packaging in one of my bathroom drawers. I picked it up, but I took my time, hovering in the bathroom until Leah was ready.

A few seconds later, as if reading my mind, Leah said, "I'm modest now, I promise."

I walked back into the room and inhaled when my eyes landed on her. God, she was gorgeous. We were close in height, but my build was broader and more muscular than hers, so the shirt fell differently on her than on me. It brushed just over the top of her thighs, a devastatingly sexy look.

A beat too late, I handed her the makeup wipe. I did it from an arm's length away, like I was worried I'd scoop her up in my arms if I took even one step closer to her.

Leah walked over to the microwave to look at her reflection while she wiped her makeup off.

"You can use my bathroom," I offered. "You know, the room with an actual mirror in it."

"This works, too."

I smiled a little bit. "Striking me as kind of an expert at removing your makeup on the go. Maybe I'm not the only one with a reputation here."

She blushed and suddenly stopped what she was doing. She locked eyes with me through the reflection in the microwave. "Have you heard anything?"

"No, no," I said and retreated quickly. "Sorry, it was just...sorry. Based on how you'd talked to me at the last party about the person you'd been seeing or whatever."

With how she'd teased me, I didn't think fooling around with other people was a sensitive spot. While I admittedly hated the thought of Leah fooling around with anyone else and just the thought filled my chest with seething, burning jealousy, I also knew I didn't own her. It was an unfair standard to expect that after I'd torn my way through most of the lesbian population at school, I'd expect Leah to suddenly drop everything and only want me just because I suddenly only had eyes for her.

"Oh god." Leah groaned, rolling her eyes. She turned back to me, her face now bare. It was my first time ever—in all of the years Leah had been around, all of the times we'd passed each other at parties—seeing her so stripped down. This somehow felt even more vulnerable than seeing her naked. I couldn't stop staring at her, taking in every detail of her face. At risk of sounding corny, I couldn't believe how beautiful she was without makeup.

It took me a second to even remember what we'd been talking about before. "Still being terrorized by your former lover?"

Leah paused. "No, actually."

I didn't ask her to elaborate—even if I was trying to play it cool with Leah, I wasn't so cool that I could hear details of her having a crush on someone else—and instead held out my hand for the used makeup wipe so I could throw it away.

Leah sat down on my bed again, this time with way less intention. Instead of posing for me and offering seductive, through-her-lashes looks at me, she was moving with seemingly no thought at all about me being there. I liked that she seemed so much more at ease.

I walked over to her, gently brushing a loose strand of hair behind her ear. She closed her eyes, leaning into my touch.

"Thanks for being so nice," she said. "You didn't have to come and get me. I think I'm going to be really embarrassed by pretty much all of this in, like, two to three hours."

My lips turned up in a smile. "You don't have to be embarrassed. I want you here. I don't mind."

Leah dropped her gaze, her lips twisted up like she was fighting off a smile. I wanted to kiss her so badly—every cell in my body was telling me to do—but I couldn't. If I kissed her now, I'd never leave the room. And as much as Leah didn't seem to mind my post-workout sweat, I wasn't so sure she'd appreciate it in such close proximity.

"I'm going to shower," I said, forcing the words out of my mouth even though I really didn't want to have to go. Everything with her felt so easy, so fun. This was only our second time being left alone here, and I could tell I was getting addicted to the thrill. I understood now why people completely fell off the face of the earth when they had a crush.

"Stay here with me. I like your sweat."

I laughed. "You can smell it whenever you want. I've just been itching to shower since I left the court."

Leah mock pouted at me, but then eased herself into bed, laying her head down on the pillow like her body had suddenly decided it was exhausted as easily as flipping a switch.

"Come back to me when you're done."

I smiled. "Yes, ma'am."

After taking a long, *stop daydreaming about Leah* shower, I toweled off and pulled on my fresh pair of clothes. In my bed, Leah was peacefully asleep, now curled up under my sheets.

She looked so sweet that it was tempting to take a picture. I'd never really liked sharing my space with other people, especially when it came to sleepovers with flings, but a sleepover suddenly sounded like the most appealing thing in the world if I got to wake up to her in the morning.

"Stop staring and come lay with me," Leah mumbled. She half opened her eyes and patted the empty spot next to her in the bed. "I could feel you looking at me."

She made space for me as I slid into bed next to her. She wasted no time resting her head on my chest.

"Hard to be sneaky when you're over six feet tall."

"People over six feet tall will always find some excuse to bring it up," she teased sleepily.

"As if you've ever been with someone before who's been tall enough that you can wear heels," I teased back. I trailed my fingers through the ends of her hair, letting my touch just barely brush over her back. The weight of her head on my chest was comforting. Rather than feeling suffocated and checking the clock, I wondered if I could come up with some kind of excuse to keep her here for a few more hours at least.

"I'm only a few inches shorter than you. For that to happen, you'd need to be closer to 6'3.""

I blinked. "How tall are your heels usually?"

"The ones I was wearing today were nothing. You forget I have pageant training; I've never been scared of a few inches."

I snorted. "I have so many comments I want to make, but I'm resisting."

Leah laughed, her body vibrating against mine as she did. The sound was starting to become my favorite hit of dopamine—right up there with game-winning shots, and every time we beat the men's team in a practice game.

After a few beats of silence, I guessed she'd fallen back asleep. I tried to get a glimpse at her face, but she'd tucked it away, burrowing into my shirt. I took out my phone and watched recent men's basketball highlights with my phone silent, my free hand making small circles over Leah's back.

After falling asleep, Leah didn't move at all for an impressively long time. I held my hand out in front of her nose to make sure she was still breathing. When I felt her soft, warm exhale against my palm, I went back to my basketball highlights, smiling to myself.

I didn't know how much time had passed when she finally opened her eyes again. The room was dark now that the sun had pretty much completely gone down, but that was the only indication that time had passed.

She woke up slowly at first and then suddenly shot up in bed. She winced and put a hand to her head.

"Oh my god, I feel awful," she moaned. She turned and looked at me and then blinked, like she couldn't believe I was actually there. Her hands went to her hair, smoothing it down. I reached out and pushed some strands gently behind her ear.

"I'm..." she blushed, her hair falling over her face. "I can leave. I'm so sorry."

"Leah."

Leah looked around, taking in my apartment. "I'm so mortified. Did I *call* you?"

"*Leah*," I said, and she turned to look at me. "Lay down. It's okay. You texted me, but I answered because I wanted to see you."

She looked at me like I'd just given her a riddle. Her eyes danced across my face, her posture poised to still get out of bed.

"I'm not testing you. Come on, lay down. I want you here."

It took a few breaths for Leah to finally even relax her shoulders. I patted my chest playfully. "Come back."

She bit back a smile. "Okay."

Leah wrapped her warm body around me, her long legs tangled in mine. She laid her head over my chest with uncertainty at first, but then eased into position pretty quickly. "I feel like I was asleep for days."

I chuckled. "Not days but definitely hours."

"I'm never drinking like that again," she said, her body now fully relaxed against mine. I could only assume whoever she'd been dating before had not exactly been the accommodating type since it'd taken her so long to believe me. But I liked that she was open to it now, open to me. Nothing ever felt like a fight or a game with Leah. I'd been caught in so many weird cycles—girls who tried to play hard to get, girls who didn't put up a fight at all, girls who wanted me but mostly just wanted the idea of me. Everything was somehow casual but exhausting.

Leah wasn't, though. Leah felt simple, straightforward. Someone who knew what she wanted and knew how to go after it. It was hot.

"Alcohol will do that, unfortunately," I said and put my phone down.

She moved off my chest and laid on the pillow next to me. I turned over so we could look at each other.

"Am I allowed to admit that I was drunk now with no judgment?"

I laughed. "I could already guess, but it's fine."

"It'd been a long morning."

"We've all been there," I said. Even though drinking wasn't the first thing I gravitated toward when I was having a bad day, I understood the feeling. I was hardest on myself when it came to basketball, so my punishment was usually pushing myself too hard at the gym, working out for too long on the court. I'd go until my body hurt, until I threw up. Whatever made me feel better in the moment. But similarly to alcohol, it usually wouldn't actually fix anything or make me feel any better.

Her eyes danced over my face. "Thanks for coming to get me. You didn't have to do that."

"Of course I did. A beautiful woman asked me to do her the honor of walking her home. I'm not saying no."

"My knight in shining armor."

"Twice now, not that I'm counting."

Leah smiled. "Just so big and strong," she teased, dropping her voice into a tone that was, fortunately *and* unfortunately for me, incredibly sexy. If I had a dick, that was about all that would've been required to get me hard.

"You joke, but I am. Got the evidence to prove it and every-thing."

"I'm not sure I believe you."

I smirked, knowing a setup when I saw one. She'd seen me play basketball too many times not to know. But I wasn't about to deny her the opportunity to see my arms again.

I propped myself up with my left arm and flexed my right bicep for her.

Her playful demeanor dropped in an instant, her cheeks flushing. She recovered quickly in the face, but I could tell the move had worked on her.

Leah exhaled. "Oh, fuck," she said under her breath. She traced her fingers over my arm and then gripped it. Her hand couldn't even wrap all the way around. "I can't believe you just have these."

I threw my head back with laughter. "I'd sure hope I have them considering how much time I spend working out."

"Not to state the obvious, but this is so hot," she said, her fingers still trailing over my muscles. "You could throw me around with these." Her eyes lit up. "You could probably lift me."

"Think so?" I teased.

Leah nodded, redirecting her eyes from my arms to my face. "Mhm," she said and repositioned her legs so one was draped over my torso.

My eyes wandered over her body, taking in the way my t-shirt hung off her frame and how I could see the fabric of her thong stretched against her hip bone.

The air in the room changed, mutual hunger growing between us. Leah bent her knee toward the ceiling to give me a better look at what was under the shirt she was wearing, tempting me to move closer. I put my hand on her thigh and then moved it down her leg, relishing in her soft skin.

She moved the shirt up higher on her torso, fully revealing her underwear and the smooth expanse of her stomach.

My mouth nearly started watering looking at her. I was too deep in it now to bother asking if this was a good idea. I didn't care; I needed her.

I repositioned on the bed, propping myself up between her legs. She locked eyes with me, silently begging.

Smiling, I pressed my lips to her lower leg and moved back up toward her thigh. As I inched closer to the space between her legs, I trailed with my tongue instead. She arched her back in response and moved herself closer to me on the bed. She moaned, her voice breathy as she gripped the sheets.

I could feel and taste how wet she already was. "Did you miss this?" I asked as I wrapped my arms around her legs to hold her in place. I just barely brushed the fabric covering her with my lips, but it was enough to make her inhale sharply.

"Yes." She rocked her hips as she tried to spread her legs out further for me.

I moved back up, pressing my body to hers. I kept my weight between her legs. "You're doing that thing again," I whispered and took her ear gently between my teeth. "We don't have to rush. Let me take my time with you."

"I don't know how to be patient with you."

Fuck. She made it impossible for me to wait, too, even though I wanted to. But just because Leah had demonstrated she had unbelievable stamina—we'd gone for so many rounds last time, I was surprised she didn't complain about being sore—didn't mean I didn't plan to drag those rounds out for as long as I could. I wasn't ready for her to leave yet.

"Take a deep breath for me," I said, my voice low. "Unless you want this to be quick and dirty. I can do that, too."

Leah shook her head. "I never want to leave this bed."

I kissed the material of her thong sitting at her pubic bone and slipped my thumb underneath the string at her right hip. "Good answer."

I moved her underwear to the side and dipped my head between her thighs. I kissed her slit, just teasing her at first with varied pressure. When her breath changed into something deeper and needier, I used my tongue to go between her lips. I trailed her opening until I reached her clit.

Her wetness covered my chin and lips. She was fucking delicious, a sexy, moaning mess at my touch. I ran my tongue over her clit, listening to her breaths get shorter and feeling her desperately clinging to my hair, the sheets, my shoulders.

I could feel her orgasm as she cried out, louder than I'd heard her before. Our first time having sex had been undeniably incredible, but this was something else entirely. There was still so much to learn about her, but I knew her body better now. That knowledge was proven useful in getting her to finish even harder than last time.

I slowed down, gauging Leah's interest in another round. When she squeezed her thighs to my face and didn't let up, I knew I could keep going.

I stripped her underwear away easily and sat up, pulling her legs to either side of me. She looked up at me, her cheeks flushed. She was panting, her chest rising and falling. I cupped one of her breasts with my hands, running my thumb over her nipple.

She bit her lip, moving her hand down her stomach to go toward her clit. I stopped her and pinned her arm over her head.

"Needy girl," I said as I leaned over her.

"I am." She tilted her chin up, and I nipped at her neck, careful not to leave any marks behind. When I trailed my tongue from the base of her neck to her ear, she moaned desperately and dug her short fingers into my back.

Her back arched as I swirled my tongue around her ear. "Oh my god."

I brushed my hand down her stomach, just barely grazing her skin. She spread her legs further apart for me in the process. She was soaking wet and impossibly sexy as she looked up at me with hunger in her eyes.

I teased the lips of her pussy apart and then slowly eased a finger inside. Leah gasped and gripped the sheets.

"GJ," she said, my name only a whisper.

"How's that?" I asked, increasing the speed of my fingers just slightly. I kept her arm still pinned above her head, her wrist flat against the mattress. I moved effortlessly in and out of her with my other hand.

"Mhm." She nodded, her eyes tightly closed. "*More.*"

I obliged, sliding in another finger and then increasing my speed even more. Wetness pooled over my hands, telling me I was finding the right spot.

Leah's breaths became quicker and more uneven. I deepened my fingers, and she gasped, moving her body against my hand to get me to go even harder. Her breasts moved with her body, her nipples hard.

I ducked my head to kiss her neck again, using the weight of my body to thrust deeper into her. We found a rhythm quickly from there, Leah's moans and whimpers becoming increasingly urgent. I bit my lip, almost shamefully turned on by her. The noises she was making, the way her body moved—everything was the hottest thing I'd ever witnessed.

She gripped harder onto the sheets as her body tightened around my fingers. Her moans became breathy and distant, and then it all came crashing down as she shuddered through her orgasm.

I slipped my fingers slowly out of her, her legs shaking as I did. I moved my hand to her mouth, and she sucked on my fingers, her eyes locked on mine. I was certain just the sight of her doing that alone was enough to make me finish.

When I moved my hand away, she closed her eyes, looking like the dictionary definition of relaxed. She might as well have just gone to a spa.

I gently brushed my thumb against her cheek and kissed her temple. As soon as I did it, embarrassment swept over me.

Leah didn't react to it, and I couldn't tell if that was a good thing or a bad thing. I was mostly grateful she wasn't acknowledging how intimate of a move that was.

"Oh my god," she finally whispered. She opened her eyes again and looked up at me, her pale cheeks flushed. "That was amazing."

I smirked. "Happy to be of service."

I laid down next to her and kept my arms open to silently invite her to lay on my chest. She laid nearby, hovering like she didn't want to get too close.

"Come here," I said, and Leah obliged, resting her head on my chest and then quickly melting the rest of her body into me.

We laid like that for what felt like hours, and I still found myself not wanting it to end. For the first time since this absolutely cursed semester started, I felt like I was able to take a deep breath.

The spell was only broken when I heard the sound of a phone vibrating. I opened my eyes and looked for the source of the sound. Across the room, Leah's phone was lighting up like crazy. It buzzed once and then fifteen times consecutively after that.

I nodded my head to my kitchen counter, where it was sitting. "Do you need to answer that? Seems important."

Leah groaned, throwing her arm dramatically over her eyes. "No, don't make me."

I chuckled. "I'm not making you, I'm just asking. I have no complaints about you brushing off whoever so desperately wants to get in touch with you. All the better if it's an ex or a fling you're choosing over me—"

Leah shut me up by gently placing a finger to my lips. I opened my mouth and playfully took her pointer finger between my teeth, making Leah laugh. "It's just my parents."

"Oh, the Morettis. Of course."

Leah scowled. "Yeah, the Morettis," she said and rolled onto her back. "I'm sure it's a bunch of texts about how they're about to leave for the airport and wish I'd respond to them before they fly out of town. It's always something with them."

I didn't know that much about the Moretti family dynamic. Their parents came to games sometimes, but they kept to themselves, and I'd never spoken to them. That wasn't totally unusual; some of the parents were chattier and more familiar with the team than others. But they had a certain kind of removed coldness that made me think they were like that at home, too, and not just at the games.

Still, it was hard for me to relate. I couldn't imagine straight-up ignoring my family's text messages after they'd just come to visit. Then again, I was just fortunate that my family hadn't done anything to warrant that kind of response.

"You think I'm a bitch, don't you?" Leah asked, glancing over at me. For just a moment, the confident demeanor faded, and she looked legitimately nervous about what I was going to say.

"What do you mean?"

"Your face. It totally changed when I said it was my parents," she said. "It's okay. I feel like kind of a bitch for doing it, too."

"I have a great poker face—"

Leah laughed harder than I'd heard her, making her nose wrinkle. The mental image of seeing her like that—the sheet pulled up over her chest, her hair falling over my pillow, her mouth open in a laugh—was immediately frozen in my memory. "Your poker face is *terrible*."

I was still so charmed by her laugh that I couldn't defend myself properly. "That's not true at all," I lightly argued, laughing as I said it.

"You can hide it during games, but you're, like, the most expressive person I've ever met off the court. I saw your face change *immediately*."

My jaw went slack. "There's no way."

"Yeah, I'll point it out to you the next time I see you out somewhere. It probably won't take long," Leah challenged, her eyes traveling from my eyes to my lips in the process.

"Oh, yeah? Planning on seeing me around?"

"Don't flatter yourself, I'm going to see you everywhere whether I want to or not."

I put my hand to my chest. "Ouch," I joked.

Leah's phone buzzed again and then again, and then started ringing.

We both looked over that way, and Leah moved the sheet higher up on her body until she was hiding underneath it.

"You're absolutely sure you don't want to check it?"

"If you saw how brunch with them went earlier, you'd understand," she said, her voice muffled by my bedding.

"It couldn't have possibly been that bad. You could just talk to them, ease the tension a little. It'll only feel worse the longer you drag it out," I said. When Leah didn't respond, I caressed her hair, the only part of her that was still exposed. "Look, I love conflict more than anyone and will hold a grudge for years, but they clearly want to talk to you. It might be worth seeing what they have to say before deciding you're not going to engage at all."

Leah moved the sheet down from her face so I could at least see her eyes. They were the most incredible shade of hazel I'd ever seen—deep brown with shades of green, flecks of yellow. I didn't hate having an excuse to look at them this closely. "I snapped at them."

"What do you mean?"

She sighed. "They were talking about how I was going to, like, follow Mags to work for whatever professional team she goes to play for—"

"Hilarious to assume Mags is absolutely going to be drafted, by the way, but whatever," I said, making Leah snort. We both knew she probably was, but I couldn't miss an opportunity to rag on her sister, especially for Leah's benefit.

"Like I was saying," Leah said and moved so I could finally see her full face again, a smile at her lips already. "Mags offered that as an option, and my parents were *thrilled* because they love being able to force me to follow Mags somewhere. I think if we could be roommates forever, they'd literally make us do it."

"I guess there's nothing that's stopping you. Your future partners might have some thoughts on that, though." I brushed off the jealous buzz in my chest at the thought of that being someone who wasn't me.

"*I'll* have some thoughts on that." Leah looked off to the wall across the room from us. "But yeah, I got really upset with them about it and for the first time literally ever in my life I actually stood up for myself."

"What did you say? Like, *fuck you* level of bad?"

"Basically just telling them they've never actually cared that much about us and they like having us in the same place because it makes their lives easier," I said. "Which is true, by the way. I've been my sister's shadow for forever. My entire schedule growing up was based around hers. And I only ended up at Lakeside Green because my parents said they wouldn't help with school if I didn't go where she went."

"Wait, seriously?"

"I mean, I don't know if they'd actually follow through on a threat like that because I've never made them do it before. But that's what they said. And I hate disappointing them, so I just rolled with it."

I took in what she was saying, nodding as I thought it over. It was glaringly obvious now how different our upbringings were. No wonder she was willing to brush off their texts. "Damn."

"Yeah. Only took me twenty-one years to finally say something to them. I probably should've played it smarter and waited until *after* I graduated from college and could be financially independent, but I don't know. Something took over me today.

I think it was hearing them yet again steamroll me and any type of independence I want to have away from my sister."

"I don't think that's unreasonable. There was probably a nicer way of saying what you said, but I also don't think it was totally out of line," I said, even though I would never in a million years speak that way to my parents. They'd hand my ass back to me without hesitation. My sisters, too.

Leah twisted her lips in thought. "You don't have to be nice to me about it," she responded sheepishly. "I regretted it immediately. I know it was stupid."

"I don't know. Maybe it's a good thing you learn how to speak up for yourself, or it sounds like you have an entire lifetime ahead of you of your parents telling you where to live, what to do."

"That sounds like them." Leah looked at me and then looked away again, quiet for a beat. "I think the part that hurt the most was that my sister was the one who basically threw me to the wolves again. I don't know if she's just oblivious or what, but she always puts herself in the middle in the worst way. And my parents *love* her. She's the golden child. If she said anything at all about not wanting me to follow her, they'd actually probably take it seriously. But instead, she's always, like, playing hero or something. It's fucking annoying."

I paused. "I want to offer you something insightful in response, but I'm still stuck on Mags being the favorite of your family."

Leah shrugged. "My parents just want to be able to brag at the country club about something, and she's the one who gives them an easy opportunity to. Everyone loves an athlete who's actually good."

"Let me in the ring. I'll let your parents know where she actually falls in the grand scheme of college women's basketball right now," I said lightly and then made myself get serious again for Leah's benefit. I wasn't dumb enough to fuck around during a conversation like this. "They really make you follow her around like that?"

"Yeah. They treat it like we're one entity. It's like they wanted to have one kid but ended up with twins, so they just decided they'd only actually parent one child."

I didn't have anything of substance to contribute. My first and only thought was *that sucks,* but I knew better than to say that.

I thought about what my life would've been like if I'd had to follow my sisters. Ada, Bev, and Vivian all followed pretty similar trajectories that were so different from my own. They'd all dabbled in some kind of physical activity at one point or another, but they'd always gravitated toward dance classes and never at a competitive level. They didn't understand team sports, and they definitely didn't understand that I'd known I'd wanted to be a basketball player since I learned what the sport was.

I couldn't imagine having to follow them wherever they went. They'd all stayed close to home, so I never would've ended up here. I probably never would've played basketball seriously enough to be a D1 athlete on the way to being drafted. I never would've actually known who I was.

"I'm really sorry," I said and then stopped. "Sorry, I actually don't know if that's helpful to hear."

"No, it honestly...kind of is," Leah admitted. "No one in my family has apologized to me for basically taking away any opportunity at autonomy I could've had. And I don't really talk about it with anyone except friends sometimes, so I've never given my family the chance to apologize or sympathize or, like, make it better." She bit her lip. "I know I have to take some responsibility. I could've put up a fight at any point, but I just don't have that kind of personality."

"Maybe you're gaining that now, considering you finally stood up for yourself today," I said and shrugged. "It's not too late."

Leah nodded, thinking the words over. "You're right, it's not," she said softly. "I've never really thought about it like that before."

I held my hands out in a confident shrug. "Here to help," I said smugly, and Leah laughed.

She half-winced. "Do you think I should check and see what my parents had to say?"

"You can't avoid them forever."

"Fair enough." She started sliding out from the bed, maneuvering over me in the process. As she was about to put her feet on the ground, she turned to look at me. "Thank you."

Her expression was so earnest, so vulnerable, that it made me want to help her for the rest of my life. Anything she ever needed, I'd do. Anytime she was scared or hurt or even just mildly inconvenienced, I wanted to be there to make it better.

It took everything in me to not lean in and kiss her.

Leah got up from the bed, body on full display with absolutely no shame. I took in the shape of her lean but strong build, the way her ass moved as she walked.

God, her confidence was so sexy.

She hesitated as she reached for her phone, but eventually picked it up. As she looked at the screen, her expression became visibly nervous. "I think I might need to go."

I was surprised by how disappointed I was. I fought off an instinct to come up with excuses for her to stay. "Oh, okay. For sure."

Leah started picking up her clothes from the ground and pulling them. "Thanks for...everything," she said, gesturing broadly to the bed I was still sitting in.

"Yeah, for sure," I said, and it took everything in me not to get up to kiss her, walk her to the door, and ask her if she was sure she had to go.

But this was casual, and I wasn't going to be the one who fucked that up—even if I really, *really* wanted to.

Chapter Eight
Leah

In their truest form, my parents hadn't intentionally blown up my phone with calls and texts. There was no frantic urgency, no yelling. The family group chat was active with my parents chatting with Mags, talking about what a lovely weekend it was and how nice it was to be back out for one of Mags's games. Mags had been the one who called, followed by texts that said *Can you please just respond to them?*

But every message from my parents was laced with a passive-aggressive overtone about how great it was to see both of us and that they hoped they could say goodbye before their flight took off. None of it made me feel particularly motivated to offer an olive branch, even though holding a grudge against my parents was categorically my worst nightmare.

Knowing that they were mad at me made me want to break out in hives—I realistically probably would. I'd never handled anxiety well, but I was also just as mad at them in return. And for once, I wanted to be allowed to be mad at them. Really, actually mad at them. Not in a quiet way, not in a *silently fuming in my bedroom* kind of way. Actively, directly mad at them.

My post-sex glow didn't stand a chance against the rage that had taken up a home in my chest.

Only adding fuel to the fire was consistently being proven right. This was *exactly* why living with my sister was a bad idea and why I hadn't wanted to do it. Even with my parents states away from me, I couldn't actually escape them. I'd gotten myself the only roommate in the world who could effectively guilt-trip me in person *and* in the family group chat.

I took a deep breath as I went up to my apartment and unlocked the door. An NBA game was loudly playing on the TV, telling me that Mags was home.

I hung up my purse on the hook near the door and placed my keys on the rack. To signify that I wasn't happy, I did the best thing I could think of, which was pathetically kicking off my shoes in a way that I hoped sounded agitated to Mags's ear.

As I rounded the corner from the entryway hallway into our open-plan living area, Mags turned to look at me. She leaned against the counter, watching the game on the living room TV from the kitchen.

"Dude, Mom and Dad are pissed at you," Mags said, her mouth full of the yogurt parfait she was eating.

Even though I knew that, Mags saying those words stirred up the worst kind of feeling—fear. I hated disappointing my parents, hated knowing that they were upset. I'd dedicated basically my entire life to being a people pleaser to every single person I ever met. My parents were very high on my list—next to teachers and bosses—of people I didn't want to ever upset if I could help it. My sister was the only exception, which went without saying.

But swirled in with the fear was a completely new and different feeling I wasn't sure I'd experienced before. I thought back to everything GJ had said to me earlier. Even if she didn't completely understand because her family wasn't a fucked up mess like mine, it was obvious she agreed that I was allowed to be upset. Having that confirmation was weirdly validating, like maybe it was actually okay for me to be scared but also be angry.

"I don't really care," I said. I didn't sound at all confident, but I hoped that I would believe it more as time went on.

"You might want to. I know they've never had to, but they strike me as the kind of people to follow through on promises about not paying for school or whatever."

"Then I guess we'll see," I responded with a shrug.

I fought off the tiniest bit of a smile at how good it felt to say that. It felt kind of badass—which was not at all something someone who was *actually* a badass would think.

Mags blinked at me. "What's wrong with you?" Mags asked. It wasn't even said rudely, which was the most impressive feat of all. She was genuinely concerned. But my sister expressing any kind of emotion at all had a way of annoying me.

I sighed, throwing my hands up. "Maybe I am mad at them. I don't know. They can be disappointed, but I'm also allowed to be. I'm a person, even if they like to forget I am."

"Okay." Mags drew the word in a way that was infuriatingly dismissive. "Where have you been, by the way? You basically ran off and have been totally MIA. And you look..." Mags looked like a man trying to figure out an answer to the question *Do you notice anything different about me?* Her expression suddenly went tight. "You're seeing someone again, aren't you?"

I didn't have an answer. It was written all over my face—I'd always been a bad liar   and the glow radiating from me. It was hard hiding a crush, but it was even harder when the sex was *that* good, and our interactions were *that* positive. So far, GJ was two-for-two in me leaving her place without me hating her, which was more than I could say about literally anyone else I'd ever fooled around with.

I knew I was playing a dangerous game—both with Mags wanting to murder me if she found out, and GJ being the non-committal type—but part of me didn't care. It was nice to be in a dream world for once that lasted past the first five minutes of afterglow. Mags didn't *have* to ever find out the truth, and things were never going to become serious with GJ. If anything, part of what made it all so fun was that there were no feelings involved.

Mags shook her head. "I don't care who the asshole is this time, just don't make me hear about it. And stop letting them affect how you talk to Mom and Dad. Giving them an attitude because your most recent lay won't call you back, just like they always do, isn't fair."Anger bubbled through me. Normally, I just brushed the feeling off and left to stew in my room alone until I forced myself to get over it. I loved compartmentalizing, loved pushing a feeling down.

But GJ was right that I still had a life to live. I'd never thought about it that way, but I had so many more years ahead of me. I didn't want to spend the entire rest of my life dodging feelings with my family. And I definitely didn't want to be someone who was still bending over backward, scared of my parents, in my forties, or when I had kids of my own. Maybe it *was* time I at least tried to be a real person around them instead of a fucking robot.

"So now you're assuming the only reason I'd ever be in a bad mood is because of the person I'm seeing? You don't think I have *any* right to be mad at Mom and Dad?"

Mags shrugged. She had the exact demeanor I'd gotten used to seeing from her—that half-removed, *you're being kind of crazy right now* shrug. I'd never been so desperate for the free will to wrestle her to the ground like we used to do when we were kids. "I don't think I really see where you're coming from. Nothing has changed."

"That's exactly my point—nothing has changed. This is exactly how my entire life has always been. Do you not see anything wrong with that?"

Mags blinked at me. "It's okay if you're scared to graduate."

"What could you even *possibly* mean by that?" I threw my hands up in the air in frustration. I missed the woman I'd been just half an hour ago, warm and safe in GJ's bed. There was no real life in her apartment. It was just the two of us in the most addictive, all-consuming kind of way. I was already itching to go back.

"I don't know. You're just acting so weird. I think it probably has something to do with how you always act like more of a bitch when you're seeing someone because you only date losers, but since you're so insistent it's not—"

"I mean, okay. Following your thinking, maybe I really don't want to graduate. And maybe that has something to do with how you and Mom and Dad don't listen to me about anything. But that doesn't change the fact that you don't take anything I say seriously."

Mags's face went hard. "Hey, that's not fair."

"I know you hate having to look at yourself in the mirror and realize that you kind of suck as a sister sometimes, but maybe it's time you do."

"Leah—"

I brushed by Mags to go to my room and slammed the door behind me.

I was out of breath and scared out of my mind being so direct with my sister, but it also felt good to finally do *something*. After years of taking every single shot my family took at me like it was nothing, it was time they started getting it back.

Leah

> *Can I come over tonight for a sleepover?*

Soph, always with her phone in her hand and always equipped for an emergency, responded immediately.

Soph

> *Of course. I'll order us delivery from that Thai place.*

Leah

> *You are my moon and stars*

Soph

> *Just get your ass over here, I'm in the middle of rewatching Grey's Anatomy and I will start this episode without you if you take too long*

I smiled, feeling better for about half a second, and tossed my phone on my bed as I gathered everything I'd need for my classes tomorrow.

But the crushing realization that I was doing this because I was feuding with my family was hard to completely shake off. As badly as being ghosted or dumped, or watching my crush flirt with someone else hurt, fighting my family hurt a million times more.

I arrived at Soph's in practically record time, wiping furious tears from my eyes the entire walk over. I'd been able to avoid crossing paths with Mags again on the way out; she'd made herself comfortable in the living room and was either too distracted by the game or too disinterested in engaging with me to acknowledge me leaving. I didn't mind; I'd had enough uncharacteristically bold moments of confrontation today to last me months, if not a lifetime.

"Thank god you're here, I was itching to start the episode. Teddy is finally making her appearance," Soph called out when she heard her front door open. Soph's house was the place to hang out—she and her roommate loved guests, and Soph was the first person to volunteer to host watch parties of away games.

It wasn't uncommon for at least one person who wasn't a roommate to be over at all times. I loved it; it all felt so warm, from their demeanors to the warm light that washed over the entire apartment. They had a strict no big light policy that they never strayed from, and there always seemed to be a communal, freshly baked snack either made by Soph or her roommate, depending on how stressful their week was.

It was so different from my apartment with Mags. It had, of course, been the place she'd picked—all 'luxury' amenities and cold, sterile feeling stainless steel. It was a new build with none of the comfort of Soph's much more lived-in place. It made sense Mags liked it; it felt a lot like our parents' house.

"Hey, Leah," Diana, Soph's roommate, called out from her open bedroom door.

"Hey, Di," I said as I grabbed a cup of ice water from the kitchen. I didn't bother trying to hide my red-rimmed eyes and puffy face from crying—Soph knew I was upset, and there was no reason to pretend like I wasn't.

We headed to the living room, where our food was already situated on the coffee table. I could see the steam rising from our bowls from across the room. My mouth watered, a reminder that I hadn't eaten since I saw my parents earlier in the day, and I hadn't exactly had much of an appetite then.

As we settled into our usual seats on the floor, Soph looked over at me. "Should I ask now or should I save it for later?"

I sighed a little, not knowing where to even start. "You already heard most of it at the party earlier."

"I meant more of, *does this have anything to do with you very suddenly leaving the party earlier?* variety," Soph clarified. She started the episode for background noise—we'd both seen the show so many times we just talked through most episodes, any-way—and dug into her food while I tried to think of a response.

"Um," I offered, the best I could come up with.

"Oh, this is worse than I could've possibly imagined."

"It's *not*."

"Who picked you up from the party?"

"You're not going to like the answer."

"I swear to god, if you tell me it was Kai—"

"No," I said with full confidence and without hesitation. For the second time that day—including after GJ had made a comment about the ex I'd been trying to make jealous—I realized it'd been at least a few days since Kai had crossed my mind. Now that they were being brought back up, I was being reminded of how much it sucked to see them at a party with someone else. But it stung less, and that was something.

"Okay." Soph dragged the word out, narrowing her eyes at me like she was studying me. She gestured her fork at my tear-streaked face. "So, what's all of this then? I find it hard to believe you left the party without meeting up with *someone* because one second you were on your phone and the next, you were gone. You're surprisingly speedy when you have alcohol in you."

"You can't say anything, okay? I'm being serious. I've heard enough from my family today."

Soph's expression went deadly serious. "Okay."

I looked down, not wanting to see her immediate reaction. "It was GJ."

Soph earnestly gasped. When I looked over at her, her hand had flown to her mouth. Rather than looking judgmental, she looked earnestly surprised. "Did you text her or did she text you?" She punched my shoulder. "I can't believe you guys have had a thing this whole time and you didn't tell me! Maybe you are better with secrets than I thought."

"We haven't had a thing, actually. We hadn't seen each other, like, *alone,* since the last time. But I texted her. I don't know. I was drunk. I'd be more embarrassed, but it worked out so well that I think I have to own it now."

Soph's eyes lit up, somehow even more surprised than she had been initially. "Okay. Wow. I was not expecting that. I know you'd fooled around the other night, but you going out of your way to text her is respectable. And with a few weeks of not speaking to each other? It's *bold*, Moretti. And she *still* responded?"

"I know."

"As much as I wish you weren't getting your rocks off with a lesbian super villain, I think I prefer this over hearing about Kai," she said and then frowned. "But wait—what happened? What's with the tears?"

"Totally unrelated. Just family bullshit. I actually had a really...nice time with GJ."

"Crazy way to refer to what had to have been absolutely life-altering sex, but okay."

I laughed. "No, I mean that genuinely. Like, the sex was really good, but that's to be assumed. She was also just so...nice. She let me, like, nap in her bed and gave me a shirt to wear. She got me water, too."

"Oh, wow. She's really pulling out all the stops," Soph deadpanned.

"You know what I mean. You've heard my dating stories."

"I will say, I *am* impressed. Hospitable and welcoming are not exactly words I'd use—or, like, any girl on campus would use—to refer to her, but I'm glad she was nice." Soph's eyes glanced over my face, still carefully studying my expression. "It's just sex, though, right?"

"Yeah, of course."

Despite my confidence, Soph's hesitance was written all over her face. "The only reason I'm letting this pass is that I kind of like that you're finally off the Kai train. But my feelings haven't changed—I don't actually *like* GJ for you, but she's better than Kai. You can't actually have a crush on someone like GJ. We've talked about this."

"I know, I know," I said, waving her off. "I've been normal at games, haven't I? And I'm not sitting here gushing about how we have some great future together. It's casual. It's a palette cleanser. She's just...a break from reality for a second. And a much-needed one with how I acted with my parents earlier. And I just now bitched at Mags, who is being so *annoying* and oblivious, which is the icing on the cake of an absolute shit day."

Soph offered a sympathetic look. If there was anyone who understood how hard it was to actually say anything to my family of substance, it was her. She'd heard years of it, seen me navigate the complicated feeling of so badly wanting to be pissed at someone while feeling I couldn't be. Our plans of potentially living together had gotten fucked over by my parents' insistence—and my cowardice—around living with Mags. Four years and she'd never even met my parents, and it wasn't for Soph's lack of trying.

"And I'm assuming the bitching had nothing to do with Mags figuring out you're fooling around with GJ? Because as much as I'm willing to give this a pass, I'm not sure she will."

"I don't think I'd even be here right now if Mags knew. She'd probably be having some kind of intervention and acting like I'm a child she has to take care of." I rolled my eyes. "She pretty explicitly told me she can tell I'm involved with someone, but that she doesn't want to hear about it, so I'm assuming I'm home free for now."

Soph offered an amused smile. "We'll see how long that attitude lasts for once she figures out what's going on."

"*If* she ever figures out what's going on," I said. Soph looked over at me, knowing I was useless at keeping a secret. "I promise I'm on my best behavior this time. It really does feel different when it's obvious who you're dealing with. I've been played before, but GJ isn't playing me. It's borderline transactional. I don't have any feelings about this, and she definitely doesn't either."

I was surprised by how sure I was of my words. Despite GJ's kindness, there was a part of me that was still walled off to her. I knew it wasn't serious, and I knew it wasn't going to be anything, so there was no reason to get myself all knotted up. And knowing that neither of us wanted or expected anything and that GJ wasn't making assumptions about doing things like randomly calling her to fool around made me feel like I could act however I wanted. It was nice to have the chance to do something casual and be able to just enjoy spending time together without it having weight to it—at least for now.

Soph nodded, thinking over my words. "I've been impressed so far by your behavior. I haven't gotten even *one* anxiety-ridden text about a girl in GJ's Instagram comments. And I've only caught you looking her way once during a game so far."

"Stop." I laughed. "And that's probably because that would be about a million girls. Way too many to send texts about." When Soph gave me a look of genuine fear, I sighed. "That was a joke."

Soph snorted but still looked skeptical. "Okay, fair." She gently picked at her food with her fork, clearly thinking about what she wanted to say to me next. "You're good, though?"

"As good as I can be." I sighed. "I can't believe I'm saying this, but I think for the first time ever, I'm not in distress about a girl. It's my family that's driving me crazy now."

"I guess I did kind of see this one coming. You've been venting to me about Mags for as long as I've known you. And I still have some beef with Mags for keeping us from being roommates all these years."

"I know," I said, thinking about how I could've just been living here this entire time instead of sharing a place with Mags. I hadn't even bothered to pitch the idea of me moving out to spend senior year living with Soph to my parents, and I definitely hadn't brought it up with Mags. I'd been so scared, so certain that I was going to get bulldozed. It hadn't even felt worth the conversation.

Now, I was regretting it. It felt so small at the time, but I could see in retrospect that it set the tone of my senior year. I should've been able to live with whoever I wanted to live with, should've been able to just tell my family no without worrying about how they'd respond.

I wasn't even worried about them picking a fight with me; I was worried about the coldness, the dismissiveness. The look on my mom's face seemed to always be there whenever I spoke in her general vicinity. I could tell her I was getting nationally recognized for an award, and she'd make an offhand comment about how I should remember to fix my highlights before it. And then, worst of all, was how she would always play it off and make me feel stupid for having hurt feelings over it.

But not all hope was yet lost. My parents might've won at convincing me to stay roommates with my sister—along with about a million other things. But the one thing I *had* gotten was having unbelievable sex with one of Mags's teammates despite all of her years of telling me I never could.

I smiled a little to myself at realizing I'd won at least one battle, even if my family didn't know.

Chapter Nine

GJ

Even though my bed felt empty when Leah left, the post-sex glow lasted for an annoyingly long time. As days went by, all I could think about was the next time I'd be able to have her in my bed. When she wasn't here, I was having dreams about her. I'd stare at my phone and debate texting her during class, or when I was lying in bed, or after practice. But I never did it, and I knew it was because I was scared she might tell me she didn't want to see me again. The uncertainty was a new feeling I wasn't sure I liked, but the high of seeing Leah in passing at games outweighed everything else.

It was like my brain and my body physically couldn't get enough. The sex—and the company—were just that good. It was undeniable; whatever spell Leah had me under was something I'd never experienced before.

But maybe it was just the absence that was making my heart grow fonder, or whatever it was that people said. I just wanted what I couldn't have.

I stared at my ceiling, willing myself to stop ruminating over this and get my ass out of bed. But I knew I needed some additional assistance. I picked up my phone and immediately FaceTimed the one voice of reason I had in this.

Theo answered almost immediately, her face flashing up on my screen. It looked like she'd just wrapped up a workout—her hair was tied back in a ponytail, and her pale cheeks were flushed pink. "Hey, what's up?" Her voice was abnormally, forcefully chill.

"Why are you being weird?"

"What?" Theo asked, blinking at me.

"I've known you long enough to know that you're being weird. What's going on?" I sat up straighter in bed and glanced at the clock. I had a morning workout soon—leave it to Theo to keep up a routine that had her up before even the Coyotes practiced in the morning—but I wasn't going to let this slide. Gushing about Leah could be put on the back burner for now.

Theo flattened her lips, shaking her head in disagreement. "Nothing's going on. Why are you calling?"

"You know something. You definitely know something."

"Is that GJ?" Maya called out from offscreen. Theo moved the camera away from her face, but I caught the tiniest look on her face.

"Dude, you're stressing me out. What the hell is going on?" I asked.

"Has she seen it?"

"*Maya.*" Theo groaned.

"I'm sorry! I thought that was why she was calling!"

My heart went into double time. "Okay, now you guys are really freaking me out. What is going on?"

"Wait, why were you calling?" Theo asked, putting the camera back on her face again.

"I was going to talk about a girl, but this is clearly way more important."

"I'm sorry, GJ. That was my bad—please don't ask!" Maya called out from off-screen.

"You're both so bad at this," I said, but I was doing a terrible job at playing off my nerves. As casual as I wanted to sound, my palms were sweaty, and my heart was racing. If they were both still on campus, I'd immediately chalk it up to campus gossip—some girl talking shit at a party, a men's basketball player who wanted to pick a fight over a comment I made about their weak ass team.

But they weren't still on campus. For them to know any gossip before me—or someone else on the team—was unlikely. This had to be something big.

"Maybe we should focus on the girl drama. The other stuff isn't important," Theo said. "Is this about Mags's sister?"

"Way to air me the fuck out, dude." I put the phone down on my bed and threw my shirt on, knowing I didn't have long until I had to leave.

"Maya knows everything I know. I can't help it."

"You're a fucking simp. Weak willed."

"Bold coming from the one with a way worse campus reputation than I ever had, but is calling to talk to me *about* a girl. Usually, it's pulling teeth to get information. And they never have names. They're just *girl in the blue shirt. Girl visiting from California—*"

I snorted. "You're so fucking annoying. But you're not distracting me—tell me what's going on."

Theo took a long breath. She went over to her fridge and pulled it open, grabbing the ingredients for a smoothie before finally responding. "It's in *Sports Illustrated.*"

My stomach dropped. I knew better than to ever think whatever she was talking about was a good thing. "You're fucking lying."

"It's not *bad—*"

I reached out for my laptop that was haphazardly balancing on my nightstand. Throwing my phone down on the bed so I could focus, I googled my name. There wasn't a single doubt in my mind when I saw it—it was the first fucking article on the screen.

"Oh my fucking god, dude," I said. I buried my head in my hands.

"It's fine. People always have something to say. You saw some of the stuff people were saying about me online while I was playing. They're *still* talking about me, and it's the offseason."

"It's different when you were named Rookie of the Year. I've been playing like shit, which means this article is *right*."

I didn't know what to do with myself. I rubbed my palms against my shirt, clenched my jaw, rubbed at the back of my neck. I didn't know where to put my nervous energy.

"I have to go," I said.

"GJ—"

I hung up the call and jumped up from my bed, jumping up and down and shaking out my arms. The article headline flashed over and over in my mind. *Pro basketball scouts talk season standouts so far, express concern over the Coyotes season led by GJ Mitchell.*

This wasn't the first time I'd made it into *Sports Illustrated*—Theo was never afraid to name-drop us directly in interviews because she knew how much it meant for our careers—but it was the first genuinely negative press I'd gotten. *Me*. Directly. By name. And not just in an article somewhere but in the *headline*.

I grabbed a pillow from my bed and screamed into it.

No one said anything to me during morning workout, but I could feel my teammates periodically glancing over at me. I knew Coach Darlene had to have seen it and the rest of the coaching staff, too. Our team was way too high profile for anything to slip by. And as much as we were told to ignore what people had to say online and focus on playing ball, *Sports Illustrated* wasn't exactly some guy on the internet.

As the day went on, I couldn't bring myself to read the entire article. The only thing I could do was continuously refresh various social media apps, curious if people were reposting it and what they were saying. A couple of fans were stepping in to defend the team and me, which I was grateful for. But mostly, it was people acknowledging that we weren't the same team that had beaten Point Brook last year during the regular season. We lacked the chemistry, the excitement, the fun that we used to have.

And most resoundingly of all was how many people were commenting on me not being able to match Theo. I was never going to replace her, never going to fill her shoes. Naturally, anyone who had any hope for us emphasized Anna as what we had left for keeping the team's record afloat.

I spent all day in a state of heightened anxiety. It swirled around in my chest and made the day feel impossibly long, and my body feel heavy. I felt like everyone was looking at me, which was typically the case; people tended to stare when they realized I was the person from the giant poster on campus. But this time, it didn't feel like they were looking because they were fans.

It didn't help that we had afternoon practice, so I wasn't going to be free of basketball until later in the evening. I spent all day waiting to be called into Coach Darlene's office like she was a school principal and I was a kid who'd done something wrong. Even though the article wasn't inherently my fault, it definitely reflected badly on us. And as captain, everything kind of felt like my fault. If people were suddenly doubting our team and the only thing that really changed was Theo graduating and me taking over, there was no one else to blame.

My teammates still not saying anything into the evening also made me feel worse and even more anxious. The group chat had been active, but with people sharing random life updates or asking about practice today.

I *needed* someone to talk to me about it, or I was going to explode.

We huddled on the court around Coach Darlene, and I glanced around to see if anyone looked upset with me. I didn't necessarily fear authority—I was too much of a self-aware class clown and an idiot to take what they said personally—but I was learning now that I could *definitely* experience fear when it came to the general fate of my basketball career.

But there was nothing. As if it were any normal day, Coach Darlene ran through positions for us in a 3v3.

"GJ, let's see you as a shooting guard for this one," Coach Darlene said, glancing down at her clipboard and then back up at us. I squeezed my hands tight and then let them go, not wanting to make a scene.

Her tone and expression were so neutral, like she didn't just say the most casually infuriating thing she could've said. The fear that had been balled up in my chest instantly turned into annoyance. That felt like all the confirmation I needed to know she'd seen the article.

I shot a glare over in Anna's direction and ignored the smug look from Mags nearby. Mags was typically our starting shooting guard, but she was—annoyingly—built to be good in just about any position. She was as versatile as a basketball player could be, which was part of the reason she had such a massive ego. She saw being trusted in a different position as a point of pride and an acknowledgment of her skills, not as a demotion.

But as someone who'd been pretty much always a point guard since I was in middle school, I wasn't interested in doing this.

"I'm a fucking point guard," I mumbled, and Nia looked over sympathetically. I could also see the fear in her eyes, worried that Coach Darlene was going to hear me.

After Coach Darlene went over who'd be playing and on which team, she told us to get into position. I did as I was told because I didn't know what other option I possibly had.

"Tough look," Mags mumbled to me, just quietly enough that no one else was going to hear her.

She was lucky I was just mature enough to know that saying *When was the last time you asked your sister who she was hooking up with?* wasn't going to help anyone.

As we got into position, I tried to get myself in the headspace to play, but I couldn't. There were too many things going on in my head to possibly be able to focus. It was hard enough when it was just that I didn't feel like I was playing well—now, it was documented in *Sports Illustrated*, my team seemed insistent on not acknowledging it, which only made it worse, and Coach coincidentally was 'trying out new positions.'

Anna looked over at Gemma and me. We were supposed to be a team for this game, but I had very little interest in having to engage with Anna directly. Just looking at her was a reminder of how far behind I was falling and how much of a failure I was this season. I suddenly understood a lot of the resentment Leah felt toward her family about Mags being the favorite. Theo had never made it feel like a competition—we played in rhythm, always together. But it sucked to be now in a position where it really felt like one, and I was losing.

We kicked off the game, the ball starting in my hands. I bounced it and moved up the court, carefully moving away from attempted steals.

I came up on Mags and thought through where I could go next on the court. "Your screen sucks."

"GJ!" Anna yelled out, clearly trying to get the ball away from Mags. She waved her arm to indicate that she was open. I could see how to get the ball to her, but in a split-second decision, I danced around Mags instead and went for the basket. I knew immediately I'd made a huge mistake—the ball bounced on the rim, almost like it was going to go in, and then fell.

"Shit," I mumbled. So much for trying to be the hero. It turned out the only thing worse than already feeling like shit was trying and failing at making yourself feel better.

I could tell immediately that my teammates were not impressed. Even Anna, who never seemed to be affected by anything, looked a little annoyed.

Mags smiled, amused. "Nice shot."

"Alright," Coach Darlene snapped. "Let's see some teamwork, alright? GJ, get the playmaker the ball. Don't hold onto it."

I took a deep breath, avoiding eye contact with every single person in the room. "Yes, Coach."

After practice, I gathered my things and left as quickly as possible, more than ready to get my ass home. I wasn't even sure what I was going to do there—maybe lift some weights or something to burn off my nervous energy. I kind of wanted to hide under the covers and never get up again, but that didn't feel like much of a solution.

As soon as I was physically back outside, I felt a little better. The air was crisp and cool on my skin, and it was quiet, so it was a tiny break from the feeling I had that people were staring at me. For the first time all day, I felt like I could relax, even just a little bit.

I headed off on my walk home and was about to put my headphones in when I heard my name from a distance. I brushed it off, but it only got louder.

"*GJ!*"

I turned around and saw Ellie sprinting after me. She'd looped her thumbs into her backpack straps to hold her bag to her body as she ran. Her red ponytail bounced, her cheeks already flushed from the cold.

I slowed my pace down so she could meet me. "Hey," I said, surprised to see her. Curiosity—and also already feeling guilty about being a bad teammate and a shitty captain—kept me from brushing her off.

"Can you..." Ellie paused and looked at me with a healthy dose of anxiety, like she couldn't believe she was doing this. She redirected to looking down at the ground as we walked. "Can you help me with my passing? I know you're busy and you already have a lot going on, so I feel bad asking. But it's my weakest skill. We have East Hill coming up and Point Brook. And with so many of y'all graduating, I don't want to wait too long to learn this stuff."

Even though I knew Ellie was a nice person, my defenses immediately went up. "Did someone put you up to this?"

Ellie looked genuinely taken aback. Her full lips fell apart in surprise. "What?"

"I know you saw the article about the team. Nobody wants to talk about it for whatever reason, which is making it worse, but I know it definitely made the rounds," I said. I stuffed my hands in my pockets, avoiding looking at her.

"I don't care about that stuff. Journalists and fans and who-ever else don't actually know you, but I do," Ellie insisted. When she could tell that the approach wasn't working, she softened her tone. "I saw the article. But my only takeaway from it was that we could improve as an entire team. There's clearly a piece missing."

"That piece being Theo."

"Kind of, but not necessarily. It was an honor to play with her, and we've definitely been missing her on the court, but we have the talent. We're leading our conference in rebounds and steals. And our field goal average has been one of the best our team has ever had. Our overall points per game have taken a hit since we didn't have anyone as solid with threes as Theo, but that's not all that matters."

I smiled a little. I'd never actually gotten to know Ellie well enough to realize she had an accent that very softly came through when she spoke. And I'd also never gotten to know her well enough to really have an opinion on her, but right now, I appreciated her certainty and no-bullshit analytical approach to the game. It was giving me a much-needed reminder—the team was more than me. I'd been so focused on my shit and how I compared to Anna that I hadn't been paying attention to any of our collective wins, just my personal losses.

We walked side-by-side down the same sidewalk Theo and I used to take walking back from practice. I used to tease Theo about Maya here, debrief practices and games here. It was nice to have someone walk this way with me again after so long.

"We're not a bad team, and I don't think it's fair that they're painting us that way," Ellie continued. "I'll own up to asking you about this now because of the article, but I also think a lot of it was for engagement. Everyone's waiting for us to fail because they keep chalking up our past wins to only Theo. We know better than that, though."

I took in what she was saying. Despite the shitty, uneasy feeling that felt like it was going to swallow me whole, Ellie's words were making a difference. The glimmer of hope was back, even if it was weak and would inevitably be short-lived.

"I think this is the most we've ever spoken to each other consecutively," I said, mostly to deflect the way Ellie's earnest support was making me legitimately emotional. I wasn't really a crier—more of a *crack jokes until the feeling passed* person—but the stress of the day was making me want to curl up in bed and let it out.

I'd never been in a position before where the critiques people were offering felt grounded in truth. Normally, it was comments online from someone comparing me to their favorite player, stacking up stats or awards or general accomplishments against each other. It'd always been things where I'd just roll my eyes and get annoyed because it was obviously biased or coming from someone who didn't actually understand basketball.

But I *was* having an off-season. No one would argue that. And it made it a million times worse knowing the critics were right about me.

I didn't want to fuck up Ellie's positive perception of me, but it was hard not to be surprised she came to me after getting such a swift and public kick in the nuts. I wasn't even sure I believed in myself anymore; I didn't see why she would. "You *really* want to work with me on it? I know Gemma's working with some of the girls on the team."

I didn't say what I really wanted to say, which was asking why she wasn't just going to Anna instead of me. Not going to Gemma was fine enough; Gemma had always been good at being the team's glue, but wasn't much of a strong personality on her own. Anna made sense to ask, though, especially now that Coach Darlene seemed determined to have her running point. I also had never thought of myself as much of a teacher or a coach-to-be. That'd always been Theo's role.

It suddenly all made sense. "Theo used to coach you."

Ellie nodded. "I don't like comparing players, but personality-wise, you match each other. And you played well together." She turned to me, and I could see how badly she wanted me to hear her out in her eyes. "I just really, *really* want to be good, and you're the best I know here."

I furrowed my brow. "Dude, you're already really good. You didn't just make the team by accident. You got yourself transferred out here and were good enough to play as Theo's shadow.

And I mean that as a compliment—a lot of people wouldn't be able to keep up with her like that."

Ellie's face remained unmoved. I realized I'd spent years making the mistake of underestimating her because she was quiet. The determination in her expression and the way she was completely serious about wanting to improve said everything.

"Alright, let's do it," I finally agreed, surprising myself. I looked at her. "I might be a little scared of you, Ellie Allison. You're hard to say no to."

"I'm a farmer's daughter—not one thing in life is funny," she said firmly.

I saluted, my lips turning up in a smile. "Yes, ma'am."

There wasn't one ounce of bullshit in her, I could tell. Suddenly, Theo's certainty that Ellie was one to watch was making more and more sense. She'd never made it onto any lists about players to watch, she didn't sell jerseys, she wasn't being whispered about when it came to getting drafted. But something told me if she did it just right, she was going to be the breakout draftee of her senior year.

"Which way is your place?" I asked as the end of the sidewalk came into view, and it was almost time for me to take the right to my apartment.

"Up this way," she said, pointing in the opposite direction of where my apartment was.

"I'll walk with you. We can talk about your turnover during the Dalton State game."

For just a moment, a whisper of a smile appeared at Ellie's lips. "Okay."

Chapter Ten

Leah

I was deep into an article for one of my marketing classes when Mags and Gemma walked into the apartment.

Predictably, Mags and I had brushed off our spat and kept acting like it hadn't happened. I got back from my sleepover at Soph's, and things had been pretty much back to normal since then—meaning I was silently fuming and Mags was oblivious.

I still hadn't been able to bring myself to speak to my parents, but Mags hadn't been riding my ass about it, which I appreciated. She usually kept to herself during basketball season; she was so busy dealing with her team and practices and travel games that she didn't have the time to be my parents' mouthpiece.

"The whole thing is bullshit," Mags said. I heard her and Gemma dropping their things near the front door, just out of view of where I was sitting. "They're just ragging on us because we're an easy target. And the person who wrote the article went to one of the schools in our conference, so it's definitely just a smear piece. It's whatever."

"Yeah. I feel bad GJ got thrown under the bus."

My ears perked up at the mention of GJ's name, and I immediately tuned in. I couldn't help it; it was like when I said the word *walk* around my childhood dog. Despite insisting to Soph that there was nothing going on, I'd been in a total GJ haze since the last time I saw her.

It was entirely casual, though, and in a very cool way. It was the side effect of having unbelievable sex and someone I could reliably text to get it whenever I wanted. That was all it was.

Obviously.

As they rounded the corner and walked into the kitchen, Mags brushed the comment off with her hand. "That's part of being a captain. She knew what she signed up for. And it'll only get worse if she gets signed to a team; she'll have to get used to this level of attention."

Gemma shrugged. "Doesn't mean it wasn't mean."

"Wait, what happened?" I asked, looking at them from my spot on the couch.

Mags rolled her eyes. "It's some article in *Sports Illustrated*. It kind of threw GJ under the bus for us not meeting expectations or whatever. Everyone's disappointed in us. Everyone misses Theo. Whatever."

Gemma and I exchanged a small smile. I'd always liked Gemma—she was the quieter half of the duo, and a lot more palatable. I didn't know much about her outside of basketball because she didn't really talk. Despite being pretty much Mags's only friend, I found it hard to dislike Gemma purely by association. She seemed actually really nice. Mags's high school team was a lot more insufferable comparatively.

I thought back to GJ's comment about Gemma and Mags having something going on between them. As I watched them move effortlessly through the kitchen, prepping dinner together in a fluid dance, I could see where she was coming from. They did spend a lot of time together, too. But then again, Soph and I were basically obsessed with each other and had sleepovers all the time, and that was earnestly platonic.

But mostly, I just found it hard to believe my sister could ever have romantic feelings for anyone. Or that someone would want her.

Gross.

"So weird how it always comes back to Theo," I said and Mags threw a look back in my direction that told me I was playing with fire. I put my hands up in surrender. "What else did the article say?"

It was my best attempt at asking what the writer had said about GJ without *really* asking. Even though there was no reason for either of them to believe I was asking for anything other than gossip, I was nervous that it would be written all over me.

Mags had made it clear she didn't really care about me or my feelings or my thoughts on anything, but I knew her well enough to guess her Protective Sister radar would immediately go off. She might not want to hear about my dating life, but she was too up my ass to stay away completely.

I was still annoyed with her for the times she used to grill me about her old teammates growing up, always assuming I wanted them because I said their name a *little* differently one day.

To be fair, some of her teammates had been really cute, and I'd kind of hoped something would line up with one of them eventually. It'd only taken most of my life, but the wait had been worth it; none of the other girls would've held a candle to GJ.

"The writer mentioned Anna being our last hope, basically. She said we were good, but it was obvious we were missing something. But the likelihood of all of us getting drafted was low, especially compared to Point Brook. She mentioned most of us by name, but GJ made it into the headline," Gemma explained.

My stomach knotted with sympathy. "That must be hard."

"No one brought it up during practice, so I have no idea. I don't think anyone knew what to say about it. And GJ and Coach Darlene don't get along nearly as well as Coach Darlene and Theo got along. I just *know* Coach was pissed when she realized GJ was the natural next pick for captain," Mags said bitterly. I resisted rolling my eyes. As if Mags had ever been a team player once in her life. She was the kind of person who would only do well as a captain for a blood-hungry, every-man-for-himself team. She couldn't give an uplifting speech to save her life. GJ was definitely less serious than Theo or Mags, but she was at least charismatic and had a good heart.

I weighed my options, wondering if I should text GJ and check in. Unwelcome doubts swirled, all sorts of little reminders of the times I'd tried to connect with hookups in the past and completely fallen flat. The ignored texts, the coldness, the sudden disappearance when they perceived me as trying to make things into something serious.

It didn't help that basketball season was *long*. If GJ blew me off now, I couldn't promise that my feelings wouldn't be at least a little hurt. And Soph had been right about how badly it would suck to have to see GJ at games if things went south.

But then again, it *was* casual. This wasn't anything at all. There were no promises about the future, no talks about what we could be. I could text her, and it would be fine. Rejection hurt no matter what, but it didn't *have* to be the end of the world. And if anything, it was probably for the best if things did get cut off—the more time we spent together, the more likely it was that Mags would figure out what was going on.

Fuck it. I wasn't going to spend my entire life paralyzed in fear over texting someone I wanted to talk to. If GJ didn't respond, that was her prerogative.

I picked up my phone and drafted out a text. And then deleted it and tried again. And again.

As Gemma and Mags wandered out of the kitchen to head back to her room, I was still staring at the screen. I bit my lip, reading it over and over. I tried to read it through GJ's eyes, wondering how she would feel about it, how she would read it. I rewrote it and then went back to the original version, hoping it sounded casual enough.

After staring at my phone for what had to have been at least ten minutes, I half-closed my eyes and then finally hit *send*. After doing it, I tossed my phone across the couch.

I tried to focus on my textbook, but it was useless. I kept looking over, waiting for my phone to vibrate. Waiting for the screen to light up. Anything at all.

And then it did.

I brushed off the relief at not only seeing a response from her, but that the typing bubble was still up on my screen.

Have you read it?

Leah

No, Mags and Gemma were talking about it.

GJ

I'm surprised you didn't hear about it sooner. It's making the rounds on social media.

Leah

I had an exam today that took up all of my attention, regrettably couldn't spend the entire day thinking about basketball

GJ

Not even thinking about me playing basketball?

I put my fingers to my lips that were turned up in a soft smile. The nerves evaporated instantaneously, everything feeling so natural between us. I suddenly felt like an idiot for even having to steel myself—of course, GJ wasn't going to be an asshole.

Leah

GJ

As I was thinking about how to respond, my phone vibrated again.

GJ

My heart fluttered. If that was a booty call text, it had to be the most vulnerable, sweetest one I'd ever received. I knew my standards weren't great to begin with, but even Soph would have to agree—not that I was going to tell her about this. I'd just have to let her guess I was over there based on where my Find My Friends would be tonight.

Leah

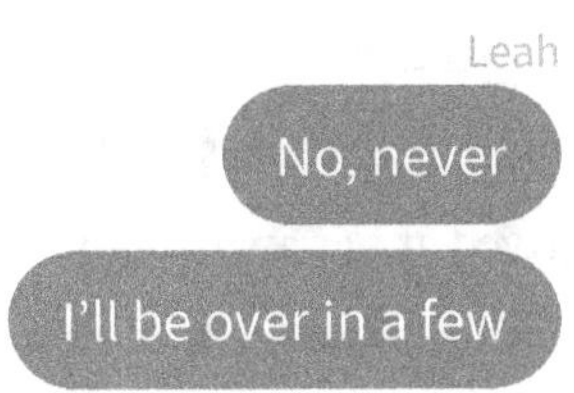

As I quickly threw together a bag of my things I'd need for class tomorrow, I'd never been so grateful that I spent at least one night a week at Soph's so Mags wouldn't think anything of me slipping out in the late evening. I was also grateful that GJ happened to live in one of the larger apartment complexes on campus, so I could've been seeing anyone if Mags happened to check my location and see I wasn't with Soph.

Before exiting my bedroom, I stopped in front of my full-length mirror to make sure I looked okay. My outfit wasn't much, just a blue matching sweat set. My hair wasn't done, and I had no makeup on. But GJ hadn't seemed to have an issue with it when she saw me barefaced before.

So for the first time ever, I opted out of putting makeup on to go see someone I was most likely going to have sex with. I still made sure I was wearing cute underwear, though.

The walk to GJ's wasn't long, but the sun set so early now that it was cold and dark. As I made it closer to Main Street, students walked past me in groups to head to a party or bar or study session.

Despite it only being a few days since I last saw GJ and there being no indication I should be nervous to see her, there was still a small buzz of nerves fluttering through me as I texted her that I'd arrived at her apartment.

She came down a few moments later, breathless. "Sorry, the elevator was taking too long—I ended up taking the stairs."

In spite of myself, I smiled as soon as I saw her face. Her body wash—I recognized the smell from when she'd showered the other day—radiated off of her, telling me she'd just showered. She held the door open for me, and all I could think about was how strong her arms were and how safe I felt being so close to her. It also didn't hurt that she was the tallest person I'd ever fooled around with; it was a refreshing change of pace to not be The Tall One.

"Thanks," I said as I slipped past her and entered her apartment complex entryway. It was small—just a hallway, a place for mail and packages, the elevator, and the stairs—but there was enough space for us to theoretically keep a distance.

GJ, however, hovered as close as she could. She stood behind me, her skin brushing against my jacket. I could feel the warmth of her skin through it.

I wanted to kiss her so badly it felt like torture.

The elevator dinged, and the doors opened soon after. A few students stepped out and walked past us, one of them double-taking when their eyes fell on GJ.

I did everything I could to stay calm and normal because other people were around. But pretending electricity wasn't buzzing between the two of us seemed impossible. I was certain everyone could tell exactly what I was thinking and feeling—and none of it was particularly PG.

GJ and I stepped onto the elevator. I was too caught up in remembering how to manually breathe to say anything. It obviously wasn't my first time over at her place, but it felt different than before. Once was casual, twice was getting it out of our systems. But three times—and so intentionally, with GJ explicitly asking for my company and not even a direct booty call—felt like the start of something. We were entering the point of no return.

GJ opened her apartment door and gestured for me to walk in. "Let me take your coat," she offered.

I shrugged it off and handed it to her. "So chivalrous."

She hung it up in the coat closet near the front door. "At your service," she said with a playful half-bow. The entryway was small enough that we were practically on top of each other. As we slid off our shoes, our shoulders brushed.

I glanced over at her for just a second, taking in the sharpness of her jaw, the smoothness of her skin. I looked away quickly, like I was nervous I'd get caught. But when I looked over at her again, GJ was looking at me.

Even though I'd come over with a specific purpose that wasn't overtly sexual, keeping GJ company could *also* mean having sex. There wasn't a strict definition.

The thought seemed to occur to us at the same time. GJ turned to me and tilted my chin up so she could kiss me. I melted to her touch, my knees immediately going weak. Her touch was ridiculously fucking hot—just the right amount of gentleness, just the right amount of pressure in her kiss. It was a kiss that told me we were taking our time.

I wrapped my arms around her neck, and she pulled me in by the waist. Our bodies fell together effortlessly, like two puzzle pieces that fit just right. I loved being able to reach up, to not have to be so aware of my partner being sometimes five or six inches shorter than me, like people I'd hooked up with previously.

GJ tilted my chin to the right and moved my hair out of the way so she could work her way down my neck. She trailed carefully downwards, using her tongue and her teeth instead of sucking, so a mark wouldn't be left behind.

I moaned, heat rushing between my legs, and pressed my weight to her. I was desperate to be as close to her as I possibly could. My body clearly remembered how good the sex had been last time—and the time before that—based on how quickly I was turned on. Just the anticipation of knowing what was coming next was getting me wet.

GJ moved her hands up my back and then around to the front. One of her hands wandered inside my sweatshirt, moving over the bare skin underneath. I might not have gotten dolled up for GJ, but I *had* made the intentional move not to bother to wear a shirt underneath my sweatshirt, and I was grateful I had. I wanted her to have easy access with as little as possible in between us.

Her soft hands worked their way up my skin, making goose-bumps bloom. When she reached my nipples, blood rushed to every sensitive part of my body. I wanted to strip off my clothes, climb onto the bed, and go for hours, not spending even one more second with foreplay.

But GJ's voice echoed in my head, little reminders of how she liked to take her time with me. And she was right for it—the sex with her was better than I'd ever had with anyone else.

GJ slid her hands out from under my sweatshirt and moved them over my sweatpants, running her hands over the curve of my ass. She then easily lifted me up, my legs on either side of her torso.

I giggled. "New move?"

"I seem to remember you making a joke about me being able to lift you." She didn't miss a beat, didn't even seem tired or out of breath. She just held me like I was nothing more than a piece of paper.

I didn't even try to hide how badly I was blushing. "You really are strong."

She smirked. "I'm good in bed, too."

I lifted my eyebrows, leaning into the joke. "Oh yeah? You might need to show me, not sure I believe you—"

Before I could even finish my sentence, GJ brought me over to the bed. As we fell on it together, I threw my head back with laughter.

"I'll have to work on the landing part," she admitted.

"No, that was hot. I've always envisioned being dropped as a form of foreplay."

GJ chuckled and pinned my arms above my head. Our bodies were pressed together, our faces just a breath apart. "I can arrange for more of that."

"That feels vaguely like a threat."

"Just let me kiss you," she said with a smile, and I happily let her.

After several perfect rounds together, I finally had to ask for a break. We curled up in bed and wrapped our naked bodies up in the sheets. Even though this was only our third time alone together, it felt like we'd been doing this forever.

I glanced up at GJ, who was staring off across the room. The distraction part of the evening was officially over.

"Are you thinking about the article?" I asked. It felt good to see the person I was with clearly thinking about something and not being nervous that it was about me. Weirdly, it was hard to imagine GJ thinking something about me and not just telling me. She struck me as someone who was naturally pretty blunt—or at least, she'd been clear with me.

"Yeah," GJ admitted and cleared her throat. "Sorry, kind of a mood killer."

"You don't need to explain yourself. It's okay. It sucks."

GJ was quiet for a beat. "You're right. It does suck."

"Do you want to read it together?" I offered. "Since you haven't read it yet?" I kept my eyes locked on her face, carefully reading what she might be thinking and feeling. I didn't want to push her to do anything, but I also didn't want her to think I didn't care.

"I don't know if I can," GJ admitted. She huffed out a long, thoughtful exhale. "I don't know if it'll help me."

"Maybe it's not as bad as what the headline is saying. People love a clickbait headline. Maybe you're not even mentioned in the rest of the article."

She scoffed. "I doubt that. I'm sure there are at least a few paragraphs talking about my shitty playing and how my chances at getting drafted are shot. Everyone is going to talk about how I was only good before because I had Theo to bounce off of. It's what everyone's been saying for years, anyway. I'm just giving them the proof."

I turned on my stomach, draping my arm over her waist so I could really look at her. "You're good on your own. You know you are."

GJ shrugged the comment off. "I've seen enough online to know what to expect. And public perception means more than actual ability to play sometimes. No one wants to draft the lackey."

I tilted my head. "Do you want me to read it, and I can give you the summary?"

GJ let out the sexiest groan I'd ever heard in my life in a non-sexual context. My entire body fluttered at the sound. "I'm really glad you're offering because it's been driving me insane not reading it. I'm addicted to reading everything I find online about myself."

I gasped. "Not a chronic self-Googler. *Naughty.*"

"I am," GJ admitted, chuckling. "I've always been really bad about it. I like to say that it makes me better, but I think that's only true when you're actually good. When you're feeling like shit and playing like shit, it changes things."

"You're so hard on yourself." I reached for my phone on the nightstand and pulled up the article. I was careful to keep the screen out of view so GJ wouldn't accidentally see anything about herself.

"I think you're the only person who's ever said that to me. Usually, the only thing people have to say about me is that I have a god complex."

"I mean that's definitely in there, too," I teased, and GJ took me into her arms, turning me over in the bed.

"Stop!" I laughed, nearly losing my phone in the process. "Okay, let me read this article! You're distracting me."

GJ positioned herself over me, our bodies caught up in each other under the sheets. Her skin was soft and warm against mine. "We could just pretend the article doesn't exist."

"You basically just told me you were dying to see what it says."

GJ rolled her neck. "I want to know, but I don't want to know. Either way, I'm going to be up all night thinking about it. It's a lose-lose." She turned to me. "Unless you want to give me another type of distraction."

Warmth rushed between my legs at the thought. I was starting to think I would never leave if GJ never asked me to. U-Hauling had never made more sense.

But we couldn't. I wasn't setting myself up for failure like that.

"You have practice," I said, which was a much more casual and cool girl response than *I can't stay because I'm worried I'm going to become obsessed with you.*

"Yeah, yeah."

I pulled out my phone, quickly needing to get my eyes off of GJ before I got myself totally lost in staring at her. "At the very least, let *me* read it, and then I can tell you how bad it actually is."

"But what if you read it and agree with what they say? How am I supposed to live with myself then?"

Her tone was light enough that she could've played it off like a joke. But I'd known GJ for years now—not well, but I'd seen her on the court. Seen her with her friends. Heard her make jokes and saw her post them online. I knew people could have a different outward presence than how they felt on the inside—I was all too familiar with that—but GJ had never been self-deprecating.

"I *actually* know you as a person; an article isn't going to change my opinion of what I see in front of me."

GJ was so uncharacteristically quiet that I was worried I'd managed to really offend her this time. I glanced up from my phone, worried this was going to be when she'd finally switch up on me and I'd be reminded that everyone really was the same.

But instead, she was staring down at her hands, deep in thought. She looked earnestly *sad,* which was breaking my heart into about a million pieces.

"Hey," I said gently. I locked my phone and put it face down, tilting her chin toward me. "It's going to be okay. I don't doubt for even a second that you will get out of this just fine. You've been too good for too long to just go out like this. You just need to get back in the swing of things."

"I don't know if I can," she admitted. "I'm scared it's never going to happen."

I nodded thoughtfully and tried to think of something nice to say, but I knew how it was. Athletes at this level, no matter how chill they seemed, were *not* chill about losing or getting drafted. Saying *You don't have to be a first-round draft pick* to an aspiring professional athlete was pointless. All of them needed it like oxygen.

Growing up, there hadn't been a single thing that could be said or done to Mags to make up for a bad game. And if Mags had been the one who played badly, it would take what felt like years for her to get over it. Sometimes it didn't seem like she ever did—she still made comments about games she'd played in high school.

"Ellie wants me to work on drills with her on the side," GJ said and readjusted on the bed. I could tell that what she'd just said, hanging in the air between us, was making her uncomfortable. "She just asked me earlier today."

"That sounds really nice." I propped myself up on my hand so I could look at her. "Are you gonna do it?"

GJ took a long inhale, her eyes fixed on the ceiling. "I mean, I told her I would. But I don't know. I feel kind of weird about it with everything. It feels kind of like a pity offer."

"Or an olive branch. She probably wanted to make sure you didn't think the team agreed with the article."

She nodded. "Yeah, I think that's what her intention actually was. But I don't know. I can't help but feel like the resident failure either way." She turned to look at me. "I'm sure Mags is loving this, though."

"Mags mostly feels defensive over the team. Somewhat surprisingly," I added with a small smile. "She's taking her shots, but pretty much everything comes down to her ego at the end of the day. She only cares about how this will all impact her."

"Well, the good news is she's probably quickly moving up in the draft pick list. I'm probably out of the first round predictions at this point."

"Maybe playing with Ellie will be a good break from it all," I offered. It was the best I could come up with.

GJ had turned back to look at the ceiling again, and I was nervous that maybe now I *was* actually overstepping. We'd gotten to know each other, but this was a conversation with weight. I didn't really *know* GJ. I knew I liked spending time with her, and I'd slowly learned about things she liked and didn't like, the things she found funny, the things she hated. But I didn't know how she was when she got annoyed or mad or frustrated. I didn't know if she was going to go cold on me because I'd asked a question that was too personal or because she'd said something she deemed too personal.

"This has been a good break from it all." Her voice was low, almost like she was telling me a secret.

My heart fluttered in my chest. There was no mistaking what she meant. "It has been," I whispered. And it was true. When I was with GJ, I didn't really think about my family at all, outside of occasionally making digs at my sister. I didn't worry about what was going to come next after graduation. I didn't feel that baseline existential fear that had really kicked into overdrive this year.

"Okay, you can read the article. But I'm not looking at your screen," she finally agreed.

"Fair enough." I picked up my phone again and moved slowly enough to give her a second in case she changed her mind. But she didn't; she let me search up the article, pull it up, and start reading.

Despite the frankly super cruel—not that I'm biased—headline, the article itself was pretty mild. It was hard on the Coyotes as a whole, and there was a lot of talking about Theo, as if any team would be able to fill the void of a number one draft pick overnight.

"They only mention you, like, twice in the actual article," I said. "And they use a great photo of you, which I feel like should count more than anything."

GJ glanced over, and I tilted my screen toward her so she could see it. "It is pretty good," she admitted.

"It literally looks like one of those pictures kids buy as a poster for their walls," I said. It was true—she was midshot, her face full of determination. Her arm muscles were also absolutely *rippling,* but I was not going to get into that with her sitting right next to me.

GJ's lips turned up in a smile. "What does the article actually say?"

"Everything you'd expect—the team is struggling, your record is good, but it's not from steady and predictable wins. A lot of *their record is from luck and not skill,* kind of thing. But you're mentioned along with pretty much every other senior on the team. I really think they did just use your name for clickbait. You're an easy target since people spent years talking about you and Theo in conjunction with each other."

GJ fixed her jaw, and I wished I could know anything at all about what she was thinking. She was sharing more with me than she ever had, but I knew she had more she could say.

"And draft predictions?" GJ asked.

My stomach knotted. That was the one part of the article that probably wouldn't feel great to hear—it was true that some people in charge were cautious about wanting to draft GJ.

There was a lot less enthusiasm now than there was last season. And it was all for predictable reasons I couldn't necessarily fault them for—they needed someone good under pressure and someone who could play consistently well.

I looked over at her. "It doesn't matter—I think you're going to prove them wrong." I put my phone down and reached for GJ to move on top of me again, knowing the best way to distract her.

Chapter Eleven

GJ

The arena was so loud that I could barely hear myself think. Despite a personally rough season, our record as a collective team was perfect, and the fans were *loving* it. It wasn't an easy perfect, and we'd only played against smaller teams so far, which wasn't promising for tournaments. At this rate, Point Brook University was going to hand us our asses when we played against them.

But none of that mattered to our fans. They cared that we were playing and that it was their favorite few hours of each week.

I rolled my shoulders from the bench, taking a second to drink some water and breathe. Despite getting experimental during practices, Coach Darlene hadn't taken away much of my time on the court. I was still putting up about the same number of minutes I always was, and I was still a starting player.

As time had gone on since the article, I was less anxious than I'd initially been. It seemed like the team genuinely didn't care that much, and no one was holding anything against me specifically. We were used to shit-talking; if we took every single negative comment someone made to heart, we'd never get anywhere.

But even so, I couldn't shake the feeling that the season might as well have been a wash. A winning record didn't mean anything if the teams we were playing were barely a competition. And we weren't even crushing them, which was the most embarrassing part of all.

The whistle blew, and Coach Darlene waved for me to go back up and switch places with Gemma. We clapped our hands together in a low-five as we passed each other.

"Go get 'em," Gemma said. "Nineteen is a shit talker."

"All the better," I responded and Gemma cackled in response as she took her seat on the bench.

I took position, carefully taking note of everyone on the court. Anna was the point guard, so we were all meant to follow her lead. No matter how much I didn't like her as a person, I owed it to the team—and myself—to at least try to fall in line with her. I'd learned my lesson during practice and really didn't need a repeat. In this moment, I needed to know where she would be before she got there, where to put myself so she could most effectively pass to me if needed.

Anna dribbled, crossing hard to her left to slide by the player blocking her. Ellie set a hard screen and didn't waver, one of her biggest strengths on the court, and the coverage on Mags was too deep to safely pass the ball to her.

I looked at Anna, seeing a clear pathway for me to get a basket. But just being able to see how we could do it was one thing; it was another to have to actually put it into action. On-court chemistry was hard to fake.

Anna saw the same thing I did, and rather than trying to get the shot herself, she passed it to me. I was too caught up in the game to be genuinely embarrassed that she was showing me up with her sportsmanship, but I knew that would haunt me later. Unfortunately, she made it really fucking hard not to like her, and I was starting to realize maybe I needed to drop the jealous, petty act.

I moved the ball up the court and then went for a quick fadeaway, knowing there wasn't time for me to think about it with a defender coming up on me.

My shot landed perfectly, only just barely brushing the rim. The crowd erupted, and despite my attempt at a cool demeanor, I was sure the relief was written all over me.

I looked over at Leah, a giant smile on her face. For a brief moment, we locked eyes, and I was certain I could see her smile somehow get even bigger. Warmth flooded my chest, and her soft, gentle voice flashed through my memory. *I think you're going to prove them wrong.*

It was such a simple statement, but it was everything. It was exactly what I'd needed at exactly the right time.

I forced myself to look away and refocus on the game, knowing I could've probably stared at her for hours if I wasn't careful. We had six minutes left in the last quarter. Just six minutes between us and continuing our undefeated record. This wasn't the time to get distracted.

When the ball was set back into motion, everything melted away. It felt exactly like it was supposed to. Moving around the court felt as natural as breathing. I didn't have to think about what to do with my hands or where to put my feet; it just happened.

For the first time all season, I felt *back*. I felt like myself. Even if just for a moment. The weight lifted from my chest, the noise that'd been buzzing in my head for weeks quieted. I felt still. Level.

I was exactly where I was supposed to be.

As the final buzzer sounded out, I was relieved to realize the win actually felt *good*. The hit of dopamine that came with knowing I'd performed to my standards was back; we'd closed the game out with a solid lead, and I'd actually contributed something to the team, which was more than I felt like I could say for every game we'd played so far.

Ellie had shown some improvement in the minutes she'd played, too. We'd been doing casual practices on the side together, running drills and working through areas of improvement.

We hadn't been able to do much in just a few short weeks, but it was something. And it admittedly felt pretty good to know I played a part in that, too, even though Ellie had already been such a strong player. I was starting to realize the power of just making sure someone knew other people believed in them, as corny as it was.

"You and Anna are good together," Nia said after we finished shaking the hands of the other team. She squirted water into her mouth and took a deep breath. "At least, when you actually let her play with you instead of playing like you're one-sided mortal enemies."

I half rolled my eyes, but I knew she was right to say it. That was exactly the difference in how this game felt compared to the others. I was used to having beef with my teammates, but I wasn't used to being jealous of them.

Even though Ellie hadn't said it straight out, I could pick up on what she was suggesting by having me help coach her. We were a team, and we were in this together, whether I liked everyone or not. Annoyingly, forcing myself to play nice was exactly what I'd needed.

"Good movement today, GJ," Coach Darlene said with a supportive squeeze of my shoulder.

"Thanks, Coach." I tried to keep my expression as professional and chill as possible, but Leah's comment about how my face gave everything away popped into my mind.

I looked around to see if she was still there and then remembered that it didn't matter if she was still here—I couldn't say hi. Not with Mags here.

Part of me just wanted to say fuck it, but that was a decision I was going to leave up to Leah. Her relationship with her family was already tense; I wasn't going to add to it until told otherwise.

If ever told otherwise.

I shook the thought away. There wasn't a universe where Leah was going to want to make this something serious. I knew better than to play that game, even as someone who'd never been in the position of having a crush before.

Before I could get myself too caught up in my feelings, I was dragged off to a post-game presser. As had been the standard for this season, Mags, Anna, and I were the featured members of the Coyotes.

As much as I didn't mind being the center of attention, I'd come to find these pretty repetitive and usually pretty dull. There were only so many ways to answer questions about games before it felt like just saying the same things over and over again. *We played hard. There's always room for improvement, but I'm proud of my team.* Occasionally, we could throw out something like *it wasn't our best, but we learned from it*. Rinse and repeat.

The same faces that we saw at every post-game smiled at us as we settled into our seats. It all felt like white noise. Reporters ran through questions, and I answered them on autopilot.

"Following the *Sports Illustrated* article about your team, we'd expect morale to potentially take a hit, but this seems to be the best game you've played all season," one of the reporters said, making me sit up a little straighter in my seat. Even though he wasn't saying my name directly, his eyes were firmly on me. The knot in my chest tightened, anxiously awaiting whatever was about to come next. "Good motivator to play hard?"

"Is there an actual question in that?" Anna asked from next to me, leaning into her mic. The room went still—Anna was a skilled player and didn't necessarily mince her words, but she also wasn't known for being direct in that way. "And the article wasn't about us—it was about recruiters' opinions of us. If it'd really been for us, they'd have reached out for a quote." Anna paused for a beat and then waved her hand. "Next question."

I glanced down the table, and Anna looked back at me, a nearly imperceptible look exchanged between the two of us.

Neither of us acknowledged it as we wrapped up the press conference, or as we went back to the locker room. But it still meant something regardless. I wasn't sure exactly what, but it was something.

I checked my phone to see that Theo had texted, congratulating me on the game and a few of the shots I'd made.

Theo

You looked back today, it was good to see

From a different text chain, my phone was vibrating basically nonstop. I smiled at the *outside!!!!* text Vivian had sent. Everyone had been texting for weeks on and off about coming, but I wasn't sure it would actually be able to happen. I was glad it did, even if I was sure my family was absolutely going to credit being at the game for the reason I played so well.

After changing into something more appropriate for a dinner out, I threw my bag over my shoulder and headed out to go find them.

I heard my family as soon as I opened the door to leave the arena. The cold air bit at my skin, the sun completely gone from the sky now. I knew they loved me to be willing to hang out in this and wait for me.

"Here she comes! Our star player!" Vivian called out as Bev did a pathetic but earnest attempt at our school's fight song. Vivian roped Eli and Shantae into it, twirling them around. Ada, in true eldest daughter fashion, hung back and laughed along at how ridiculous they were being.

I walked over, and my family wrapped me in one hug after another. My nervous system immediately felt so much calmer in response. As much as I could handle my shit on my own, there was nothing like having them around.

"That was a solid game, GJ. Looked like you had a lot of fun," Dad said. He'd never been much of an athlete—he played ball here and there, but mostly because that was what people thought tall kids should do with their time. From what he'd told me, he'd never been particularly coordinated or very good at actually playing, at least not to the level that he would've needed to play past JV.

Mom wrapped me in a warm hug, immediately making me feel like a kid again in the best way. "You did good, baby,"

"Thanks," I said, even though what I really wanted to say was *still wasn't good enough*. Despite the game ending on a high note and joking with Theo, the presser had put me in a weird headspace that reminded me of how fragile it all was. Things were fine right now, but I didn't know how they'd be next game.

But my parents didn't like it when I was too hard on myself, so I always tried to keep the negative talk to myself when I was around them. I knew they were just proud of me in general; the specifics didn't have to matter.

Across the way, I saw a familiar figure that I knew could only be one person. I didn't know at what point I'd memorized the curves of her body, the way she walked, well enough to spot her from a distance, but I wasn't complaining.

"Leah!" I called out without thinking. The cheerleader she was walking with waved and headed off as Leah walked over toward me.

"Who is that?" Vivan whispered to my sisters from behind me and I brushed the question off. I met Leah halfway—ideally a decent enough distance from my family that they couldn't overhear me. I didn't necessarily mean to blow my family off, but I'd seen Mags and Gemma leave so I knew this was my chance to talk to Leah, even if just for a second. I had the rest of the night to be with my family.

"Hey," she said with a smile as she approached. I could see her breath in the cold, and the bright exterior stadium lights caught her makeup just right, making her practically glow.

I couldn't stop myself from smiling. I could feel it through my entire body just standing next to her. "Hey."

Leah and I stood there smiling at each other for so long that it started to get weird. I realized a beat too late that she probably thought that I had something to say to her since I was the one who had called her over.

"Not a bad game, right?" I teased. I could tell there was a part of me—probably a big part of me, if I was being honest—that wanted to hear a compliment from her.

"It was really good, you looked confident out there," Leah said. She looked behind me. "Is that your family staring at us and whispering?"

I laughed, embarrassed. "That would be them."

"Cute," she said, her face softening. There was an undertone of sadness to it that made my heart ache. She looked past me at my family. "Your niece and nephew are so cute."

"Do you want to meet them?" I asked without thinking.

I hadn't introduced a girl to my family since I was in high school and even then, I was so weird about labels that she was just *the girl I was going to prom with* or *a friend*. I didn't know what the fuck had come over me, but it was too late to turn back down.

Leah looked equally as surprised, but when I didn't take it back, she nodded. "Yeah, I'd love to."

As we walked over together, I saw my sisters exchange a look.

"Thank god, I was worried you weren't going to bring her over here," Vivian said to me, always the first to speak and the biggest personality of the family. She turned to Leah. "It's like she's embarrassed of us or something."

"With good reason," I offered and Vivian held her hand up to tell me to shut it.

"I'm Leah."

"You are so *cute*. Well, I'm Vivian, this is Bev and the one who looks like she never smiles is Ada," Vivian explained, pointing to each sister as she spoke. "And then, of course, you already know Georgia Jane."

"*Vivian*," I said, fighting off a groan. She was going to be getting an earful from me.

"Georgia Jane." Leah turned to me with a smile. "Beautiful names."

"*Very* southern," Vivian widened her eyes to add emphasis. "Our cutie pie parents can't resist a theme."

I would've been more annoyed at this being Leah's initial introduction if this wasn't so quintessentially Vivian. She'd behaved the exact same way when she met Theo even after she'd confirmed Theo was still not my type. "Cutie pie is one way of describing them."

"They are extremely successful professors and academics, by the way," Ada called over. "Just to put Vivian's words into context."

Vivian nodded. "Daddy is an engineer, too, in addition to teaching," she bragged proudly.

I glanced over at Leah to gauge how she was feeling. I hadn't been prepared for her to meet my family—hadn't even been prepared for *me* to see them today—so I hadn't had the chance to prep her for any of it. It felt especially shitty right now, considering she was in the middle of a cold war with her entire family.

But instead of looking uneasy, she was all smiles.

"And then who are these two?" Leah asked, lowering to meet my niece and nephew at eye level.

"Eli and Shantae, my babies," Vivian said. "I was going to leave them back home with my husband, but the kids have a way of going everywhere I go."

Bev laughed. "You say that like it's his fault. Vivian can't go anywhere without them."

Shantae looked at Leah through her round glasses. Her hair was done up in two puffs, and she was dressed like a little librarian—more Shantae's taste than Vivian's. She hovered close to her mom's side, always the shier of the two kids. "Are you a cheerleader?" she asked quietly, looking at Leah.

Leah fully squatted. "I am. I was a dancer first, though. Do you dance?"

"I have ballet every Wednesday."

"Oh, ballet is so fun. I did ballet and contemporary dance growing up. I did a little bit of jazz, too," Leah said. "I can go teach you some cheerleading moves if you want, so your mom and aunt can catch up?" She glanced up at Vivian and me to ask for confirmation that it was okay.

"Please, I'll never say no to someone watching the kids. Even an obsessed mom needs a breather sometimes," Vivian said and gently guided Shantae away from her side so she'd go with Leah. She gestured for Eli to go with her, too. It never took him much convincing to do anything, though, so he followed easily behind.

Leah headed off with the kids nearby, talking to them. It was impossible to keep my eyes off of her. I wanted to watch her every move, see how my niece and nephew responded to her. I didn't want to miss a single second of it.

"She's very pretty," Vivian said, pulling her attention away. Her face was lit up, practically glowing from the inside—this was the kind of thing she lived for.

I waved her off. "You're always in my business."

"Oh, so you *like* her," she teased.

I groaned and threw my hands up. "Can you not?"

"I'm just calling it like I see it."

I looked back over at Leah, where she was showing the kids her pom poms and how to hold them. It made me think about what she might've been like as a kid in dance, so young and so excited. It made me sad that it didn't seem like her parents understood it.

"Can we get moving to dinner, please? I'm freezing, and I need to get off my feet," Bev said, hand to her stomach. The last time I saw her, she hadn't had a baby bump at all, but now even her heavy winter coat was having a hard time concealing it. "Ada? Need you to wrangle everyone. Use your bossiness."

Ada threw her hands up. "I'm not bossy," she said, immediately annoyed. She had been deep in a conversation with my partners, probably talking about something grown-up I didn't want to have to think about yet. She and her boyfriend were always talking about plans for buying property and making investments and planning for retirement. Even though she was only six years older than me, she felt like she was light-years ahead.

"Okay, well, then be *useful* and get everyone moving." Bev smiled sweetly.

Ada looked at me. "Tell GJ the only person missing is her girlfriend."

"Oh, okay, hold on now," I said, hands up. "Roll that one back."

"You're going to tell me I'm wrong?"

"We are, by definition, not dating," I said and looked back over at Leah. Seeing the way that she was acting with my niece and nephew didn't particularly help my case. Even as I was insisting she wasn't my girlfriend, she was taking the time to teach them basic cheerleading moves. There was a smile on her face, and even Shantae seemed to be having a good time, her shy smile having turned into one that almost looked like enjoyment.

Vivian looked at me and then between my sisters. I knew the unspoken sisterly language between us well enough to know they didn't believe me. "Okay."

I waved them off. "Man, whatever."

Bev and Vivian cackled in response. When they were done laughing—wiping tears from their eyes and everything, because they weren't already annoying enough—Vivian called her kids back over. "Let's go, we're hungry and cold. I don't know how your aunt survives out here. I've never missed Alabama so much in my life."

"Dramatic as hell."

Vivian rolled her eyes and held up her hand in my direction. "Bye."

Her kids hurried back over, Leah following closely behind.

"How were they as students?" Vivian asked proudly as Shantae wrapped her arms around her mom.

"The best. Stellar," Leah said with a smile. Despite her heavy winter coat, her cheeks and the tip of her nose were bright pink from the cold. She looked ridiculously cute, the kind of cute that would've made me want to introduce her to my family if she wasn't already standing next to them.

Vivian beamed with pride as if Leah was ever going to be dumb enough to do anything but praise the kids. "Exactly what I'd expect of them," she responded and turned her attention to Shantae and Eli. "Okay, gloves still on, no coats or scarves missing—you look good. I think we're ready to head out."

"We're good?" Ada called out, using her typical project manager voice.

"She always speaks to us like she's wrangling a classroom of twenty rather than a group of adults," Bev joked lightheartedly, knocking her shoulder into Leah's. Leah cracked an amused smile. When Leah realized I was looking at her, she turned her attention my way and her smile softened even more. It was a smile just for me—the best kind there was.

"Are you coming with us?" Ada asked, looking at Leah. Leah's eyes broke away from mine, and it felt like getting pulled out of a trance.

"That's her way of inviting you," Bev explained.

Leah's face softened again. "Oh, no. I have some homework to catch up on and some things to get done, unfortunately. But it was amazing to meet you all."

"It was wonderful to meet you. I'm sure we'll see you around soon," Vivian said, and I didn't bother to argue with the interpretation. There was no use in trying to get through to my sisters—they were too stubborn to let something like that go.

They started heading out to their rental cars in the parking lot. Before following behind, I turned to Leah. "Do you need me to walk you back? Did you take your car here?"

She took a step closer to me. "I won't take away from your time with your family. I can find my way home." She watched as they walked out to their cars, talking and laughing. "They're really nice."

"Yeah, I'm very lucky."

Leah and I stood there for another beat, neither of us moving or speaking. I looked at her and debated whether I could kiss her—if I *should* kiss her. It felt natural at this point in knowing each other, but I also knew how much I wanted her, and that made all the difference. I didn't know what she wanted yet, and it wouldn't benefit either of us if I tried to push it.

"Have a good night, Leah," I said.

"You too," she responded, and we both slowly began walking in our respective directions, our paces slower than usual as if one of us just might change our minds and insist on going with the other one. I was tempted. But I wasn't going to blow off my family just because I had a crush on a girl, even if that girl was Leah.

But even so, I didn't take my eyes off of her until she was too deep into the parking lot for me to see her.

Chapter Twelve

Leah

I woke up the next morning with a ball of light in my chest and a literal pep in my step. It was the only way to describe it. I felt like a Disney princess—birds literally chirping outside, warm light streaming through the window.

As soon as I opened my eyes, I got out of bed and pulled on some clothes to go for a run. I could hear Mags banging around pots and pans in the kitchen as she put away the clean dishes we'd left out to dry.

Despite GJ and me just having spoken last night, I felt like we might have as well have had absolutely filthy sex. I'd never experienced this before, even with my biggest crushes—I was *happy*. As I brushed my teeth, I leaned into the mirror to inspect my skin. My cheeks were rosy pink, and I didn't even have bags under my eyes.

This was ridiculous.

But it also felt...good. It was the kind of feeling I didn't want to go away. I wasn't interested in bringing myself back to earth or thinking about what all of this meant or how stupid it would be for me to lean into having a crush on GJ; I just wanted to enjoy this for a minute. I could let myself be a little naive without it ruining my whole life.

After putting up my hair, I headed into the kitchen.

"Did you end up picking up more frozen strawberries?" I asked as I opened the freezer. Mags didn't respond, but I brushed it off; she wasn't much of a morning person to begin with. When I found the giant family-sized bag in the freezer, I pulled it out and shut the freezer door behind me.

"When are you leaving for your away game?" I asked. Mags was quiet again, which was now enough to trigger my annoyance. It didn't take much. "Mags? Hello? Anyone home?"

She kept her eyes fixed on her phone. "Why? Are you asking because you want to know when GJ is going to be leaving town?"

My blood ran cold. I'd never been a convincing liar, but I was about to have to put on the performance of my life. "What are you talking about?"

"I know you were with GJ."

The statement was so vague that it almost felt like a trap. It was just asking for me to walk into giving Mags more information than what she knew—or thought she knew.

"At the game? Along with the rest of the basketball players?" I asked, trying as best as I could to play it off. My sunny disposition from earlier was quickly melting away into something much heavier and guiltier. And something more nervous, too. All of the worst-case scenarios were playing out in my head in rapid succession as I waited for Mags to respond.

"Funny." Mags crossed her arms and leaned against the counter. "Gemma and I saw you after the game. She drove me home because you had the car, and it was too cold to walk. You were with GJ's family."

I nearly let out a sigh of relief. I wasn't exactly *thrilled* Mags was potentially onto us now, but just seeing me with GJ's family was nothing. A friend would do that; Theo used to do that all the time.

"Yeah, I ran into them outside. I was just trying to be friend-ly."

"By teaching GJ's niece and nephew different cheers?"

"They're kids. That's like, what you do with kids," I said, scrambling to find explanations that didn't make me sound guilty. I knew in the grand scheme of things, disobeying my sister and fooling around with someone was pretty low on the list of unforgivable acts. But still, I knew how my sister was going to feel about me fooling around with a teammate. And not just any teammate, but GJ, who Mags infamously had never gotten along with. Even if I didn't like the rule, my sister had always communicated it clearly and made it known that she wouldn't approve. I'd intentionally chosen not to give a fuck about her feelings, or to even try to talk to her before jumping into something. And no matter how annoying those feelings were, Mags probably deserved better than that.

Mags leaned her back against the counter and looked at me. "I don't like the idea of you being close to GJ."

"It wasn't even really about GJ; it was about GJ's family. I was just saying hi. You're spinning this into something bigger than it was," I insisted. My heart rate picked up. I hated the idea of upsetting Mags so much that I was already playing out in my head how I was going to call this whole thing with GJ before it went too far. I was sure GJ would understand. It was the right thing to do—even if the thought of it opened an unexpected pit of sadness in me.

"GJ doesn't let girls meet her family. Ever."

I fought off my lips turning up at the thought. I'd gathered based on her family's teasing that they didn't meet many of GJ's conquests—and that made sense, considering it would be a constant rotation. But I assumed there'd been at least a handful that had been serious enough to justify meeting her family. I turned my head quickly away from Mags so she wouldn't see the thrilled expression on my face. "Maybe you should take that as a good thing, then. She views me more as one of you guys than some girl she's interested in."

"I don't think so," Mags said. "Twin-tuition."

I rolled my eyes. "We haven't said that since we were, like, twelve years old. Maybe now that we're older, you don't know me as well as you think you do."

"No, I think I see exactly what's happening. Even with you insisting it's nothing, I know you, and I know that you have a tendency to latch onto people. Your taste has always been bad, and someone like GJ is exactly that—"

I frowned, immediately offended even though she was right to say it. Mostly. Just minus the GJ part since GJ has demonstrated to actually be different so far. "What's that supposed to mean?"

Mags threw her hands up. "You like them emotionally unavailable and difficult to reach. You like the chase and the feeling of someone wanting you. You have so many people who've had crushes on you over the years, and you have never paid attention to any of it because you're always fixated on the person you can't have."

I scoffed. "*So many people* is an exaggeration."

"I've had, like, basically entire team rosters I've had to fight to keep away from you. People ask all the time at parties if I know if you're seeing someone. But you still make it *so hard* for yourself for some reason."

I was annoyed—both by how much she was simplifying the situation, and how she wasn't lying. I *did* make it difficult for myself. I didn't have a shortage of options, and I was sure I could've found a nice partner by now if I'd really wanted to. But I never wanted them nice. Mags was right to say it; she was just being intentionally dense about why that would be the case.

"For some reason?" I snapped. The guilt I was feeling earlier was washed away by bold-faced annoyance. "It doesn't take a fancy therapist to realize that I chase shitty people because that's how you guys make me feel."

"What the fuck do you mean by *you guys*?"

"You know *exactly* what I mean. I have never been anything to our parents because of you. I am always in your shadow. All I know is chasing people down for approval and wanting them to care about me." I put the frozen fruit back in the freezer, not wanting it to melt over the course of our conversation. My smoothie was long forgotten by now. "You don't get to play dumb on that. I know it's hard for you to see because Mom and Dad have always loved you and made it clear how much they love you. You probably don't even realize how hard and awful and distant they're capable of being. And I'm so happy for you that that's the case, but you don't get to act like this is all some big surprise. My dating history sucks, and it's self-inflicted, but it's not out of nowhere."

Mags shook her head. "You are so stuck on this idea that Mom and Dad secretly resent you or something. It's honestly kind of crazy. They take great care of us. We've had so many opportunities—"

I groaned into my hands. "I'm not getting into this with you. I can't. I have things to do today. You've never listened to me, and you never will."

"Oh, great. Here we go again with the fucking melodrama—"

"God, you are the *worst*." I took a deep breath, doing everything in my power to calm myself down. My hands were literally shaking.

"What is going on with you?" Mags asked, dropping her voice back down to a normal speaking volume. "You've been so *weird* this year."

I shrugged, less from a place of uncertainty and more from a place of *I don't know, leave me the fuck alone.* "It's senior year. We're preparing for a big transition."

"I just want to make sure you're okay. I want what's best for you," Mags said, her voice raised again in an effort to really make me hear her. But it was such a familiar refrain that it didn't mean anything to me anymore. My parents also always insisted that they wanted what was best for me, but they'd never actually asked me what that meant to me. There was no concern over what I wanted.

I lowered my voice. I didn't have a fight in me—there was no use. I'd been trying my best to figure out how to communicate with my family and how to finally stand up for myself, and it was becoming abundantly clear that maybe my issue wasn't that I didn't have a backbone—it was that I knew the people I was talking to sucked at listening. "Yeah, okay."

"And what's best for you starts with not surrounding yourself with shitty people anymore. Okay?" Mags said, ducking her head so she could meet my eyes. I refused to look at her, turning my head so my eyes were fixed on the subway tile lining our kitchen walls. "I don't like seeing you go through all of that. You deserve better than to be crying over people. And GJ is the last person you want to get yourself caught up in. You fall hard and fast, and if you think the people you've been down bad for before are awful, GJ is a million times worse. Even if you just picked her because you knew it'd drive me insane, you need to stop before it goes too far."

That stopped me in my tracks. "What the fuck are you talking about?"

"I mean, it's obvious that this has to do with me. The person I hate most on my team and my sister? Either one or both of you is doing it vindictively. You can't tell me that's not the case."

I was so caught off guard that my mouth just hung open, no words coming out. I didn't even bother trying to keep up a convincing lie anymore—it didn't feel worth it. I blinked and shook my head. "You think this is *because* of you?"

"Literally, what other reason would there be? You just got mad at Mom and Dad and are basically fighting with them. And based on how you're talking to me now, you seem to harbor some kind of resentment over being treated unfairly in the family. I don't know. I know you think I'm stupid, but I can connect dots. It's an easy form of revenge."

I looked at her, locking our eyes so she knew that I really meant it. "Right now, I don't think you're stupid—I just think you're self-centered."

Mags rolled her eyes, never capable of taking anything I say seriously. "Whatever. I have to go. Sorry for trying to help you."

"Yeah, fine. Whatever." It wasn't the most clever closing line I'd ever had, but it was the best I could come up with. My body was buzzing with adrenaline and agitation and hurt. And there was the tiniest bit of fear in there too—the fear of how close Mags was to figuring out the whole truth and the fear of how she would act if she ever found out everything.

In a way, I understood where she was coming from with wanting to keep me away from GJ. On the surface, it looked like an awful match—even Soph had been skeptical and probably still was. I was always chasing someone who I knew would inevitably go on to hurt me, always seeking the approval of someone I didn't even really like just because I wanted the satisfaction of knowing they liked me.

But despite Mags's insistence that GJ was no good for me, there was one person who listened to me and supported me between the two of them, and it wasn't Mags.

Chapter Thirteen

GJ

Despite my last game being a good one, I went into practice cautious. I didn't want to overestimate myself and believe that the season was really about to turn around, but it had felt really fucking good to feel like myself again. It was a feeling I wanted to hold onto.

It also didn't hurt having my family around—or Leah—even just for a little bit. As supportive as my family had always been, it was from a distance for most of the season. Theo had always been my go-to whenever I needed someone to talk some sense into me or congratulate me on doing a good job. I'd forgotten how good it felt to have someone who could be there for me immediately after a game and help take my mind off things. My mom always talked about the importance of a village and community, and I was seeing that now. Theo used to be basically my entire village at Lakeside Green, but I'd been forced to find something new to keep me going.

And the fact that Leah was part of that definitely didn't hurt.

It'd taken every ounce of willpower I had not to bother her for the rest of the weekend. Part of that was enjoying the limited amount of time I had with my family, but I also didn't want it to feel too intense and too sudden. It was a lot for her to have so suddenly and accidentally met my family, and it was new territory for me. I didn't know the exact protocol, but I couldn't think of anything more mortifying than deciding immediately after meeting my family was the time to get clingy and weird with her.

Despite the good mood I was in—an extremely fragile one, but one either way—I could always count on Mags to ruin it in about half a second.

"What's up your ass?" I asked as I opened my locker to drop my stuff off for practice. She was sitting on the bench, her foot up so she could tie her shoe. She rolled her eyes, and I could think of about a million things it might be—including her just feeling like being an asshole. She liked to make it everyone's problem when she was having a bad day. "Good talk," I said when she didn't respond.

As we all went out to the practice court to stretch before practice, Nia walked over to me and sat down on the ground to work on her hamstrings. "Nice work at the last game, Mitchell."

"Someone has to carry the rest of you to the finish line," I joked.

"I'd ask if you're feeling okay after that article, but it seems like you're just fine." She flipped her hair over her shoulder as she moved to stretch her other leg. "I'm sorry about that reporter, though. That was fucked up."

"It's alright. Someone's always saying something."

"That was profound."

"Here for you if you need some philosophical guidance."

Coach Darlene then walked out with the other coaching staff, their steps echoing through the gym. "Alright, huddle up," she said, waving us all in. "We played a good game, but I don't want to see you all getting cocky. Our defense needs work, rebounds especially. And I need to see more conversation on the court; there's a lot of dancing around each other, and we can't afford to make mistakes."

After getting a general overview from our coaches, we broke out into groups for passing drills. As I crossed the court, Mags shoulder checked me so hard that it knocked my body forward. Nia glanced over at me, and I shrugged. It was about what I'd expect from her.

We took our positions on the court for a criss-cross drill. Just to be an asshole, I stood across from Mags, knowing she'd hate having to be partners for this.

"Can anyone else do this, please?" Mags asked, rolling her eyes.

I bounced my basketball, unfazed. "You're stuck with me, partner."

"Whatever," she muttered. She rolled her ball between her hands and bounced it a few times, looking down the line in Gemma's direction. Gemma was too busy chatting with Anna to notice.

Our offensive coach blew the whistle, and we started. The drill wasn't anything particularly complex—we stood in two lines facing each other, all of us with our own balls. I never minded the dribbling and passing exercises because it was something I'd always been good at as a point guard.

In unison, Mags and I bounced our individual basketballs twice and then tossed them to each other. But Mags tossed the ball *hard* in my direction—really hard. It was subtle enough that anyone watching would just assume Mags was super focused on the drill, but I knew better. She was clearly pissed at me.

"You good?" I asked, looking back toward her. She just scoffed and rolled her eyes. Even though this wasn't new behavior for her, something about this felt different. Intentional.

It seemed like more than just being in a bad mood; it seemed like she might actually be mad at me. Realistically, that could be about anything since Mags was always on one—she didn't like a decision I'd made during the game, she thought a joke I told was annoying.

But I had a gut feeling that I knew what it was about.

I wasn't sure enough to say something, and there was always a chance I was just paranoid, but something told me that it had to be her sister. I'd played on the same team as Mags long enough to know her different attitudes, and this one was a new one.

But it didn't make any sense why she'd know something—or even just think that she knew something. I'd seen her and Gemma leave the arena after the last game, and Leah and I were intentional about not hanging out otherwise. We were dumb, and I didn't give a single fuck about Mags's feelings, but we weren't *that* dumb or that malicious to rub it in her face.

But I would just have to wait until someone said something, because I wasn't about to accidentally expose myself if Mags was mad at me about something else.

We ran through the drill until the whistle blew again and we transitioned to shooting. As we broke out into different parts of the court depending on where we were assigned, I turned to Mags. "You got something to say?" I asked.

Mags turned to me, her blue eyes practically burning holes into me. "What are you talking about?"

"Your panties seem extra twisted up today. Just checking in. Captain shit." It was a dick move to throw in the last part since I knew how badly Mags had wanted to be captain this year. But if there was anyone else less equipped than me to be the team's glue, it was her. I was an asshole on the court, and Coach Darlene wanted to strangle me more often than not, but Mags was a difficult teammate to work with. It was the kind of thing that was going to catch up with her later if she wasn't careful.

Mags's jaw tightened. My stomach knotted when I realized it seemed like she actually did want to say something to me and was just debating whether it was worth it to go there or not.

"I saw you guys. You and Leah. What the fuck is your problem, dude? You finally run out of random girls to fuck on campus, so now you have to go after my sister?" Mags snapped.

There it was. I was definitely playing with fire, engaging with her when she was this mad, but she also definitely didn't know the full story. If she did, she would've thrown a punch by now. "What are you even on—"

"I saw you guys together after the game yesterday."

I nearly scoffed at her. If she was that worked up over a simple conversation outside in a public setting, she'd be *pissed* to hear about what went on behind closed doors. The opportunity to get smart with her was right there, but I wasn't going to do it. I liked Leah too much to risk throwing it away like this, all as a way of proving some kind of stupid point to Mags.

Unfortunately—inevitability—our scuffle was catching the attention of our teammates. It wasn't unusual for words to be exchanged—as much as we all cared about each other and were teammates, we were athletes first. There was a lot of ego involved in playing a team sport ,whether we wanted there to be or not, and it could get ugly sometimes, bad enough that it could fuck up the chemistry of the entire team on and off the court. We were fortunate to usually keep our heads on straight enough to play well, but sometimes things got more heated than just some offhand smack talk.

"Mags, it's fine. None of us would want GJ dating our sister, but she can be trusted to talk to women without it meaning anything," Nia cut in.

"I'm a little offended by that, but thank you," I said.

Gemma looked between Mags and me. "Maybe we should stick to focusing on practice."

Mags still had a look in her eye like she was a dog ready to bite, but I could see her posture visibly relax in response to Gemma. If Mags didn't realize she was into Gemma, she was even more of an idiot than I'd chalked her up to be, and that was saying something.

"Whatever." Mags bounced her basketball and headed back to a different side of the court, away from me.

"Can you chill, please?" Nia asked me. "Do not disturb the wild animals, do not tap on the glass."

I put my hands up defensively. "She started it."

Nia looked at me for a beat, like she was sizing me up. "Right."

I brushed off the look—Nia was a straight shooter, so if she really had something to say, she would just say it.

After running through practice and just barely managing to avoid bodily harm at the hands of Mags, I walked over to the army of water bottles on the floor and found mine.

"Mags is kind of on one today, no?" Anna asked and then took a sip of water. She dabbed sweat from her forehead using her shirt.

I was a little surprised Anna was initiating conversation with me, but I wasn't in the mood to be a dickhead to her. I wasn't so awful that I was going to brush off someone who'd saved my ass very publicly in front of a bunch of reporters. "She's always on one."

"Yeah, so I've gathered since transferring here." She put her water bottle down. "Whatever is going on, I'm on your side."

I nearly laughed. "Without even knowing what's happening?"

Anna shrugged. "You're a loudmouth, but you back up what you say. I can appreciate that. Even if you were on the wrong side, you'd be loud and wrong. It doesn't even seem like you know what you did." She rolled out her shoulders. "And anyway, her sister is a grown ass woman. You guys can make your own mistakes."

The one thing I really didn't appreciate about Mags bringing everything with Leah up was that now everyone on the team was going to know Leah was on my radar. And while I normally didn't mind being associated with girls, the last thing I needed was for everyone to be on high alert if I was anywhere in Leah's vicinity. We'd gotten away with slipping away together at a party once, but that was definitely never happening again.

I didn't want to tell Anna that I actually knew *exactly* what I did, and it was even worse than Mags was imagining. As far as my teammates and Mags were allowed to know, nothing was actually going on with Leah.

But that didn't mean I couldn't agree with Anna that Leah was allowed to do her own thing. Because she *was* right, Leah should be allowed to date whoever she wanted. Or even just sleep with whoever she wanted. My reputation had never been a secret, so it wasn't like Leah wouldn't know what she was getting herself into.

Now, if only Mags would just see it that way.

"I really didn't want to like you," I admitted.

Anna grinned. "Finally, some confirmation. I've been pretty sure since the first day we met at practice. Feels good to finally have you say you've had beef."

I fought off a smile. "Don't get too soft on me now."

I was surprised by how much better I felt after letting myself warm up to her. It was almost like being jealous of one of my teammates didn't actually accomplish anything.

What a corny ass discovery. At least Theo would be proud.

Chapter Fourteen

Leah

Despite Mags being up my ass about things with GJ, it was impossible to stay away from GJ. When she texted me after my run, and I saw her name pop up on my phone, my heart legitimately fluttered. There was no way in hell I was going to call things off with her for the sake of my sister's feelings.

As I opened GJ's message, I turned on the shower in my bathroom, a smile already on my face.

GJ

I think our cover is blown

Even though that text should've been enough to send me into a full-blown panic, I was surprisingly calm. Mags had already bitched me out, so it wasn't exactly surprising she'd also gone after GJ. And since my phone wasn't blowing up, I could only assume GJ had done an equally good job at downplaying what was going on between us.

I felt bad that GJ was caught up in the middle of what should've been a feud between sisters, but I also kind of liked the thrill. It felt good to finally be doing something for myself—and there was something kind of hot about sneaking around.

And Mags being so insistent that all of this was because of her and just a way of getting revenge made me all the more determined to see it through. It was hard to bring myself to care about her feelings when she very clearly didn't care about mine.

I bit back a smile just thinking about it. I was having by far the best sex of my life, to the point where I understood why people literally craved being with their partner. I was practically crawling out of my skin when I went too long without seeing her—and that was going to have to be the case because of the away games coming up.

When GJ and I had first started hooking up, I hadn't realized that the biggest problem I'd run into was not being able to get enough of her. If anything, I would've assumed that, by now, things would've fizzled. With everyone else, it was so obvious what there was to not like, and I'd just ignore it.

But with GJ, I couldn't find anything to get icked out by, or any real reason to end things. Even with everything about her laid out so clearly—her dating history and her ego, the way she could barely be around for most of the school year because of basketball—I still wanted her. I still couldn't find anything that I didn't like.

As I put down my phone, I allowed myself one small squeal before forcing myself to be cool again.

As much as I appreciated having a quiet house while Mags was away for basketball, I really wished I could have GJ over to keep me company. In all of my years of quietly fantasizing about what it would be like to date one of Mags's teammates, I'd never considered how annoying it was that they were on the same exact schedule.

It also didn't help that I was prone to getting restless when I was left alone for too long. Soph was busy working on a group project for class, Mags wasn't around to bicker with, and GJ wasn't around to sneak off to, so it was just me for most of the weekend.

I leaned against the kitchen island, scrolling through my phone to see what I could do to pass the time on a Saturday. A party invite was getting passed around in the group chat, with some of the girls planning on going out early and staying out through the night. A few other girls talked about potentially hitting up The 151 or Stephen's—which I was still avoiding like the plague after everything that happened with Kai.

I looked at the digital party flyer for a day party at a nearby frat. It wouldn't exactly be my favorite scene in the world, but my friends would be there, and it was never a bad time with them.

But as much as I liked going out and drinking, I think I liked getting picked up and walked home more. And GJ wasn't here to do that.

I nearly rolled my eyes at myself. What kind of person had I turned into? Potentially skipping out on parties all because the person I wanted to kiss couldn't pick me up at the end of it?

The sex really was that good, so I couldn't *entirely* blame myself. But that was obviously the only reason. It wasn't like I was genuinely looking forward to seeing GJ and talking to her and maybe even coming up with some kind of weak excuse to sleep next to her again.

Not at all.

My phone vibrated and part of me—stupidly—hoped that maybe GJ was texting. But it was the group chat again instead.

Reese

Teaching a class today, sorry guys. I'll catch you next time

After reading her message, I nearly locked my phone and put it to the side, not thinking twice about it. But in the middle of doing so, I paused.

It had been amazing to meet GJ's family—they were warm and kind, and I could see where GJ's sense of humor and bold personality came from. They were everything I wished my family could be.

But beyond that, it had been so nice to meet her niece and nephew and remember what it felt like to just *dance* again. I'd taught them some basic cheer moves, but I'd mostly fallen back on the things that I'd learned in my dance classes around their age. There were so many cute basics that I hadn't thought about in so long because I hadn't really needed to. I used a different skillset for cheer than I did for dancing, and I was over a decade and a half out from my first-ever dance class; it was easy to forget how fun it had been at the beginning.

I smiled, thinking about their little giggles as they practiced a mix of jazz and ballet and random moves I only vaguely remembered. It was a challenge to be on the teaching side of things for the first time ever, especially for kids, but they also didn't seem to care that much. They didn't need to know that I was making it up as I went; all they knew was that I was having just as much as they were.

I pulled up the class schedule for the Lakeside Green gym, knowing exactly what it was that I wanted to do this weekend.

For the first time since I started as a student at Lakeside Green, I took the hallways toward the dance studios at the gym. I hadn't been inside a dance studio in general since I was in high school, and it was weirdly intimidating. The entire walk over from my apartment, I was convinced that I was making a stupid mistake and I should just turn back around.

But another part of me remembered how much I used to love it, and how stupid it was for me not to just let myself enjoy it all these years.

"Leah! Do my eyes deceive me?" Reese cried out when she saw me walk in the door. She ran over and gave me a hug. "I had no idea you were coming!"

"Yeah, I saw your text in the group chat and decided it was probably time I actually came by."

"I'm so glad you did. This class is *so* fun, and you'll love the regulars. We've gotten a really good group going since the semester started," Reese bragged proudly. "Are you ready to do some intermediate jazz?"

I'd been so caught up in seeing that Reese was teaching that I hadn't even paid attention to what the actual class was. "I guess I'll have to be," I said and put my bag down against the front wall under the mirrors. I hadn't taken a jazz class at all in so long that I wasn't sure intermediate was the place to start, but it was too late now.

"You're going to do great," Reese said with a wink. She tightened her curly blonde ponytail and then looked up at the clock before turning her attention back to the room of about six people. "Okay, five more minutes and then we'll get started."

I stretched out my body, mostly to put my nervous energy toward something. Even though I could tell it made Reese happy, I was nervous about having to actually dance again. And knowing it was an intermediate class made me want to run for the hills; I might not have a beginner's technique, but I no longer had the skills of a trained dancer.

After five minutes of me half-stretching and shyly smiling at everyone who came in, Reese clapped her hands. "Alright, let's get moving. We'll start with our stretches first, and then we'll go right into what is one of my personal favorite routines."

The class felt like it was over in a blink. I was sweating from pretty much every part of my body, and despite years of cheer practices, I had a feeling I was going to be sore in ways I hadn't seen in a long time. Reese had me using muscles I forgot I had.

I wasn't the only one who'd been left breathless and sweaty from the class. Everyone around me looked visibly exhausted. But they also looked so *cheery*. Pairs of friends who came together congratulated each other on surviving; the girl next to me smiled to herself as she grabbed her water bottle, probably running off a post-workout endorphin high. It was hard for me to keep the smile off my face, too.

Despite also doing the routine with us, Reese hadn't broken a sweat at all. "That was great, guys. Good work keeping up the energy. Alondra will be teaching a class later tonight if you didn't get enough, or I'll be back on Wednesday," she said. "Have a great rest of your day."

"That was amazing," I said as I walked to the front of the classroom where Reese was waving goodbye to everyone.

"You think so? You're not just saying that because you're my friend and you have to?"

I laughed. "No, that was genuinely so much fun. And it's obvious how much you love teaching the class."

Reese glowed from my praise. "Not to brag but I do have the best part-time job in the entire world." She bumped her shoulder into mine. "You looked good out there. Almost like you love dancing, and you should keep coming back to classes."

"Oh, I don't know," I said, laughing it off. "I really liked it, but it's..."

Reese raised her perfectly gelled eyebrow at me and crossed her arms, waiting for me to finish the sentence. "You can't even finish the sentence," she teased after I left my thought hanging in the air for a beat too long.

"I just, I don't know. I don't think I know how to dance in a way that isn't my entire life. I've never danced for fun, ever."

"You literally just did. And you'll never learn how to fully enjoy dancing if you don't just start dancing again." Reese turned away from me to gather up her things to leave. Everyone else in the class had cleared out, leaving just us behind. She flicked off the studio lights as we headed for the door. "I'm just saying that you're allowed to have fun and you're allowed to love something. No mean teachers and no pressure to compete. Just love of the game."

She described it in a way that seemed so simple, but I was skeptical that it actually would be. Untangling all of the complex feelings I had about dance was hard—it was basically a decade and a half of my life. It had been my attempt at getting even an ounce of parental approval or support outside of Mags, so it'd been hard to ever enjoy it.

But Reese was right that I'd loved it. For the entire fifty-minute class, my brain had gone completely radio silent. It was just me and the music and Reese guiding us through the dance routine. It was nothing like cheerleading practice, which was mostly only fun because my friends were there. It was so *whatever*, so integrated into my routine, that I just showed up like I had to and didn't think about it, like it was a job.

But this class hadn't felt like a job. And maybe it was time I finally learned that I could do things with no actual end goal or award at the end. I could just do them because it made life more enjoyable.

Chapter Fifteen

GJ

Even though the crowd was roaring, it was all white noise to me.

My feet pounded against the court as I got into position to catch Gemma's rebound. She'd been on it tonight—the entire team had. Even though we were playing an away game and the crowd wasn't interested in letting us forget it, we hadn't slowed down at all.

Gemma passed the ball to me, and I surveyed the court to see who was open. Defense had been tight on us, but we had one of the best offenses of the season in women's college basketball, so we were hard to pin down.

I locked eyes with Ellie down the court and knew she was ready. Having to make a split-second decision—my body moving before my brain could even fully process what I was going to do next—I sent the ball flying her way. It was an effortless pass, and our opponents hadn't been prepared for it, setting Ellie up well.

Ellie fired a ball up the court and swooshed effortlessly through the net. She'd been so smooth with it that she looked like a starter, exactly what we'd been working toward during our one-on-one practice sessions. As the ball fell back onto the court, caught by the other team, I let go of a breath that I'd been holding.

"Good! Good!" Coach Darlene shouted, clapping her hand against her clipboard. "Keep that momentum, ladies!"

Ellie and I caught each other's eye on the court, the two of us exchanging a small nod. Ellie's face, serious as always, didn't betray much, but I was pretty sure I saw the smallest smile forming at her lips.

The adrenaline from that game carried us through to the next. This was one of our hardest weeks—not that any part of our schedule was ever actually easy—since we had a game in Ohio, basically one and a half days of rest, and then a game in West Virginia. Time zone changes like that were fucking killer.

But bouncing from Colorado to Ohio to Colorado to now West Virginia, hopefully, wouldn't slow us down. We were still miraculously undefeated, but there were some games coming up later in the season that I was nervous about. There was still a lot of time to go—enough time for us to blow it all.

But it was easy to feel confident, mostly because we were playing a smaller program. There'd most likely be a crowd because name-recognized schools were a huge draw, but it wouldn't be anything like what we were used to back home. We never framed a game as an easy win because that was asking for trouble, but it definitely helped keep my confidence up.

"I'm exhausted. I can't believe we have a game tomorrow," Nia groaned, throwing herself down on her hotel bed. We'd gotten paired up as roommates this season because our typical travel game roommates both graduated. I was fine with it—I would've picked her a million times over Anna. Or rooming with some random on the team that I didn't know as well. I was all for building a team bond, but I didn't want just anyone in my space like that. "I'm definitely hitting that slump. Travel games are becoming a hell of a lot less fun now."

I looked over at her from my bed and shrugged. "We don't have that many left."

"Yeah, there's a reason one of us is aspiring to go pro and one of us isn't." She took a deep breath, draping her arm over her forehead. "I love this sport, but I love my bed more."

"You're not planning on declaring?" I asked, surprised. Nia was really good; she wasn't necessarily at the top of prospective draftee lists, but I could see her easily being a second-round pick.

She groaned, turning her head to look at me. "I don't know. Maybe. Maybe I'm just talking out of my ass because my body is so sore that the thought of ever having to move again makes me want to cry. And I'm so fucking luteal. I can't believe we have to play even when our period hormones are acting up." She took a beat. "Talk to me again in a few weeks. There's still time to figure it out."

"Not that much time." I snorted as Nia waved me off and then reached for the remote to turn on the TV.

My phone vibrated on the nightstand, and I reached for it, hoping the person texting was the person I'd been hoping to hear from. When I saw just a singular heart emoji pop up on my screen as the contact name—the best way I could think of to avoid accidentally exposing that Leah and I had been texting—I fought off a smile.

You've been looking good out there, how are you feeling about your game tomorrow?

GJ

Oh I looked good out there?

I'm sick of you

GJ

You miss me yet? I'll be back soon to keep you warm in bed, don't worry

Maybe a little but if you ever bring this up I'll pretend someone else sent that text

I snorted, unable to help myself. I was so lost in texting Leah, thinking about her being here with me and what she was doing right now.

And also how she looked on the other side of the phone. Maybe she was wearing that shirt that I liked...

"You seem awfully giggly over there."

I put my phone down immediately like I'd just been caught smiling at my phone by my teacher. "I have no idea what you're talking about."

Nia looked at me sideways. "For being someone who has broken every heart on the Lakeside Green campus, you're a terrible liar."

I mulled over her words. "I mean, I own up to breaking hearts, but I've never identified as a *liar*. I might just stretch the truth sometimes." Realizing I was thinking about it way too much, I waved the comment off. "Man, shut up. Stay out of my business."

Nia snorted. "Oh, so you really like this one."

I sucked my teeth, refusing to answer.

"Mhm. That's what I thought."

"Whatever."

Nia snorted to herself. "She must be pretty amazing."

I didn't even have to think about how to respond. "She is."

"Does she know that you feel that way about her?" She glanced over at me. "Don't give me that look, I know how you are."

"I think so. It's complicated."

She shrugged. "You'll figure it out. Your ego makes it impossible to stop you or slow you down. You always manage to figure it out."

"That almost sounded like a compliment." I ran my hand over the bedding. "Thanks for defending me the other day, by the way."

Nia frowned, confused. "What?"

"With Mags, when she was talking about Leah and me. I know my dating history doesn't exactly reflect positively, so I appreciate you backing me up."

"You haven't been the most relationship-forward person on the planet, and you might *stretch the truth* or whatever bullshit you just tried with me, but it doesn't mean you're a bad person. There is such a thing as just dating around."

"Yeah." I looked up at Nia and thought about the years we'd spent on the same team together. We'd always gotten along, and she was probably the person I liked the most and trusted the most as a friend outside of Theo. "Leah is the girl. But you can't tell anyone."

Nia threw her head back with laughter. "Oh, trust me, I know. I knew once Mags got all pissy about it. Mags might kind of suck, but that sibling intuition doesn't lie. *But* I do genuinely believe you can handle being friends with women either way—I wouldn't defend it if I didn't believe it." She looked over at me. "I'm happy for you. Don't fumble."

"I'm doing everything in my power not to," I said, not one bit of that sentence was me stretching the truth.

After an easy win on the road, we got back home, and as soon as I physically could—outside of exams and getting some homework done—I invited Leah over. I hopped down my apartment complex steps two steps at a time just to get her more quickly.

When she saw me, she smiled. "Hi."

"Hey."

I was careful not to touch her in public, even though I wanted to. It was one thing to sneak away from a party together, but if I'd learned anything from Theo's time at Lakeside Green, it was that people *would* take random photos during the day like amateur paparazzi. The thought of Mags seeing a picture of her sister and me making out in my hallway was hilarious, but I didn't want to deal with that inevitable shit storm.

Leah seemed to be thinking the same thing. She looked around the hallway and back at the front entrance, and then bit her lip. "Just one kiss?" she whispered.

I grinned like a fucking idiot. "Okay."

There was nothing quick about our kiss—we took our time, treating this like a reunion where we'd been apart for weeks instead of a few days. Her lips were soft and inviting and felt like home. I literally, physically, could not get enough of her. I'd never minded having to be off campus for away games, but the thought of having to do this all over again in just a few weeks fucking sucked.

At least coming back home to Leah was nice.

We finally broke apart when the elevator dinged, and the two of us pulled from our daze. Leah blushed as the doors opened, and we saw the students on the other side. None of them even looked at us, all too busy on their phones to care.

We slipped on and headed up to my apartment. As soon as we walked inside, Leah gasped. "You didn't."

Not to suck my own dick, but I was pretty proud of the surprise. I knew how much Leah loved the Thai food place near campus, so after digging a little to get her order from her while I was away, I ordered it for us today.

Leah genuinely looked like she might cry. "You ordered my favorite. That is so thoughtful."

I shrugged smugly, knowing I did a good job. "Just a little something."

She put her arms around my neck and kissed me again, even more deeply this time, now that we weren't at risk of getting caught. I let myself fall into it and didn't stop my hands from wandering. I moved her hair to the side and kissed down her neck, making her giggle.

"I know you so nicely ordered us dinner, and it smells *so* good, but I think I'm distracted."

"It'll still be good in twenty minutes."

She cackled. "As if anytime we've had sex it's only been for twenty minutes."

"Fair point." I slipped my hand up Leah's shirt, running my hands over her bare back and then bringing one around to cup her breast. She leaned into me, moaning softly.

"The food can wait," she murmured against my lips.

I nodded. "The food can wait."

We didn't make it more than two steps before we were pulling each other's clothes off and falling onto the couch nearby. Even with the bed no more than a few feet away, it didn't feel worth it to waste any time.

Leah laid on the couch, and I got comfortable between her legs. She pulled me as close to her as she physically could, our bare skin pressed together, and traced her hand down my stomach. With our eyes locked on each other, I slipped my fingers against her slit.

She inhaled, gripping my skin. "*Oh,*" she moaned softly. She was already soaking wet to the touch. I trailed my thumb over her clit and then moved down, teasing her. Her back arched in response, and she bit her lip.

"Miss me?"

She nodded desperately, her nails digging into my back. I slowly slid my fingers inside of her, taking my time. Leah's eyes nearly rolled to the back of her head, and her body relaxed into the movement, enjoying it without rushing it.

"You're so wet," I whispered, and she moaned in response. As I thrusted my fingers in and out of her, I let myself enjoy the view—her body stretched out over the couch, her nipples raised.

She reached out for me, pulling me in closer by the waist. "Can I?" she asked, as her hand slowly started drifting south.

I nodded and repositioned so she could get her hands between my legs. The sensation of her finding my spot sent a shockwave through my entire body. Being touched during sex had never been a priority for me, but right now, I was more than appreciative of the release of tension. The only thing I wanted, other than for me to get Leah off, was for Leah to get me off.

I kissed her as she eased a finger inside of me, both of our breaths catching. We moved slowly, kissing each other deeply. It was a feeling I'd never experienced before during sex, and I really, *really* liked it.

Our moans became increasingly desperate, every touch bringing me closer and closer to the edge.

"*Please*," Leah begged breathlessly, gripping onto me with her free hand. We both kept going until the tension was too much—when I saw in Leah's face that she was about to finish, it brought me to the edge. I tightened around her touch, and my breath went shallow.

"Oh my god," I moaned softly as I came, and Leah laughed. My body felt so light and easy; every single one of my muscles relaxed.

We laid together on our couch, our bodies soft and limp together, like we physically didn't have the strength to keep going.

But the feeling was still swirling; Leah's hands were traveling my body in a way that suggested she wasn't done yet.

"Would you want me to use the strap on you?" I asked, and Leah's eyes lit up.

"You're serious?"

"Yeah, of course."

She looked at me, lust in her eyes. My body buzzed with anticipation, the two of us fantasizing about the exact same thing. "I would love that."

I got up from the couch and went into my dresser. After finding the dildo and lube, I pulled on the briefs I preferred over a traditional harness and positioned the strap.

When I turned around, Leah looked at me like she couldn't wait to devour me.

She stood up and walked over to me, the dim lighting of the room reflecting beautifully off her naked skin. Just as she seemed like she might kiss me, she ducked her head down instead and kissed my shoulders, my chest. She kissed down my stomach, moving further and further down until she was resting her weight on her knees. Her kisses were featherlight, just enough to make me want more. She looked up, a teasing, perfect smile on her lips.

She moved her head forward and wrapped her lips around the head of the strap. Even though I couldn't actually feel it, I might as well have. She lifted her eyes, looking at me through her lashes. My heart literally skipped a beat. The type of need and desire I was feeling for her in that moment was unlike anything I'd ever experienced before.

"Oh, fuck," I mumbled. I let out a small breath as she took the strap deeper into her mouth. I took her hair in my hands, watching her. Even though she was technically in a submissive position, she was entirely in control.

She trailed her tongue over the silicone, spit visibly left behind. She reached between her legs and leaned her weight against her hand, softly moaning as she rubbed against her clit.

I didn't know how much longer I was going to last. Looking at her like that—cheeks flushed, hair tousled, ready and waiting—was almost too much. I moaned softly as she pulled away and wiped the corners of her mouth. I didn't have to actually feel any of it for it to have really fucking turned me on.

"Couch, now," I demanded, my voice rough. Leah giggled, but obeyed. She got on the couch and looked up at me, her body on full display.

"Turn over" She obliged, looking back over her shoulder at me in the process. She wiggled her ass slightly in the air, taunting me.

"Like this?" she asked, as she moved to lean her weight on her elbows.

Fuck. "Yes." I took her by the hips and slipped my hand between her legs to make sure she was wet enough to still take me. When my fingers slid in and out of her with ease, I removed them and replaced them with my strap. I'd already put lube on it, but it didn't hurt to be sure. I moved slowly, practically by the centimeter. "Is this okay?"

"Yes." Leah exhaled, gripping the couch cushions. She moaned as I made it deeper inside of her. I knew I'd hit a good spot for her when she cried out in pleasure, her pussy tightening around the dildo enough for me to notice.

"Jesus. You look so fucking *sexy*," I groaned as I began moving in and out of her. That was usually a line when it came out of my mouth, but I really meant it this time. The way her back was arched, the way her hair fell over her shoulders, the way she moaned. I couldn't get enough. This was a high I was going to be chasing for the rest of my life.

Her perfect ass bounced with every slow thrust back in. I knew why I hadn't fucked around with a cheerleader before—I was messy but not that messy—but I was starting to realize the oversight on my part.

And not just a cheerleader, but Leah in general. I couldn't believe I'd never imagined this. All this time, Leah had been right there, always this hot, always right in front of me. I didn't know how I hadn't seen it before, how I hadn't spent the entirety of college genuinely shooting my shot with her.

But then again, there was an obvious answer; I didn't go after girls I knew I couldn't have. But when she'd made it clear she wasn't, and she didn't care about following the rules anymore, all bets were off.

I picked up speed, thrusting harder this time. Leah wasted no time orgasming, her wetness streaking over the silicone. She moved her hips back against me, picking up the pace and taking me even deeper inside of her.

I let her go, watching her take herself to another orgasm. "You look so good, baby," I said. I could've watched her for hours; it was so good that I was nearly brought to orgasm just from watching her.

I reached around for her clit, barely able to keep my spot with how wet she was. She moved against me, moaning and begging and whimpering.

"Oh my god," she cried out and then gasped. She slowed down, her body tensing. Her legs shook as she lost the ability to hold herself up anymore.

She fell into the couch, and I slipped out of her. She turned over, and I looked over her face to figure out if she wanted to go another round or not. When she pulled me down to kiss her, moaning softly and desperately, I had a feeling I knew she wanted.

"Should I keep going?"

"Never stop," she begged.

I pinned her arms above her head as I eased the strap back inside of her. Her impossibly long legs squeezed tight to my torso.

"Oh, GJ," Leah moaned. "Oh my *god*. Just like that."

I maintained my rhythm, my grip tight around her wrists. Her back arched, and as much as I wanted to take in every single perfect detail of her, I couldn't tear my eyes away from her face. Her mouth was open, her moaning becoming increasingly desperate. I knew her well enough by now to know that meant she was close.

I moved my hands from her wrists to her hips, pulling her against me. As I slid deeper into her, Leah's hands trailed over my abdomen.

"Kiss me," she said, breathy and desperate and sure.

"Whatever you want," I said, meaning it. Anything she wanted from me, anytime—I was there. And it wasn't just the sex talking.

I repositioned her on the couch, Leah's motions fluid and easy as she slid further up to give me more room. I could see the bliss on her face and written all over the softness of her movements. Leah gripped the couch cushions and her breasts, her eyes squeezed shut with pleasure.

Once I was comfortably inside of her, I positioned myself over her with my elbows on either side of her head.

"How's this?" I asked.

Leah gasped, her eyelashes fluttering as she gripped onto me. She then nodded as she came back to earth. "Yeah, that's good," she said, making us both laugh.

I leaned down and kissed her exposed collarbone, trailing along the bone and then up her neck. I was careful to be light with my touch so there weren't any marks left behind, even if it was tempting to leave something behind that suggested she was mine. I could tell I'd found the right spots when Leah began grinding against me, moving against the strap for relief.

"You want something?" I asked, lifting my hips and then rocking back into her. My motions were small, just enough to create some friction but not enough to really even qualify as a thrust.

It seemed to more than do the trick with her. She brought her hands to my back and clung to me, nails digging into my skin.

It wasn't until I began picking up speed and deepening my thrusts that I finally kissed her. Her lips were soft against mine, open and desperate but still somehow gentle. Caring. Almost *loving*. I'd never kissed anyone like that before, even Leah. It was new, different.

I liked it.

We took our time together on this round, teasing each other and slowing down when it seemed like Leah was too close to finishing. Even Leah seemed to have finally figured out how to slow her pace with me, no longer rushing me to some finish line.

I slowly increased my speed again until Leah was moaning against my mouth. I kept us physically close enough for our lips to still brush, just shy of kissing her. I could see her face had gone tight, brows furrowed.

"You're so fucking beautiful, Leah," I breathed out. I had zero concern over my stamina—I didn't train sometimes four hours a day for me to ever get tired in bed. There was only one reason I was this breathless, and it had everything to do with how Leah made me feel. "I could look at you like this all day."

Even though it was meant to be hot, my stomach dropped. That felt way too far. Telling her she was sexy, beautiful, the best I'd ever had in bed—any of those were acceptable. But telling her I could look at her? Telling her she looked fucking beautiful?

I wasn't going to take it back—taking it back would've been a lie—but if she asked, I was going to have to find a way to somehow downplay that. That felt more like a confession than dirty talk, and I didn't have the capacity to work through that. Not while I was literally inside of her, at least.

Fortunately, Leah seemed unfazed. She either didn't even really hear me, or she was doing a really good job of ignoring me and pretending she didn't hear it.

Leah then closed the gap between us, kissing me again. We moved our bodies together, nearly every inch of available skin touching. I'd never felt so physically close to someone. Sex had always been a good time, but I now understood what people meant when it came to sex with someone who mattered. Nothing could ever compare to this.

She held on tight, but kept her eyes open and on me instead of closing them. I didn't look away, either. Even as I readjusted hers and my hips to get as deep into her as possible, she seemed determined not to take her eyes off of me.

"Oh," she softly moaned. Her breath caught, her body tensing around mine. As her orgasm built up and then came crashing down, she still kept her eyes fixed on me.

Her legs trembled around me, but the rest of her body relaxed. I brushed the hair away from her temple and gently kissed it. Before I could move my hand away, she reached up and held her own hand against mine, leaning into my touch. She turned her head and kissed the inside of my wrist, by far the most intimate thing anyone had ever done to me before.

And I couldn't lie—I loved it.

I slipped out of her slowly, and she softly gasped again from the sensation of the strap leaving her body.

After taking my boxers off and leaving them and the strap in a pile on my floor, I got into bed and took her in my arms.

"Oh my god," Leah breathed, her chest still rising and falling. "That was unbelievable."

I kissed her, overwhelmed by how badly I wanted to. She kissed me back deeply, her lips warm against mine. She opened her mouth for me, and we let our tongues explore. It was hot—*so* fucking hot—but it didn't feel like foreplay. It was honest, true-blue intimacy. It was something shifting between us; I could feel it. It was so undeniable that I knew she had to feel it too.

When we finally broke our kiss, I looked at her and just knew that I was in trouble. I could feel it in every inch of my body. For the first time ever, the girl in my bed wasn't just some girl in my bed. She was someone who actually meant something to me. And even though that was the scariest fucking feeling in the world, I was dying to say that to her.

But I couldn't. It felt too soon and too weird—this was meant to be casual. It'd never been said to be anything else otherwise. And bringing feelings into hooking up was the fastest way to ruin a good thing; I didn't know from having done it before, but I knew how it felt to be on the receiving end.

Suddenly, I had a lot more sympathy for the girls who'd been brave enough to shoot their shot with me. This was a nightmare.

I pulled my attention away from her face, thinking about anything else—the homework I needed to do, the games that were coming up, what Ellie and I were going to work on during our next training session—so I didn't say something that would mess everything up.

"Should we finally eat now?" I offered, the best I could come up with.

Chapter Sixteen

Leah

In a rare moment of silence between the two of us, Soph and I were completely focused on our work. We'd just wrapped up a morning cheer practice and grabbed food, dragging the meal out as long as possible to avoid having to do any work. But with the holidays coming up just around the corner, we were deep into midterms and then preparing for finals.

As much as I loved college, I was absolutely not going to miss how the fall semester felt—the anxiety, the deadlines, the nonstop practices, and hopping between cheering for different sports. Even though I'd been able to give myself a slightly lighter workload for my senior year fall, writing paper after paper and cramming for exams was not my favorite thing in the world.

I clicked through the digital flashcards I had up on my computer and fought off a sigh. Across the table, Soph was significantly more locked in than I was. She was so focused she didn't even sense me staring at her, willing her to look up and chat for a few minutes, or what I would tell her would be a few minutes, and then would end up being at least an hour.

As if knowing I needed a break, my phone vibrated next to me. I glanced over to see that it was GJ and smiled to myself. A little spark fluttered in my chest, but I let it be—if I picked up my phone now, there was no way I was getting this practice test done.

Of course, *that* got Soph's attention.

"GJ, hm?" Soph teased, apparently not getting the memo that we were letting the text go. "Still going strong?"

"If by *going strong* you mean *still casually hooking up*, then yes." As I said the words, I had a flashback to the marathon of sex we'd just had. My body *very* much remembered it and was not being particularly cool about it. But just because the sex was so good I could basically still feel the orgasm days later, didn't mean we weren't *casual*.

Soph nodded, narrowing her eyes slightly. "Right. I see."

I half-sighed, half-laughed. "Do you have something you'd like to share with the class?"

"Just seems awfully serious. Way more serious than what I would ever consider to be nothing."

I shrugged. "We haven't talked about anything, and I like where we are right now. And I mean, it's not like it can be anything because of Mags anyway—"

As soon as I said it, I knew I had made a mistake. Soph's eyes lit up. "Oh, you're *so* into GJ."

I hid my face, absolutely mortified. "Wait, no—"

"You're not getting out of this one. Once you get to the point where you're using your sister as the excuse standing between you and making it official, it's *something*." Leah leaned forward, closing her textbook. "Oh, this is juicy."

"You're not even supposed to approve of this. GJ is a player, remember? The enemy? Would absolutely break my heart if I tried to turn this into anything?"

"I can hear in your voice that you don't believe that for even a second," Soph said, and she was right—annoyingly. Everything with GJ felt totally different than what I was used to. She was available and kind and warm. She listened to me and took what I said seriously. She even remembered my order from my favorite restaurant and got it delivered for me.

I didn't want to set myself up for failure, but the most logical part of my brain could recognize what was going on—GJ had to have a crush on me. Even the best actor in the world couldn't put on a performance that convincing. Beyond just my own gut feeling, the stories about GJ getting caught up in drama with girls at The 151 had stopped, meaning I was pretty sure we were exclusive.

But none of it mattered since we were never going to date. It was in my best interest to ignore it and let the crush-like feelings I was experiencing pass—because they definitely would. Eventually.

"You're supposed to be talking me out of this. Remember how you felt at the beginning: GJ was only getting a pass because she was better than Kai. I feel like there was a wise woman in my life who had *really* emphasized that and didn't want me to forget it."

"My feelings have changed since clearly whatever I thought was going on was not actually what was going on at all," Soph explained. "Maybe you guys won't ever like, fall in love, or whatever, and maybe it'll just be a college fling, but you seem *happy*. And that's all that matters to me. You haven't come to me once, stressing about what GJ is doing or where GJ is. You're not obsessing over whether she might be dating someone else. Literally all of the things you used to do every time you were hooking up with someone you haven't done at all. And I know you're not just keeping those feelings to yourself because you can't hide anything from me."

I immediately jumped to be defensive, but then quickly realized I had no counterargument. Soph was totally right—I hadn't behaved at all like I usually did when I had a crush. I was acting like a sane, level-headed person would—or how a person who was receiving kind, consistent communication for the first time ever in her dating history would. I didn't have to worry because I *knew*, all without asking. As time had gone on, GJ kept me updated on her travel schedule and when she wanted to see me next. I never left her apartment wondering if it would be the last time.

"Okay, maybe you're right," I admitted. Leave it to my best friend to be able to see right through me before I could even put all of the pieces together.

"Of course I'm right. But seriously, happy you're learning how to date normally either way. I wasn't strong enough to spend even another week hearing about Kai."

It was funny to have Kai's name brought up in conversation again—I hadn't thought about them in what felt like forever. And in retrospect, everything with Kai had felt so...stupid. It was nothing. Just two people who weren't compatible and didn't actually like each other. I didn't know why I'd gotten so wound up over them in the first place.

"Yeah, I guess things have been good," I admitted, which felt like an understatement now that I was really thinking about it. Things with GJ had been going better than good. Good enough that I—maybe stupidly—hadn't experienced any anxiety at all about it. I'd just communicated what I wanted and texted her when I wanted, and she'd done the same. No games, no weird back-and-forth.

"Have you guys had a sleepover at your house yet?" Soph asked.

Just the thought of that alone was enough to give me a heart attack. "Absolutely not. There's no way to sneak GJ into the house. Besides being like, six feet tall and impossible to hide, I know Mags is on high alert now.

Soph shrugged. "It could be kind of hot, sneaking around like that."

"It already is hot sneaking around in the way we have been, but I don't have a death wish," I said and Soph snorted.

Midterms came and went, which meant the first month of the basketball season had come to a close. The girls began fluttering during practices about how they couldn't believe it was almost the end of the season or almost the end of their college cheering career. It still felt like there was so much time left, but I understood where the feeling was stemming from—December might as well have been the new year, and then once the new year started, the regular season only went until early March.

I, however, was doing everything in my power to ignore what the holidays actually meant and how soon graduation was. I wasn't so much sad about finishing my career as a cheerleader, but I was sad to be graduating. The fact that things were still tense with my parents helped take my mind off of it. I couldn't stress about how I was less than a semester and a half from graduating when I was stressed about finding a middle ground with my parents.

"Oh, they're calling," Mags shouted from the living room. I considered blowing it off, but it was stupid of me to do something like that. As mad as I still was at my parents—who hadn't even attempted to call me or text me individually to check in—the likelihood of getting an apology from them or talking things out increased if I spoke to them. I had to at least give them the chance to try.

My heart rate immediately skyrocketed, but I brushed it away. Things had felt really weird—they never spent Thanksgiving with us, but it had felt intentional this year. I hadn't gotten any of the customary, *Are you sure you and your sister don't want to come home, even for a weekend?* texts, always with a little twist of mom guilt thrown in there. All I'd gotten was a photo in the group chat of my parents at the massive family Thanksgiving my extended family hosted every year, and that had been two weeks ago.

"Hey, miss you guys," Mags said, her voice booming through the apartment as I opened my bedroom door. I walked over to meet her, sitting on the arm of the couch that Mags was sprawled out on. "Are you at the beach right now?"

"Miss you too, sweetie. We decided to escape the winter weather for a little bit between the holidays. You know how stressful this time of year can be." Mom propped her hand up over her eyes. I didn't state the obvious—*winter weather* didn't apply to San Diego like it did to most other places, and the holidays didn't have to be stressful for her because she never actually contributed anything to them or traveled that far. "Is that your sister?"

"Hi, Mom."

Mags shifted her phone camera over my way but did a poor job of it, cutting off most of my face and mostly showing my shoulder.

"Did you get your roots touched up recently?" she asked. My heart sank immediately, knowing that this call wasn't going to be fixing anything anytime soon.

"How's the resort?" I asked.

"Beautiful, warm, sunny. Your father is off somewhere doing some kind of activity, scuba diving or something, who knows." She waved the comment off. "I'm assuming Colorado is cold?"

Mags brought the camera back to herself. "Yeah. Sunny during the day at least. We're having a snowy season so far, but none of it has been sticking. Kind of a bummer, I could go for a snow day."

"Not during the season—you need all of the time on the court you can get."

Mags nodded. "Totally agree. Draft predictions have looked good."

"Tabloid fodder, just keep focusing on the game. I know you can do it, just don't fly too close to the sun."

"Yeah, I know."

"And what has your sister been up to?"

I resisted rolling my eyes just in case she could still see me. "Just studying, school stuff," I said. It was a simplification—I was cheering at games, making it to practices, coordinating a winter volunteer event for the team. But I knew my mom wasn't going to be impressed by any of that. It was all par for the course for her—she not only expected that from us, but wanted more. And I knew her well enough to know that her asking wasn't from a place of curiosity but from hoping I'd added something new to my plate that she could brag about.

"Lots of free time, then." Her tone made it clear it wasn't a question. "Well, that's good. Take a breather where you can, I guess. Can't be go, go, go all the time."

I took a deep breath, trying to level myself out before I got myself into deeper trouble with my family. But none of it felt fair—I pushed myself so hard to pad my resume in a way that my parents would approve of, only for them to not approve of any of it. And then when I took a step back, I was lazy and wasting my time. I didn't know how to win with them.

"Okay," I said, the most neutral thing I could come up with in the moment.

Mom closed her eyes and inhaled, visibly agitated. "What now? Did I manage to somehow upset you already?"

"No, I just—" I stopped myself. *No* had always been my answer, even when I knew I was upset. All of the times where my parents skipped my dance recitals because of my sister's travel games, or when my parents would pointingly praise my sister and didn't say anything to me, I'd just stayed silent. Sometimes, my parents could tell that I was upset, especially when I was a teenager, and would say something, but they'd do it exactly how they were now, like it was an annoyance rather than something to resolve. "It just doesn't feel fair to call it a breather when I'm still doing all of the same extracurriculars I usually do. I'm busy too, it's just not D1 basketball."

"My schedule's pretty intensive." Mags said it like it was an observation, not even with the clear intent of hurting my feelings, just like always. And just like always, it still managed to hurt my feelings.

The threat of tears made my eyes sting. "Not helpful."

"Mags has always been the one with the busy schedule, nothing to get defensive over. When you're this good at a sport, it's like working a full-time job on top of school. And all of those brand deals she does—it's a lot to stay up on."

I resisted the urge to make a bitchy comment about how Mags didn't even usually take on brand deals during the season—basically the entire school year—because it was too difficult to coordinate.

But that was about as far as I was able to go with stopping myself.

"I don't think that's fair." I stood up from the couch, knowing there wasn't anything else to say. I'd given it another chance to try and have any type of productive conversation, and it hadn't gotten me anywhere. "I'll talk to you later. Tell Dad hi for me."

"Leah—"

I ignored Mags and headed back to my bedroom. My hands shook as I twisted the door handle open. From the living room—basically just steps away—I could hear my mom bitching about me.

"Your sister is just being so difficult right now."

"I know, but I don't know if acting this way is going to help anything."

For the first time, maybe ever, I appreciated Mags doing the best she could when it came to standing up for me. Maybe, somewhere in her, there was the desire to be a good sister.

The conversation about me continued on, muffling as I closed my bedroom door. I didn't need to hear the rest of it to know it was most likely going to be my mom bitching about how she didn't know why I was acting like this, and then eventually switching the conversation over to Mags and basketball. I wasn't even worth dwelling on to complain about, never more than a passing thought or feeling compared to Mags.

My eyes stung with unwelcome tears. Typically, this was where I'd call in the big guns—Soph—to bitch to, but she was deep into a *do-not-disturb* multi-day study session, and I didn't want to drag her into the middle of my mess right now.

Leah

What are you doing right now?

I put my phone down on my bed and pulled my knees to my chest. I felt like I was thirteen all over again. The weight of my parents's disappointment was the heaviest feeling I'd ever had to bear and it never seemed to actually lift. I'd forget about it sometimes, downplay it sometimes, but it was always there. I'd think that I'd finally cracked the code and done something to impress them, and it would get immediately overshadowed or downplayed or ignored.

My phone vibrated next to me, and I picked it up immediately.

GJ

Just about to wrap up practice with Ellie, is everything okay?

That was enough to make me actually start crying. I wiped the tears away before they could fall, not wanting to be puffy in case I saw Mags again today.

Leah

It's my family

GJ

Come over, I'll be home in no more than twenty

I have premade cookie dough with little christmas trees on them, a comfortable couch, and a big TV

I cracked a smile.

Not a single thing in the world sounded better.

I threw together a quick bag of things, constructing the story in my head as I did it in case I ran into Mags. *Staying at Reese's.*

Yes, you probably have met Reese. It's not my problem that you don't bother to remember anything about my friends.

Needless to say, by the time I had a bag together and was exiting my room, most of my hurt had transformed into anger.

Mags was still sitting on the couch in the same spot as when I left. When she heard my door open, she immediately turned around like she was waiting for me. "Hey, Mom wished you guys could've talked longer. She sounded sorry."

It was the one thing Mags could've said that I wasn't prepared for. I froze in place. "I mean, I'm glad she sounded sorry, I guess."

"They're trying. Can you give them a little bit of a break? You have to admit you've been acting super out of character so far this year—they're probably not used to it." The emphasis on *super out of character* didn't slip by me; I knew she was referring to thinking I was revenge flirting with GJ. It was all so ridiculous and self-centered that it made me mad at her all over again.

"What, me actually standing up for myself?" I readjusted my bag on my shoulder and rolled my eyes. "I'm going to a friend's house. I'll see you later."

"Leah—"

"Bye, Mags," I said as I headed to the front door to put on my shoes and finally leave.

Chapter Seventeen

GJ

There were a handful of games throughout the season that we—both the team and the fans—looked forward to. Any game against Point Brook was an immediate sellout, whether home or away. Before Theo, people mostly came to the big-name games because they wanted to see the best of the best play, even if we got pummeled. But now, people actually expected us to win against the big-name schools. Having fans who were optimistic about the season was always a good thing, but it also meant each game got bigger and bigger.

East Hill, one of the schools we'd been preparing all semester to play against, was one of those games we were expected to win. There was no way they were going to make it easy, but I'd never minded a challenge.

We kept up a good pace throughout the first quarter. It wasn't our strongest scoring—we were up against some really intense defense—but we were holding our own.

"Keep pushing, ladies! Pressure! Pressure!" Coach Darlene yelled from the sideline, putting her hands up to her mouth to help her voice carry.

I fought off an annoyed groan as a shooter from East Hill fired off another perfect jumper. I took it back—their defense *and* offense were really good, and the small lead we had over them was quickly slipping away.

"Maybe we really do need Ellie out here. That sophomore is kicking our fucking asses," Mags bitched as we took a breather at the end of the quarter. It was a general statement directed at everyone, but I was kind of glad to be included—it felt like the closest Mags would ever offer to an olive branch.

"Yeah, this is a lot. I don't know if we'll be able to keep up." Gemma's cheeks were bright red, and her forehead was slick with sweat.

"You guys are totally killing the vibe. We're doing fine," I said. "We're just giving the fans something to talk about." I draped my arm over Mags's shoulder, and she scowled, brushing me off. "Ball up top, baby!"

Mags looked as over it as she always did with me. "I kind of miss the depressed version of you."

I threw my head back with laughter. "Who needs smear pieces when I have teammates like this?"

We got into position and went again, keeping our attitudes up. Or at least, I was—it was easy when I had Leah out of the corner of my eye. It'd been impossible to keep a smile off my face; she had me riding on the most insane high. If I wasn't with her, I was thinking about the next time I'd get to see her.

The game moved quickly—I wasn't completely out of the woods yet, but I was back to basketball games moving in the blink of an eye instead of feeling like I was wading through sludge. I felt about as back as I ever had, almost to the point of not even thinking about it anymore.

Just as Anna was about to pass me the ball to shoot a three-pointer, all of the momentum suddenly stopped. I heard the crowd before I saw what happened; up in the stands, people rose to their feet to look down at what happened. The cheerleaders had their hands up to their mouths in surprise; Leah looked shellshocked and earnestly scared.

"Oh fuck." Gemma gasped.

"Nia?" Ellie called out, her already pale face as white as a sheet of paper. She stood up from the bench along with the rest of the players who'd been sitting out.

I turned to look and saw players hovering around and checking in on each other, mostly from East Hill. One of them was holding their head and looking at their coach, most likely hurt.

Nia was still out on the floor, sprawled and unmoving. I ran over to her and squatted down. Her nose was gushing blood, and her eyes were only the tiniest bit open.

"Can you hear me?" The crowd was so quiet that it was hard to believe they were even still there.

I was careful not to touch her or move her, maintaining a slight distance just in case she'd hurt herself beyond what we could see.

"Ouch," Nia finally said as she blinked her eyes open. She lifted her hand to touch her face, and I stopped her just as she was about to coat herself in blood. "What?"

"You might not want to touch it yet. Wait for a tissue. Or twelve."

She groaned. "Is everyone staring at me?"

I snorted. "Yeah. You look good, though. Badass."

"I always look badass."

"Agree to disagree," I said, making Nia laugh. She stopped, wincing.

"My head is killing me."

I cracked a smile even though it was weird and hard to see her like that. We'd had some injuries last season, but nothing that included visible blood. I didn't think of myself as particularly squeamish, but I was starting to think that maybe I was. "Yeah, I bet."

Coach Darlene put her hands gently on my shoulders to tell me that she was there, along with the medical staff. She offered a hand to help me stand up from the floor.

"Good work, captain," she said softly. "Go talk to the rest of your team."

I nodded as she took my spot on the floor, and the medical staff started their exam.

I headed back over to the team. Everyone who'd been on the court had gone over to the bench to see what we were going to do next.

I accepted a water bottle from Gemma. "She got knocked around and probably has a broken nose, but no formal diagnosis yet."

"I'm assuming she's out?" Mags asked.

"Yeah, I don't think she's coming back. Broken nose is one thing if the bleeding stops, but I think she hit her head on the way down."

Gemma winced. "Ouch," she said softly.

"We'll figure it out. She's being taken care of."

We took a moment of heavy silence, worried about Nia, and then also thinking about ourselves. An on-court injury was scary for a multitude of reasons, one of them being the reminder that we weren't actually superhuman.

I turned to look at Nia again. She'd been moved to a stretcher, and the crowd politely and supportively clapped as she was moved off the court.

"Love you, Nia!" Gemma called out behind her.

Coach Darlene walked back over to us and took a deep breath. "Okay. First, is everyone okay?" We nodded. The energy was way down—injuries had a way of killing momentum—but we were capable of playing. "I know that was hard to see, and it's hard to lose a starter. But we'll see this one through."

"For Nia," I said.

She nodded. "For Nia." She turned to Ellie. "Ellie, you take over for Nia. How's your passing been?"

Ellie glanced over at me. "Okay?"

"She's good." I looked over at her, and when we locked eyes, I nodded. I'd never considered myself much of a coach, but I could see the difference in Ellie's playing. I didn't credit myself as much as I credited how badly she'd needed a cheerleader to remind her she'd earned her spot on the team. Theo had always been that person for her, so losing her had been a change. I understood.

"I'll take it," Coach Darlene said. She ran over the play with us and how we'd approach the game moving forward now that we were down Nia. It would be me, Ellie, Anna, Mags, and Gemma. Ellie had obviously played with us on the court before, but she didn't get as much play time as the rest of us since we were all starters. It was a tough spot to be in against a tough team. And getting back into the swing of things after an injury was always a challenge.

But I was optimistic. Ellie had great chemistry with us, and the only reason she wasn't a starter was that we were fortunate to have a stacked lineup; she'd absolutely be leading the team next year.

"This works for everyone?" Coach Darlene looked at all of us, and we nodded. "Okay. Make me proud."

We grabbed our waters for one last sip before we had to get out on the court. I rolled out my shoulders and jumped to warm myself back up.

"I've never played more than a quarter, and we have basically three left," Ellie said, turning to look at me.

"This is the kind of thing we've been preparing for," I responded, putting my hands on her shoulders.

Anna looked over at me. More than ever, we had to rely on each other. The rhythm we'd been building all season was going to be tested by a major change, and Anna and I couldn't afford to be out of rhythm. I couldn't be a dickhead—our team couldn't afford it.

"We're good?" Anna asked, the weight evident in her question. There was nothing backhanded about it, no aggression—purely checking in to make sure I'd be able to play in line with her. She'd proven to be the hardest person in the world to have any type of beef with, even when I was really trying.

I nodded, holding my hand out for her to dab. "We got this."

Anna twisted her lips in a smile as she slapped her hand against mine. "Hell yeah, we do."

We went back out onto the court, ready for whatever East Hill might have in store for us. Ellie and the sophomore eyed each other up immediately, but Ellie's expression never wavered. She might've been the sweet one on our team, but she could be a fucking monster on the court.

The game was set back into motion, and we played through, figuring out a flow. There were a few shitty passes and a few bad calls almost immediately, almost to the point that it felt like maybe the game was going to be a wash. But it wasn't over until it was over.

"Breathe, Ellie," I reminded her as we jogged together to the other end of the court.

Eventually, after a tough start to the second quarter, things clicked. I was worried halftime might kill what we had going for us, but the third quarter breezed by. There was something almost beautiful about the way we were playing together, a genuine trust and mutual respect between obvious between each other.

The game was close until the very end, but we just barely edged by with a win. When the final buzzer went off, Gemma practically leaped into Mags's arms. "Thank god!"

"Really nice work out there," Anna said and glanced over at me, smiling softly.

Coach Darlene looked thrilled, but she mostly looked relieved. "You were good today, GJ. You're a genuine leader when you stop fucking around."

A laugh flew out of me, surprised to hear something so profane from her. But I knew she was serious—probably more serious than she'd ever been with me. "Thanks, Coach."

"I see a lot of promise in you. I don't doubt you're going to get drafted and you're going to be an amazing asset to a very lucky team. I just hope they're prepared for you." She cracked a smile.

"I'll make it work even if they aren't," I said, and I was surprised by how much I meant that.

Leah met up with me later that night, both of us able to quietly slip away from The 151—and our friends—under the guise of being tired.

She laid between my legs with her head on my chest, the two of us sprawled out on the couch. My hands lightly combed through her hair while we both half-watched some TV show I'd been wanting to see. It was a new kind of post-game ritual for me, but I really liked it.

"Is Nia going to be okay?" she asked quietly.

"Coach says she's concussed, so she'll probably have to sit out the next game or two at the very least to recover."

"That's so scary." She gripped my shirt as I was the one who'd gotten hurt.

"It happens sometimes. Contact sport lifestyle."

"Still scary." She lifted her head from my chest so she could look at me. "I guess it just made me realize that you guys do actually get hurt out there. I've seen it before, but it feels...different now."

I trailed my hand down to her face, tracing my fingers over her jaw. "Yeah?"

"Yeah," she responded softly. "Can I ask you something without you thinking too much about it?"

I'd be lying if that wasn't the second scariest thing I'd ever heard, only ranked behind my mom yelling out my full name when I was in trouble. But I wasn't a coward. "What's up?"

"Okay, maybe it's a multi-part question, actually." She was quiet for a little bit after that, but I didn't want to interrupt whatever she was thinking about and rush her. "Is this like...a thing? Like, are you seeing other people?"

I blinked, surprised by the sudden vulnerability. In a way, I'd been expecting her question—or questions—to be connected back to us and what we were doing in some way. But Leah actually asking the question felt like a glimpse behind the curtain. For just a moment, she wasn't the confident girl at the party with the effortless smile and friends in every corner of the room.

And even though it was a question I'd heard what felt a million times from a million different girls—all of whom had gotten some variation of the *I do not want anything serious* talk before we started fooling around—I suddenly didn't have an answer. Usually, I was quick to write it off. Of course, there were other girls, and of course it wasn't a thing, and of course it wasn't anything serious.

But with Leah, I hadn't felt the urge. I hadn't even really thought about how she was the only woman I'd wanted in my bed, or thought about how weird that was for me. It'd just felt *natural*. There was no forcing myself to do anything, or second-guessing what I was doing. Not even an ounce of self-sabotage had taken over my decision-making. I enjoyed her company so much that the idea of spending time with anyone else felt like a waste.

"I'm not seeing anyone else," I finally admitted. It was so stupid, but saying those words made me almost sick to my stomach with nerves. As soon as I said them, I thought about how maybe I should've just lied and pretended it wasn't anything. That felt a hell of a lot less scary than telling Leah she was the only girl in my life right now.

For the first time in my life, I was leaving room for rejection that would actually hurt.

Leah was quiet again, and this time, I was a little less inclined to give her a second to think. Every second that went by made me increasingly nervous. "I'm not, either," Leah finally said. There was an instant rush of relief, followed by a heavy dose of fear.

Those words officially made me a one-woman woman. It wasn't theoretical anymore, or something I'd quietly wish for with Leah but never actually ask for. We weren't necessarily *official*, but we were exclusive, and that was new to me.

I'd never done this before, never been so close to having what could be considered a relationship. I had no idea what the hell I was doing. Talking about it like this made it feel really fucking serious and *really* fucking grown up.

"What's your follow-up question?" I asked, hoping I sounded cooler than I was feeling. I subtly wiped my sweaty palm on the side of the couch and played it off as coolly tapping my hand against it. No one had ever been more slick.

"Um." Leah took a breath. "Honestly? Like…why me? You've had so many girls and so many options over the years. You're not exactly known for being monogamous. Or, like, properly dating at all. Not that this is really properly dating, I guess, since we've really only been able to hang out at your apartment."

My initial instinct was to get defensive, used to years of girls reading way too much into things and getting disappointed when the friends with benefits situation they signed up for only had—as they knew before going in—the benefit of sex.

But I could tell from Leah's tone that it was different. And unlike the girls before Leah, I literally *couldn't* take her on a date anywhere. I'd thought about how beautiful she'd look all dressed up at a restaurant, or how much fun we'd have going to a pro game together. But I didn't let myself think about it for too long because it wasn't possible with Mags in the picture.

"Where's this all coming from?"

"I don't know." Leah bit her lip. "I guess I saw Nia get hurt and kept thinking about if something happened to you and how I'd want to be there. And that didn't feel like something someone who was being totally cool and casual would think. But it also seems like maybe we…haven't been super casual? At least, not for a little bit."

"I agree," I said and met her gaze. "I'd love to take you on a date even if I have to wait fifty more years." I could tell Leah really felt the words by how quickly she looked away, focusing on my studio kitchen, the window behind me, and the door to my bathroom. "Leah, look at me."

She inhaled but slowly did as I asked. I could see in her face that she had to fight looking away from me again.

"You are the most incredible, most confident woman I've ever met," I said, ducking my head so I could meet her eyes again. "You're consistent and level-headed, and I know you'd check me on my shit. And, honestly, I really like that you've never gotten weird about how I've been playing this season. You make it clear that you like *me* and you want to get to know me, and everything else is just...nothing. Or I guess it's still something, but you view me as human in the middle of it. It's easy to want the right-hand woman to the WNBA Rookie of the Year, but it's not so easy to still want them when they suck."

She snorted. "You don't suck."

"It maybe hasn't been my best season."

"It hasn't been mine either," Leah admitted.

I looked at her, taking in the flush of her cheeks and the way her hair fell over her shoulder. She was effortlessly funny, and I loved every second of having her around, but it was obvious the happy exterior she was good at putting on wasn't the full story. Navigating everything with her family probably was really hard on her, whether she vocalized it or not. "I hadn't noticed."

The corners of her lips turned up in a smile. "That's nice of you to say."

"I mean it. I'm sorry you've had so much shit to deal with, but you handle it well."

"I think *you're* handling it well. I just have to deal with my family. It's all dumb stuff between us. But you're dealing with, like, an entire sports fanbase and commentators and scouts."

I shrugged. "Just part of the job."

Leah propped herself up on her arms. She looked so beautiful, like a literal painting come to life, even in the glow of my TV. It was hard to believe she was real. "It sucks either way."

I nodded, never really having thought of it that way. "Yeah. It does."

"I...went to a dance class recently," Leah admitted. "After meeting your niece and nephew, I felt inspired to revisit."

"Oh shit, really?" I was surprised to hear it, but happy for her—I'd heard her talk about dance in passing, and it seemed like it'd really meant a lot to her.

"I think I really enjoyed the class. My friend has been encouraging me to keep going back. I haven't yet, but I can't stop thinking about it."

I smiled and laced my fingers through hers. I did it without thinking, without worrying. "Are you thinking you'll go again?"

"I might. It was nice to get back into it. And I'm sure the promise of me becoming even more flexible is a big motivator for you to encourage me, too."

"You won't hear any complaints from me," I said, making Leah laugh. "But I'm also being serious. You've mentioned dance here and there, and it's obvious it meant a lot to you. You might just really love it. Just because you started doing it for your parents doesn't mean you can't keep doing it for yourself."

Leah nodded, twisting her lips in thought. "You're right. But is it all kind of...ridiculous?"

"For you to have a hobby? No, some would say that's actually really healthy."

Leah snorted out a laugh. "Okay, fair. I've just never really done something for fun before. It's weirdly kind of daunting." She rested her head on my chest and sighed.

"I guess I haven't really either, so maybe I'm not the best person to ask about this. But I also always knew that I loved basketball. I didn't need anyone to tell me that I did. Even when it's giving me hell, it's still my favorite thing in the world. I love it enough to do it for free during the off-season. That might be what dance is for you."

Leah nodded and then smiled. "It's nice to hear you talk about basketball. I feel like you were skirting around it for a while."

I nodded, thinking about how the season had played out so far. She was right—I hadn't really liked talking about it. Or thinking about it. But very slowly, the knot in my stomach that formed whenever I thought about basketball or talked about it or played—basically every second of my life—became less and less tight. I wasn't at the point yet where there wasn't a knot at all, but things were better than they had been. It'd been so subtle that I hadn't noticed.

"Yeah," I said, pulling Leah closer to me. "You're right."

Chapter Eighteen
Leah

I took GJ's words to heart and kept showing up at Reese's dance classes. It went from being something I cautiously enjoyed doing to my favorite part of the week, going to sometimes two or three classes. It even made GJ going out of town for games easier because I had something that filled the void. Even if I wanted to start freaking out and getting anxious about whether things actually were serious with me and GJ, there wasn't the time. I was going to take GJ at her word and believe that she was into me and I was the only girl in her life, and that was that.

It felt good. It felt like growing up.

After a morning class on a Saturday, Reese and I went out to get smoothies from a place nearby to catch up. We'd seen each other at dance classes, but hadn't actually had the chance to be one-on-one and catch up.

The smoothie shop was unsurprisingly pretty quiet; most students were still rolling out of bed and recovering from last night's parties at this hour. A handful of students were working quietly on their laptops, the sounds of them typing and pop music playing quietly from the shop's speaker filling the room.

"It's been nice having you around so much," Reese said and headed up to the counter after her name was called. She picked up her order with a smile, thanking the barista before walking back to me.

"Yeah, it's been really nice. It feels good to get back into it and do something other than cheer. And with football season being over now, my schedule feels a little lighter."

"I just can't believe you have the time or energy. I've always known you were capable of finding hours in the day no one else had, but I'm legitimately impressed."

I shrugged. "It doesn't hurt that I like to stay as busy as I can. I don't really know anything else."

"Leah!" the barista called out, and I grabbed my smoothie from the counter.

"Thank you," I said, and then followed Reese to a sunny spot in the corner of the shop. "It also turns out it's really easy to make time for things you like to do once you just let yourself enjoy them."

"I knew you'd come around eventually," Reese sing-songed. "Dance isn't evil. I'm sorry the influences you had growing up made you feel that way."

"It kind of feels like a canon event."

Reese snorted. "Fair enough." She took a sip of her smoothie and leaned back into her chair. "Have you put much thought into what's going to come next?"

"Oh, I don't know," I responded, half-groaning. "It's not even Christmas yet. There's still time. Kind of."

It was easy to pretend that approximately five months was a lifetime if I just didn't think about it, but graduation was definitely looming. Having to pick classes for my last ever semester of college was really putting me on edge.

"Kind of?" Reese asked.

"I mean." I bit my lip, not sure if it was really worth saying out loud. "I don't know. I guess it could be cool to maybe get involved with a dance studio or something after graduation. I don't know if I'd teach, and I definitely don't have the skillset to work with teenagers or adults, but maybe like...kids? A kids' dance studio? Train to be a kids' dance teacher?" I shook my head. "It feels stupid. Like, I don't know how I'd ever find a job like that."

Reese looked at me, her lips turned up in a smile. She didn't say anything, but I could read her expression.

"Dance is supposed to be fun. I know, I know."

"You don't have to find a way to make it your career. You can just work for a studio as, like, a receptionist or something. Or volunteer for a studio, even. Or take adult classes for a while. Not everything has to be some big grand plan. It's okay."

"But isn't that so scary? Like, I don't have *any* plan at all in mind."

"Leah—you are so incredibly smart and talented and driven. Our entire friend group admires you so much. You *will* be able to figure something out. And then if that first thing doesn't work out, you'll have about a million other things. I'm not worried about you being able to find some source of decent income, but I am worried about your ability to actually have fun and enjoy life after graduation." Reese leaned forward in her seat and looked at me. She was so gentle that her words felt like the equivalent of a hug rather than a lecture. "Obviously, I'm not here to tell you what to do since I know we both hate that. But it doesn't hurt to start doing a little audit and figure out what makes you happy. You've tried a million things. Now you get to find what you like and keep it around, and replace the stuff you don't like."

I twisted my lips in thought, stirring my smoothie around with my straw. "I guess you're right," I said, even though there hadn't been a single time in my life that I'd never had a plan. It felt a little bit like free-falling, and I wasn't sure I liked the feeling.

But it probably was about time I learned how to relax. I'd already started removing myself from the grip my family had on me; being the person in charge of my own schedule for once was a step further in the right direction. Maybe at some point soon, I'd actually be fully in charge of my own life—living where

I wanted with whomever I wanted. Dating the person of my choosing. Working where I wanted to work and not wasting even a second looking at LSAT prep books.

Lightness filled my chest at the thought. Maybe the person I'd always wanted to be actually *was* there, and I actually could be her—I just had to grow up and demand it.

After saying goodbye to Reese, I cut across campus to where GJ said she was practicing today. I'd only ever driven to the court before, and only ever in an annoyed rage because I had to pick Mags up, so I was surprised by how far off campus it actually was. I followed walking directions that ducked me through trees and by the quiet, tucked-away lake the campus got its name from. The weather out here was always changing, but today, it had settled on a temperature that almost felt warm. And the sun, as usual, felt amazing—that was the one part I'd miss the most about Colorado.

Eventually, I found the court and GJ. To my surprise, Ellie was still with her, the two of them hard at work. From a distance, I watched the two of them interact. GJ was a surprisingly effective coach—I could see it in the gentle way she encouraged Ellie, while also pushing her to try harder. She passed the ball to Ellie in motion and then talked Ellie through passing it back to her, going over and over again until it was just right.

Even though I could've watched them play forever, I knew my staring was going to border on creepy if I didn't say something soon. I waited until they were in between plays to finally interrupt.

"Hey," I said, trying to keep things casual so I didn't accidentally tip off Ellie. I had no reason to believe she'd run to Mags and rat me and GJ out, but teammate loyalty ran deep.

GJ broke out into a smile. "Hey. Alright—I think we can call it."

Ellie caught the pass from GJ easily, placing it under her foot so she could tighten her ponytail. "I'll probably practice a little longer."

"I mean, hell yeah. Do your thing." GJ looked at me with an impressed shrug. "Ready to get out of here?"

"Yeah," I said and looked between GJ and Ellie like I still wasn't sure what to make of this.

GJ waved me off like she could read my mind. "Ellie's cool." She turned to Ellie, who was now dribbling the ball. "You know not to tell Mags about this?"

Ellie looked over at us, almost seeming annoyed that we were distracting her from shooting. "Why would Mags care?"

GJ gestured to Ellie as if to say *See what I mean*. "She keeps to herself. I don't even think she knows you're her sister—let's go home," she said, and I laughed. As we started walking back, GJ slipped my tote bag off my shoulder so she could carry it instead. "How was dance class?"

"It was really good. Reese has been absolutely kicking my ass, but in the best way. I leave feeling *so* refreshed and *ugh*. It's just the best." I inhaled and hugged myself to GJ's arm. "Thanks for being the push I needed to go."

"Hey, I won't take the credit," she said and kissed the top of my head. It was nice for it to feel like just us—Mags and Gemma had taken the car off campus today to go shopping, so there was no chance they'd accidentally end up on the outdoor court to see GJ and me. And we were so far off campus that the likelihood of anyone who'd actually care seeing us was low.

It made me want to just say fuck it and have GJ, not worrying at all about what my sister had to say. But there was no need to rush it—GJ and I weren't even officially dating yet. And I liked where we were. I wasn't necessarily anxious that putting a label on things would ruin everything, but I *was* nervous that Mags knowing the whole truth would put a damper on it. And I didn't want to risk ruining it. Not yet.

"It looks like things with Ellie are going well," I said.

"Yeah, she's a quick learner. She's always played well from a technical standpoint, but I can see the improvement here and there."

"Coach GJ Mitchell, reporting for duty."

GJ chuckled. "Maybe I'll worry about playing professionally first."

I looked up at her as GJ laced our hands together, my heart fluttering. "I like the sound of that."

Chapter Nineteen

Leah

The following weekend, I found myself in the same spot I pretty much always was. Soph and I were going out for yet another party, but rather than being nervous, I was hopeful I'd run into GJ.

I used my fingertips to blend out the blush on my cheeks and then exited the bathroom to find Soph locked in on her phone. She was dressed and ready to go as usual, her look always more lowkey than mine. Her effortlessness and the way she never seemed stressed over what to wear only added to her cool girl factor. "Ready?"

Soph looked up at me like she was surprised to see me. "You're really ready to go? Really?"

I blinked at her and looked down at my outfit. She was making me feel like I forgot to put on pants or something. "Yes...?" I grabbed my purse that I'd tossed onto the bed earlier while getting ready. "Is something wrong with my outfit? Oh my god, wait, do I have lipstick all over my teeth like that one time?"

"No, no—relax. Sorry, I didn't mean to stress you out. This is just usually a much more complicated process. I've only read, like, fifteen pages of my book, waiting for you to do your 'finishing touches.'" She held up her phone, showing off the eReader app she'd been so focused on.

"How much do you usually read?"

"You don't want to know," Soph said and stood up from my bed. "Shots?"

"Yes, please."

I flicked off my bedroom light as we headed to the kitchen. Soph connected to the speaker, and I grabbed the tequila from the freezer, a well-oiled machine from our many nights out together.

"Is Mags here?"

"No, she and Gemma went out to grab dinner together. I'm sure they'll be at The 151 later."

"Perfect," Soph said and then blasted our shared playlist—the one that Mags rolled her eyes at every time she heard it—at a volume probably more appropriate for a full house party instead of a pre-game of two women. "How have things been with you guys? I haven't really wanted to ask, but it's been a little bit since you talked about it."

I shrugged. "Kind of how they've always been. I don't know. I'm not excited to graduate, but I am excited to get out of this apartment."

"Have you thought any more about what city you might be going to?"

It was a weighted question—I hadn't really, because thinking about moving out meant graduation and moving and giving up the life I had here. It also meant a bunch of very adult things, like getting my first job and figuring out how to keep up with my bills. I wasn't so up my own ass that I didn't recognize how lucky I was to not have money worries because of my parents, but I was still scared of the change to come. All of the enthusiasm and hope in the world weren't enough to *completely* erase my anxiety.

"Not specifically," I answered. "Have you?"

Soph carefully poured out two shots for us. "I'll let you know when I make a final decision. I'm weighing some options right now, but I might just end up wherever a job is."

"Would you still want to go together?" I asked, nervous for some reason, like I was confessing romantic feelings for someone. But not being able to be Soph's roommate over the years had been a mild point of contention for us. It was never enough to actually get in between our friendship, but I could tell Soph had been disappointed every time I fell back on our plans and lived with Mags instead.

Soph gave me her scariest *you need to be honest with me* best friend face. The high-energy pop music playing in the background did not match the intensity of our conversation. "You actually want to this time?"

"I've always wanted to, I've just always been scared of my family above anything else," I admitted. "But I'd really like to try this time. Genuinely. Following Mags everywhere has only made me miserable. I want us to have our time together, too."

Her face remained neutral and tight until, finally, she cracked a smile. "I always knew you wanted a life with me. I can't wait to grow old together."

Relief flooded my chest. There was always a chance things wouldn't line up like we were talking about—one of us might not be able to find a job, or Soph might find work in a city not much larger than Cedar Creek, which absolutely would not work for me. But I was glad to know it wasn't entirely off the table. "Our spouses are going to be so sick of us."

"Yeah, GJ better get used to having me around."

I threw my head back with a laugh. "Right," I said with a playful eyeroll, as if I hadn't been falling asleep to the mental image of GJ with her niece and nephew, thinking about what our own kids might look like, every night since I'd met her family.

After taking enough shots to get us sufficiently giggly and tipsy, we wandered out and headed off to The 151. It was very much the kind of mountain winter night that I'd gotten used to—the air was so cold and dry that my lungs were practically hurting—and it made me sad to think about how there would only be so many more times that Soph and I would be able to do this walk together. There was Christmas, the New Year, and spring. By the time the basketball draft rolled around and we knew what Mags's future looked like, the school year—and our time at Lakeside Green University—was basically done.

I had an urge to shake the feeling away and continue pretending none of this was happening, but instead, I wrapped my arms around Soph in a hug while we walked. She leaned into me, still talking a mile a minute and completely unaware of the solo sentimental moment I was having. I smiled, not wanting to have it any other way.

We began defrosting as soon as we stepped inside The 151. Bodies were packed practically wall to wall, and everyone's voices blended in with the music playing.

"Good to be home," Soph shouted over the music, and I snorted as I put our coats in our usual hiding spot, hoping that no one would steal them—or more likely, accidentally take them home thinking they were theirs.

As we walked into the party, I felt uncharacteristically level. There was a small buzz of wondering if GJ was here already or she'd ended up somewhere else for the night. But typically, I was a *palms sweaty and feeling uneasy* kind of nervous walking in here. It felt like every single party I'd gone to, I was at risk of running into an ex, or I spent the whole night wondering if the person I had a crush on was going to go home with someone else. Or most embarrassing of all was spending the night nervously trying to hype myself up to approach a crush.

But I didn't have a reason to be nervous. If anything, I was hoping I might get laid tonight if GJ was around.

Maybe this was what it meant to actually be in something stable with someone.

Soph dragged me over to where the girls were all standing. Nearly everyone had been able to make it out tonight, and they looked like they'd also pregamed about as hard as us.

Reese pulled me into a hug as soon as she saw me. "Hi! Do you want a shot?"

"You brought a bottle?" I asked, surprised.

She reached into her purse and pulled out a water bottle, shaking it for me.

I grimaced. "Oh my god."

"It's as cold as the inside of a refrigerator outside—you can literally feel how cold the liquor still is through the bottle."

I looked at the water bottle skeptically for a beat but knew immediately that there was no way I was going to say no. It wasn't hard to convince me of anything—something that had obviously bitten me in the ass before, but was a trait that I didn't mind so much when drinking with my friends. They were the only bad influences I needed in my life. "Okay, fine."

Reese cheered as I held my head back so she could pour the shot into my mouth. She was right that it'd been kept pretty cold, but it was still just as awful as I'd imagined it would be going down.

I forced myself to swallow, nearly gagging along the way, and then laughed. "Oh, that was awful."

"Without fail," Reese said.

As I wiped the tears away I'd formed from laughing and dabbed at my chin where some of the shot had spilled, I felt eyes on me. I looked up and saw GJ looking over. She was standing with some of her friends who weren't on the basketball team, all of them talking and laughing together. But GJ's eyes were firmly on me, a smile at her lips.

My heart skipped a beat, and I got suddenly nervous in the best way. I looked away, biting my lip to keep myself from smiling like an idiot.

I grabbed Reese's hand and waved to the girls. "Let's dance!" I yelled over the music.

Finding a spot on the living room floor where some people were already dancing, I moved freely. There was no dance training required here, nothing to feel self-conscious about. I threw my arms up, sang along with the song, and twirled Reese around just because I wanted to. People who I'd really only ever seen in passing at parties here joined us, singing along and laughing.

When the song switched to a new one, I took a beat to breathe and glanced over at GJ again. Her eyes were already on me when I found her. Something about seeing her across the floor, the two of us pretending we didn't have history, was wildly hot to me. I loved the little secret we had going on—the smiles, our eyes catching.

Soph pulled me back onto the floor, and we kept dancing without a care in the world. I was acutely aware of GJ most likely still looking this way, but I liked the feeling of putting on a performance just for her.

After long enough, I needed an actual break to grab a drink and take a second to breathe—and also maybe try and sneak a moment with GJ if I could. Even just a second of conversation, a brush of our hands, would be enough to keep me happy for the night.

I headed to the kitchen, lifting my hair from my neck in the process. In a way that was absolutely not as coy as I wanted, I looked around the room to see if I could find GJ—and checked if she'd followed me.

As I grabbed a canned drink from the cooler, GJ appeared out of nowhere and leaned against the wall. I fought off a smile and fixed my eyes on the cans in front of me.

It was so stupid of us—anyone paying attention would be able to tell that we were talking to each other. But I was just drunk enough—and just baseline mad enough at my sister—to not mind playing with fire. It was plausible deniability to just be talking to each other. Mags could get mad if she saw, but there was nothing specific to get mad about.

"So, Kai was the person you wanted to make jealous?"

I blinked at her, too caught off guard to try to come up with a convincing roundabout answer. Even just hearing Kai's name was a jumpscare—that whole thing felt like a lifetime ago. "How did you even piece that together?"

"They've been looking at you all night. And you've been friendly with everyone, but you haven't even acknowledged that corner of the room," GJ said. "I was just taking a guess, but now I know for sure since you're not denying it."

"It's fine, just ignore her."

"I wish I could kiss you right now to make them jealous without risking Mags seeing it," GJ whispered, leaning toward me.

The thought of GJ kissing me right here in front of everyone to make it obvious that I was hers was officially the hottest fantasy I could think of. The sex with GJ was unreal, but loudly and proudly being together was *hot*.

I turned to look at her, my eyes traveling to her lips. What was the worst that could really happen if we just did it...

"Don't even think about it—I don't think either of us is ready to deal with the wrath," GJ said, and my lips turned up in a smile even though I was the tiniest bit disappointed. She then scoffed. "Kai just looked over here again. I'm gonna kill them."

"Stop." I laughed. "Are you jealous right now?"

"I just don't want her looking at you like that."

"They're only paying attention to me now because I haven't been paying attention to them. And I'm sure I'm practically glowing because I'm actually getting regular orgasms now, something that they were never able to achieve even once."

"Honored to know I'm better in bed than them, but the thought of you two having sex makes me sick," GJ said, her tone mostly teasing.

I turned and looked at GJ, too distracted now, thinking about having sex with her to give a single fuck about Kai. I thought about the last time GJ and I had been in bed together and how I'd left her bed practically floating.

GJ was still looking out over the room, her jawline ridiculous from this angle. It felt impossible not to kiss her.

I brushed my hand over her arm before remembering that we were in public and might as well have had a target on our backs. As much as I liked the Lakeside Green team, not all of them were going to know how to mind their business as much as Ellie did.

GJ being stupidly, blindingly hot also didn't help—I'd never been quite so aware of all of the girls who casually eyed her from across the room as I was now. And now, those eyes felt like more of a threat to me than anyone telling my sister about me and GJ. The thought of seeing anyone try to make a move on GJ brought out something truly evil in me.

"Come on," I whispered and nodded for her to follow me. GJ locked eyes with me, silently asking if I was being serious. I turned on my heel, looking over my shoulder to make sure she was following behind.

I went straight to the first-floor bathroom, too tipsy to care about how people were going to see us going in together. There was really only one person who wasn't allowed to know, anyway, and I was tired of letting Mags get in the way of everything. I wanted GJ; I wasn't going to let the risk of an argument take that away from me.

Inside the bathroom, GJ quietly closed the door and then turned the lock. We took turns quickly washing our hands—a good idea considering I could only imagine the germs floating around on the sticky, liquor-soaked surfaces at The 151.

"We have to hurry, I feel bad making people wait," I said as GJ closed the space between us. She picked me up and placed me on the counter effortlessly, her arms firm on either side of me.

"Make them wait." GJ tilted my chin up so I was looking at her and then kissed me. Her lips were soft and familiar and tasted faintly like beer. Everything around me completely melted away as she put her hands to either side of my face, her thumbs brushing against my cheeks. She pulled away for a moment and locked eyes with me. "You look really beautiful tonight."

"GJ." My voice was soft and quiet.

"I mean it. I wanted to say it from the second I saw you walk through the door." She brushed a piece of hair from my face, and I pulled her in, kissing her again. As our kiss deepened, I slid closer to her from my spot on the counter until the only thing separating us was our clothes. Her body was warm between my legs. "It was nice of you to wear a skirt for me," she said as she ran her hands up my bare thighs. It was a bold look for winter in Colorado, but that was what the alcohol jacket was for.

"Oh, you think this is for you?" I teased. I gripped onto GJ's firm shoulders as she slid her hands dangerously close to where I was most sensitive—and already wet for her. I didn't even have to check to know.

"If it's for anyone else, I'll fight them," she said. "Unless you just decided to wear a skirt because you wanted to look nice. I'd never take that right away from you."

I snorted. "Yeah, femme rights or whatever. Nice save."

"I'm not in the business of being possessive."

I looked up at GJ through my lashes and reached for the button of her pants. "You should start—it's hot." When I dropped the zipper, GJ's breath caught; it was music to my ears. "And of course I wore the skirt for you; it's just an added bonus that I look so fucking hot in it."

GJ inhaled, her eyes tracing up my body. "Great news for me," she said. She brushed her thumb over my bottom lip, and I opened my mouth for her. I swirled my tongue around her thumb and then her middle and pointer finger. GJ was in such a daze looking at me that she didn't look away once—I wasn't even sure she was still breathing.

GJ's undone pants sagged off her narrow hips, showing off her briefs. I slipped my hand between her waistband. Her skin was soft and warm, and I worked my way further and further down.

She gripped my thighs, letting out a quiet moan. The music was blasting through the house at the kind of volume that would drown out anything we were doing in here, but I liked the intimacy. This was just for us.

With our foreheads pressed together, I moved my hand down until I found her clit. We breathed together, barely any space between the two of us, as I used soft pressure to bring her toward orgasm. I kissed her, nibbling on her bottom lip.

"*Leah*," GJ moaned, increasingly wet to the touch. With my free hand, I brought her hand to my body and under my shirt. She gripped my waist and then moved up toward my nipples. Just touching me seemed like enough to bring

"I need to taste you," she whispered in my ear with her cheek against mine. She kissed my temple and dropped down, pulling me toward her until I could feel her breath on my bare thighs.

I had to press my hand to my mouth to stop myself from announcing to the entire party what was going on in here. I was sure people could guess—we'd already gotten a knock or two. But right now, I just wanted to be a little bit selfish.

GJ moved my thong to the side and slid her tongue against my folds. I moaned into my hand, nearly kicking my legs out from the shock of pleasure that one little motion sent through me.

As if knowing I couldn't be trusted to sit still, GJ held me by the waist and increased her speed and pressure. This was a feeling unlike anything I'd ever experienced; every part of my body felt it.

I looked down at GJ, and she looked up at me, her eyes locking on mine. Without a doubt, I wanted us to do exactly this forever. I wanted to go on dates and text her during away games and jump into her arms when she came home. I wanted to keep having the most delicious, intimate, perfect sex ever recorded in human history.

I bit down on my palm as my orgasm ripped through me, nothing subtle or slow about this one. It came down in a hard, crashing wave that left me breathless. My entire body felt lighter afterward, and my legs were shaking in a way that they never had before after sex.

"Oh my god." I exhaled and then laughed. GJ wiped her mouth as she stood, and I pulled her in to kiss me, wishing we didn't ever have to leave this bathroom. I wanted to live in this exact bubble for as long as I could. "I think you'll need to help me stand up."

GJ chuckled. "Come here."

She eased me off the counter, her hands lingering even after I was on my feet. I leaned into GJ's strong, impossibly safe feeling chest, and she wrapped me in a hug.

"I already want to go again," I whispered, and GJ laughed again.

"Come find me later tonight. We can sneak away together again."

I bit my lip, already knowing I would definitely be following through on that. "Okay."

After getting ourselves back together and presentable enough to be seen, we stepped outside the bathroom, flushed and unmistakably fresh off a hookup. We apologized to the people who flipped us off for making them wait so long, too giggly to care. I was so caught up in GJ and being with her and the post-orgasm glow that I entirely forgot where we were.

And who might be paying attention.

Mags turned to look at us, making my heart nearly completely stop. She was tucked into a corner with Gemma. It was obvious the two of them had been in the middle of a casual conversation, entirely unaware of what happened in the bathroom nearby.

At first, she'd glanced up probably just to see who'd stumbled into the room. I could see in her expression when it registered who exactly she was looking at. Her eyes bounced between me and GJ, the pieces coming together. I hoped maybe she'd just let it go and wouldn't think too much about it. But if there was anything that was going to give it away, it was the guilty expressions on my and GJ's faces, and the way our bodies were still leaning toward each other, even when we knew we'd gotten caught.

Almost like neither of us really cared that much about keeping the secret from her.

I expected Mags to do a lot of things—yell, make a scene, throw a drink, cause a problem. But instead, she turned around and headed straight for the door.

"Mags! Wait," I called out after her. I turned back to GJ, who looked at me with a *tell me what you want me to do* expression. Despite the anxiety already building in my chest, just looking at GJ was enough to level me out. "I'm going to talk to her."

"Do you want me to come?" she offered.

"No, it's okay." I turned to Gemma. "You should be on standby, though. I think she's going to need you after this."

"I'm already prepared," she said. She smiled softly at me. "This is just Mags being Mags, though—I'm happy for you guys. I think the rest of the team will be, too."

I fought off a smile. I wasn't sure I liked how quickly the word would inevitably spread, but I also shouldn't have expected any differently. "Thanks."

I looked back at GJ one last time—my steady rock, the one who looked ready for anything at all that might come of this. For the first time ever, I was dating someone who I knew was worth fighting for, and that was what mattered most to me.

I pushed through the front door and was immediately greeted by freezing Colorado air. It wasn't hard to figure out which direction Mags had gone in because I could see the outline of her sneakers in the snow flurries sticking to the ground.

"Mags," I called out as I followed her down the sidewalk. She kept up her pace, not even turning around to look at me. "Can you please stop and look at me? Can we talk? Please?"

She continued on in silence, and I rolled my eyes. She couldn't see me, but she was only a few paces ahead, so I knew she could at least hear me.

"Look, I feel bad about lying to you, but I don't feel bad about pursuing things with GJ on my own time. I should be allowed to make my own mistakes and date who I want to date. I appreciate you trying to protect me or whatever, but it's not your job. I never asked you to do that."

"I asked you not to date my teammates," Mags finally said, turning to look over her shoulder.

I hugged my arms around my body, the cold catching up with me. The snow was starting to come down in heavier, wetter flakes now, too, which wasn't helping. Unsurprisingly, the sidewalks were almost entirely empty, too late for people to be just heading out and too early for people to be going home. We passed by deceptively cute family homes, all of them lit up different colors on the inside from parties students were hosting, as we walked further and further from The 151.

"And I understand why you established that rule, but you also don't get to hold me to that forever. And, by the way, you've been on about a million different teams with a million different people, and this is the first and only time I've broken your rule. Shouldn't that tell you something?"

"All it tells me is that you're acting out or something. You still haven't even properly apologized to Mom and Dad. Clearly, something weird is going on with you. You might think things with GJ are real, but I promise in, like, six months, when this blows over, and you're burned by her, you'll realize they never were."

I groaned, not believing that for even a second. And even if it was true and things crashed and burned with GJ, it was my business. Not that Mags would ever in a million years understand that. "You are so convinced that something is wrong with me, but this is who I actually am. I've spent my entire life trying to appease you guys, and it hasn't worked. So you are right that I'm behaving differently now, but it's because I've learned better. I'm *finally* acting and feeling like an independent person with my own personality. I found someone who has made me realize I am capable of handling my own shit, and I'm trying my best to embrace that."

Mags finally stopped and turned to look at me. I stopped where I was standing, maintaining a distance between us. "Yeah, because GJ is such a positive influence?"

"She *is*, actually. I know you have a bone to pick with everyone on the team because you worry you're not as good as them or whatever, but you're letting it get in the way of everything else. GJ is a wonderful person. Theo was a great teammate—"

Mags scoffed. "I don't think they're better than me."

"Then whatever your fucking problem is with them, it's not *my* problem. I don't have to fight your battles for you. Especially since you have never fought them for me. You have never cared about what's best for me. You *never* stand up for me when Mom and Dad are being assholes."

"I just don't get what your problem is with them. I've been trying to understand, but I don't see it."

"Probably because you don't know how to think about anyone other than yourself," I snapped. "And that might not be fully your fault because Mom and Dad taught you the world revolves around you when we were, like, five, but you're also an adult now. It might be time to figure it the fuck out."

For possibly the first time ever, Mags looked legitimately hurt by my words. And although my initial gut reaction was to feel bad about it, I fought it off. I probably could've said it in a nicer way, but I meant what I said. I couldn't avoid conflict for my entire life with my family; it was making me miserable. I was beginning to see the appeal of temporary discomfort over being trapped in a life I was too much of a coward to get myself out of.

"I really like GJ, and I think GJ really likes me, too. What we have going on isn't just some stupid fling. I'm not blowing everything up with her just to make you happy."

"How long has it been going on for, then? You were so certain not too long ago that you were just being 'nice' saying hi to her family."

"Okay—"

Mags slowly nodded, taking everything in. I could see the wheels turning as it all clicked into place for her. "You guys both lied to me. This has been a thing, hasn't it?"

"It's been a few months," I admitted.

Mags guffawed. "A few *months*? Jesus. What was even the plan?"

"To...fool around? I don't know. There wasn't a plan. We're just two people who happened to be interested in each other, and then it turned into more. Not everything is some kind of scheme to ruin your life. This isn't about you. Not even a little bit."

"Right."

I threw my arms up, entirely out of things to say. We hadn't gotten into a physical altercation since we were literal children, but I was feeling close to it. "You are so obsessed with being the center of everyone's universe. You think you are so much more important than you actually are, and I'm *so* tired of it. I can't *do* this anymore. Mom and Dad might've set me up for failure, but at least I'm figuring it out—I don't know if you ever will."

Rather than reacting in any of the ways I thought she would—anger, annoyance, hurt—Mags just blinked at me. "I don't know what you mean by that."

I sighed, my breaths appearing as a cloud in front of me. We needed to get out of this cold soon, or we were both going to get sick. We also needed to get physically away from each other before this really got ugly. "You will eventually. It might not be me who makes you realize it, but one day you will realize you think you are way more important than you are to everyone around you. When you're ready to deal with that, I'll be here. But for now, I don't know if I have much else to say to you."

Mags, never one for reflection, let the comment slide right off. I took a deep breath, recognizing that it wasn't worth the fight. She was an adult—it was up to her if she wanted to listen.

"Okay, well, any other secrets I should know about? Old teammates, you had things with that you never mentioned?" Mags asked.

I winced, knowing it was now or never. It wasn't exactly the kind of secret I could tell she was digging for, but it was something I'd been holding onto. "I didn't want to live with you this year. And I don't want to live with you anymore once we graduate."

To my surprise, that seemed to be what impacted Mags the most. Her face crumbled with genuine hurt. "You don't like living together?"

"Do you actually like living with me? Or do you just like the comfort of living with your sister rather than someone random?" I asked. "Because we don't really get along. We bicker constantly—"

"Yeah, that's like, what sisters do."

"But they don't *have* to do that all the time. We're adult women now and about to be college graduates. You're, like, ninety-five percent of the way to getting drafted to play a professional sport. We're not sixteen and forced to cohabitate under our parents' roof. We don't need to go everywhere together anymore."

The words felt so ridiculously good to say that it almost felt like a high. A weight I didn't even realize had been there immediately lifted from my chest.

There were so many things I'd wanted to say to Mags over the years that I hadn't, but that was probably the one that had been the hardest for me. I knew it would disappoint her, and there was no way it wouldn't cause strife. But it just didn't feel as important as being selfish and doing what I wanted to do. "I know it sucks to hear, and I'm sorry I've been holding onto it for so long, but I can't keep it to myself anymore. I need to start making my own decisions, even if they end up being mistakes."

It all felt so good to finally say that I hoped that the feeling would transfer to Mags. This was her chance to finally redeem herself and see where I was coming from. I hadn't given her the chance before because I'd been too scared to actually say how I was feeling, but now there was no excuse.

"Do what you need to do," Mags finally said, and then turned to walk away.

I was so stunned that I didn't even yell after her this time. It was obvious she didn't have anything left that she wanted to say.

"Okay," I whispered, brushing away the hurt of yet again feeling rejected by someone in my family. I was prepared to a certain extent, but this hurt the worst of anything so far. I'd finally given Mags and me a chance to connect, and she completely brushed me off.

But as I walked back to The 151, I realized I was angry—unsurprising—but not guilty. I didn't regret anything I'd said. And I didn't regret going back to the party rather than wasting my night trying to make up with Mags. I'd said my piece; it was up to her now on what she wanted to do.

At the end of the driveway down the street, I saw someone standing outside in the cold. It didn't take long for me to realize it was GJ.

All of the fury melted from my body in an instant. "You waited out here for me?"

"Of course I waited for you," GJ said, and I hugged her, leaning my head against her firm chest. "Dude, you're *freezing*. Here, put on your coat."

GJ held out my coat, and I slipped my arms into it. There was so much I appreciated—she knew which coat was mine, went through the trouble of finding it for me, waited outside for me just in case I came back to the party and needed my coat. It was the sweetest, most wonderful change of pace from people who couldn't even be bothered to offer me water after sex.

Up at the front of The 151, I could see Soph standing outside with a few of my other friends. It was so cold that I could see their breath from a ways away. Illuminated by the front light of the house, Soph's lips turn up in a smile. She nodded, telling me it wasn't just the Lakeside Green Coyotes—minus Mags—who approved of me and GJ.

GJ put an arm around me, speeding up the process of warming me back up. I could've stood there forever with her, just taking in the smell of her cologne and feeling so warm and so safe. But it was cold, and the snow was getting too heavy for that.

"Can I go home with you?" I asked.

"You're sure?""There's nothing left to say to Mags tonight. I'd rather go back with you. And we have another episode of that sitcom you introduced me to."

GJ smiled and kissed the top of my head. "Whatever you want."

Chapter Twenty
GJ

I'd been prepared for any and all emotional responses from Leah—tears, anger, annoyance—after fighting with Mags. She'd given me the play-by-play on the way home, and it sounded intense. But to my surprise, Leah seemed...okay.

Even in the days following, she didn't seem that worried about it. She kept telling me she felt good about what she'd said—even with the cold war going on in their home—and felt good about us, and that was that.

Mags, on the other hand, had taken it upon herself to be even more of an asshole during practice than she normally was. But if the trade-off was that I didn't have to keep things a secret with Leah anymore, it was more than worth it to me.

The only problem was that Mags being a little bitch made it impossible for the rest of the team to mind their business. Fortunately, they all cared a hell of a lot less.

"That explains her attitude," Anna joked during practice while we were stretching. She was on the floor, her legs on either side of her body. She leaned over to touch her right toes.

I held my arm over my head and counted silently to twenty. "She's always had one, even before this."

"Oh, I'm not saying it's justified." She switched sides, moving her hair out of the way in the process. "I hooked up with a teammate's sister at my last school. I get it. It's not a big deal if you're both able to be cool about it."

"Is that why you transferred?"

Anna snorted. "Funny."

As I exited practice, my phone rang. When I saw Theo's name pop up on my screen, I immediately grinned to myself.

"Hi, who is this? I don't think I have this number saved," I said after answering.

"Yeah, yeah, okay, I get it. I'm sorry I've been MIA."

"I saw your commercial running during the men's game the other night—your acting could use some work."

"Oh god," Theo groaned. "My management has been booking the most insane shit for me. I always say yes for some reason, and then it actually comes to doing it, and I have no idea why I'm there."

I headed the same way I always walked home, my phone to my ear. It was cold, but the sun was blinding and hot, making it almost bearable. "Oh, my name is Theo McCall, and I'm the new face of women's basketball, and my life is so hard because I just got paid several hundred thousand dollars to do a commercial."

Theo laughed. "I'm humbled, thank you. I needed that. How are you feeling about the Point Brook game?"

"Easy work."

"Yeah? Feeling okay?"

I wasn't sure if *okay* was the right word. I'd started feeling pre-game anxiety now that it was inching closer. Point Brook had lost some of its momentum when their Theo Mc-Call—Cam Kerr—graduated and was drafted. Even a legacy school could feel when they'd lost a genuine superstar. But they were also undefeated, like us, and much more consistent than we'd been.

Meanwhile, every time I picked up the ball, renewed fear that I'd lose all of the progress I'd made in the last few weeks knocked me on my ass.

Our biggest saving grace was that this was a home game; we'd play them again later in the season at their arena, which was even more daunting.

"It's...you know." But trying to connect with Theo on that was impossible—Theo was known for her dependability on the court. She knew how to balance out a bad shooting game with assists, knew how to get her shit together when defense was riding her. I'd never jinx her by saying she was immune to having a bad season, but so far, she hadn't gone through the slump I had.

"Yeah, I know," Theo said. "Well, you still have a few games at least until then. There's time to prepare." She took a breath. "Anyway. I miss you, dude. I'm hoping I can get to another game before the end of the season."

"I hope so, you and Maya need to see me again now that I'm back. I have to make up for my performance at the last one."

"Yeah, we'd love that. I never thought having to coordinate being, like, an hour away would be such a pain in the ass. We're going to see each other more after you get drafted than we do now, living in the same state."

I smiled. I knew Theo was probably just doing it to be nice, but hearing her so confident in me still going pro was exactly what I needed right now. "Yeah, I think you're right."

With Nia still out on concussion protocol, I had a room to myself during the next away game. It was pretty luxurious—and I *definitely* didn't mind the texts and pictures Leah was teasing me with because she knew I was alone—but it was also kind of lonely. I'd gone from my studio apartment to an empty hotel room, and I didn't even have Leah here in person like I did back on campus.

I was flipping between TV channels and considering an early bedtime when I heard a knock on the door. I got up, curious who was stopping by. To my surprise, Anna was standing on the other side.

"Hey," I greeted her after opening the door.

"Hey. I brought some snacks, thought you could use the company."

God, she was so *nice*. It was ridiculous. The only saving grace was that I was feeling a little more normal about it now, finally. "You actually have perfect timing."

I stepped aside to let Anna in, and she settled into the chair in the corner of the room. "The vending machine had some kind of issue and gave me a bunch of stuff I didn't pay for."

I snorted and sat down on my bed. "Of course it would. You being, like, weirdly super lucky totally makes sense. Do you find money on the ground all the time, too?"

Anna blushed. "No comment."

I snorted. When she held up a bag of candy, I nodded, and she tossed it to me.

"You looking forward to this game with Mags tomorrow with the way she's been acting?"

"It's whatever. If she wants to be a brat about it, she can be a brat about it. I'm not going to dump her sister over it."

"It's nice you finally hate someone on the team more than you hate me," Anna said.

"I guess I can't really *hate* her since I'm seeing her sister," I said, and then brushed it off. "Wait, no. I'm not going to be diplomatic about it—I don't think I ever even liked her that much as a teammate, so now I really don't have to pretend to like her."

Anna snorted. "Sounds serious. With her sister, I mean."

"I guess it kind of is," I admitted, which felt both like a minimization of how much our relationship meant to me and an overstatement since Leah and I hadn't officially talked about what we were doing. We knew we were exclusive, and my feelings for her felt so big they were almost overwhelming, but that didn't mean Leah was ready for more yet.

"She'll come around. I'm sure the initial shock is weird. But the power of friendship has gotten us far this season, so I'm hoping she gets it together soon."

I laughed. "I don't know if I'd say we're benefiting from the power of friendship, exactly."

She shrugged. "I mean, we all started playing better once we got into a groove. It's amazing what happens when you have fun on the court with your teammates. It's, like, basically proven by science. And sports stats."

I tossed a few more Skittles into my mouth. "Well, then I guess I'd better keep it together because I almost blew it for all of us."

"Shooting slumps happen. You figured it out, that's what matters."

"Yeah, I guess. Let's just hope that article was overstating people's reluctance to draft me." When I glanced up and saw the look Anna was giving me, I shrugged. "I'm just saying. It's not like you have to be worried—you're definitely getting drafted if you declare."

Anna brushed my comment off. "I'm just not worried about it, period. I had a really good run in college. If I'm talented enough to continue playing, that's amazing. If I'm not, I've gotten to do what a lot of people haven't." She paused for a moment. "I do really want to go pro, though. I'm trying not to get my hopes up and whatever, but I don't know."

"How do you keep yourself so cool about it?" I finally asked. It was the question I'd been dying to get an answer to ever since Anna transferred here. I'd been too caught up in being annoyed by how effortlessly she'd fit in and taken over the role I wanted to see her as the asset—and teammate—she was. "Like, you transferred here your senior year and haven't missed a beat. You've been one of the best players in college women's ball this season. It's kind of crazy, if you think about it."

"It is crazy. It's also a lot of years of training. And talking to the right people," Anna said. "Lots of time in regular therapy and with the team therapist, too. Coach Darlene was really big on making sure I was mentally and emotionally prepared to come here and deal with the level of attention that I'd be suddenly dropped into. I spent, like, most of the summer working through all of the shit I was seeing online because I wasn't used to it."

I quietly mulled over her words, thinking back to what Theo had said so many months ago. "The therapist actually helps with that stuff?"

"Honestly, yeah," Anna admitted. "It feels kind of...embarrassing, I guess, to admit. Not, like, going to therapy. But having to go to therapy because people suddenly know who I am and really care about how well I play ball feels kind of dumb. It feels like such a non-issue in theory, but it's hard. People can be mean."

I inhaled slowly, not sure I was ready to admit to myself yet that Anna was probably right about it being a good thing.

Anna stood up and headed to the door. "I'm not going to speak on your season or tell you what to do because that shit's really annoying, but it helped me. You haven't been given a lot of grace this season by the coaches or the fans, and sometimes you just need a place to put all of those feelings," she said. "But that's all I'll say. I'll see you tomorrow for the game."

After another win, we were quickly shuttled off to the airport to go back home. In our typical *hurry up and wait* fashion, we were ready to go, but our plane wasn't. I bounced my leg, checking the time. We flew in and out of games on commercial flights—we weren't well funded enough yet to have access to fly private like some other bigger schools, so delays weren't uncommon. We were usually fortunate enough to avoid them, but Mother Nature had other plans today.

"I'm grabbing a snack," I said, kind of to my teammates and kind of to no one, since everyone was busy doing homework or on their phones, and pushed myself up from my chair.

I wandered the terminal, keeping an eye on the time. As I headed up the walkway, past the various stores and restaurants and bars, I realized that there was really only one way that I wanted to kill my time.

I ducked next to a convenience store to get out of the way of people walking by and pulled up my last text conversation with Leah. My finger hovered over the keyboard, thinking up something to say to her to continue past the *good luck* message she'd sent me before the game.

But instead of typing on the keyboard, my thumb went up to the call button.

It rang once and then twice, long enough to really make me second guess. Maybe this was too far. Calling someone out of the blue didn't feel casual.

But then, she answered.

"Hey." Her voice was so bright and warm, it made me want to run back home to her instead of waiting for the plane.

"Hey."

"Oh, wait, sorry—it's loud in here. Let me go to my room."

On the other end of the phone, I could hear some shuffling around, some voices.

"Who are you sneaking off to go talk to?" someone teased, their voice just barely carrying over through the phone.

"You already know who," Leah said, making the rest of the girls she was hanging out with squeal and cackle with laughter. Her confidence that I'd always been drawn to literally radiated through the phone. I stood by it—there was nothing sexier than a woman who knew what she wanted and exactly who she was. Leah only continued to confirm it day over day.

I heard Leah walk, the sounds of other people's voices getting further and further away. She then closed the door, and I could hear her perfectly now, no interruptions.

"Okay, try again," Leah said.

"Hey."

"Hey," Leah repeated, laughing softly to herself. "It's nice to hear your voice."

"Yeah, yours too. I was thinking about you."

"Oh, yeah?" she teased. "What about?"

"That I…wished you were here," I said honestly. I'd flirt with Leah any day of the week—I practically flirted with her even in my sleep with the dreams I had about the two of us—but what I really loved about her was that I could call about nothing at all. She was someone I wanted to call, just to say hi and talk about my game. "I played really well."

"You really did—the girls and I were watching it at Soph's apartment." Her voice softened. "I'm really happy for you. And proud of you."

My heart fluttered at the praise. "Thanks," I replied softly. It was possibly the only time in recorded history that I just took a compliment as it was, instead of making a stupid joke. That was who Leah was to me—the person I could be soft with, the person I could be a fuck-up with. Being with her was fun, and the sex was unlike anything I'd ever had before, but she was also just my favorite person to be around. My safe space. I hoped she felt the same way about me.

"You're happy we're doing this, right? You're sure?"

Leah chuckled. "What do you mean?"

"Like, all of the stuff with your sister. And then I don't know how your parents will feel about it, but I'm preparing for the worst if Mags is their favorite child," I said. "I'd understand if it was too much for you and you wanted to focus on them instead of me."

Leah didn't even hesitate. "Absolutely not. I've spent my entire life focusing on them. It's been hard for me to stand my ground, but I also haven't really had anything I felt was worth standing my ground on before. I don't have any regrets at all; I'm more than happy." She was quiet for a beat. "Are you okay with it? You still have to play with Mags for a few more months."

"Mags and I have been ragging on each other since the day we met for no reason. I can definitely keep it up for the sake of fighting for you," I said, and Leah laughed.

"GJ!"

I looked up and saw Nia waving me back to the gate for boarding. I lifted my chin at her in acknowledgement. I did the best I could at hiding my disappointment that I had to hang up, but I was sure it was all over my face.

"I have to go but I'll text you when I land," I said. The truth was that I'd text her pretty much immediately after hanging up and then keep texting her until the plane took off.

I could practically hear Leah's pout over the phone. "Okay. Have a safe flight."

It took all of my brain power to stop myself from saying *love you* as I hung up.

Chapter Twenty-One
GJ

The season continued to roll along at a breakneck speed, and while I wanted to hold onto it, part of the reason it felt so fast was because of Leah, and I wouldn't trade that for anything. My life had become a blur of basketball and seeing her whenever I could. We still avoided her apartment like the plague—seeing Mags at practice, and games was enough—she was over at least a few nights a week when I was in town for home games.

It wasn't until the week of our first Point Brook game of the season that time slowed down. If anything, it didn't just slow down—it slammed so hard on the brakes it gave me whiplash.

"You okay?" Leah mumbled. It was three in the morning, which I knew because I was on my phone. I'd fallen asleep for about an hour earlier in the night, but had woken up to a heart-pounding nightmare I couldn't remember.

I readjusted my phone, worried the light might've woken Leah up. "Yeah, I'm alright. Did I wake you?"

"No." She curled up against me, sleepy and warm. "NBA highlights more important than sleeping?"

"Can't miss a clip."

Leah didn't even have to look at me for me to know what expression she was making. "GJ."

"I can't sleep," I admitted, folding with absolutely zero pressure. The only downside to having Leah in my life was that I'd become possibly *too* comfortable with her. Eventually, I'd probably start talking to her about my feelings without her even needing to prompt me.

"Stressed?"

I locked my phone, realizing the same Anthony Edwards reel had been playing on repeat during our entire conversation. "Yeah. It's the Point Brook game. I'm nervous our luck is going to run out."

Leah laced her fingers through mine. "I'm sorry."

The nerves in my stomach lightened. I was so appreciative of so many things about her, but I really loved how she knew how to talk to me. I didn't have to explain to her that telling me things would be fine probably wouldn't be enough; she knew how much this meant to me. There was a very good chance things *wouldn't* be fine, and I liked that she was prepared for that. It made me trust she'd know how to be there for me if things really went to shit.

When I was having a hard time sleeping like this, it was hard not to go down the rabbit hole of wondering if Leah would still want me if I went undrafted. When I was feeling logical, I knew she wasn't doing this for status. But when I wasn't feeling logical, I was worried that maybe I wouldn't be as interesting to her if I didn't make it.

"You're spiraling," Leah said gently, like she could read my thoughts.

I took a deep breath, trying my best to slow it all down. "Maybe I need to talk to Dr. Licht after all."

It ended up not being difficult to schedule an appointment, unsurprising since Dr. Licht was on the school's payroll to only work with student athletes. She was a new addition who had been added when everything with Theo blew up, and we went from regional favorites to basically internationally recognized. The newness of her role was mirrored in the way the office was decorated—she had a few Lakeside Green items up and her degrees up on the wall, but that was about it.

I was immediately surprised by how young she was, and how she looked like she must've been—or currently was—an athlete herself. She was even taller than me and built with the lean muscle that typically developed from years of playing basketball.

"You can take a seat wherever." Dr. Licht gestured around the office. Her blonde bob moved with her as she walked through the room. I settled on the love seat, and she took a seat in the chair across from me.

"Did you play basketball?" I blurted out. I was nervous, almost like I was on a first date or something. But it was a first date where I was going to spend the entire time sharing my innermost thoughts, which felt like something out of a nightmare.

"I did. I played for a rival school in the division, actually. But not here to sabotage," she joked lightly. "I was never going to get drafted—I didn't play at the level you girls play at. But I do know what it's like to be a student athlete, which is what made me pursue this type of specialized therapy."

I nodded, bouncing my leg and then readjusting to make myself stop. "That's cool."

She turned her lips up in a smile. "Have you seen any kind of mental health professional before?"

I shook my head. "New to this."

"That's alright, everyone has to start somewhere."

"What am I supposed to do? Do I just start talking?"

"You can start wherever, and we'll go from there. How's that sound?" she asked.

I took a deep breath and went into it the only way I know how to do anything—headfirst.

I went through the rest of my day after my appointment with Dr. Licht, not sure I felt all that different, but not dreading seeing her again. I considered it as close to a victory as I could get right now.

I was standing in the kitchen, replaying my therapy session and wondering if Dr. Licht thought I was a loser, when the door to my apartment opened.

"God, today was so long," Leah said as she walked inside. She dropped her bag by the front door and kicked off her shoes. "I have been looking forward to this all day. I had an exam from hell, and then I accidentally spilled my coffee *everywhere*—"

She stopped when she saw me standing in the kitchen. I leaned against the counter, eating some kind of organic snack Theo had always kept around and gotten me into.

"What?" she asked.

I laughed. "What?"

"You're giving me a look."

"A *look*? What kind of look?"

Leah walked over and kissed me, every inch of her feeling like home. "Hi, by the way," she said. I pulled her in close to me, my snack bag crinkling against her back.

"Hi," I responded before kissing her again.

She inhaled and leaned her weight against me. The smell of her hair oil and perfume immediately relaxed me. "This is exactly what I've been waiting for all day." She looked up at me. "I missed you."

"I missed you, too."

Her eyes danced around my face like she was looking for something.

"Are you still trying to figure out the look?"

"So you agree that there *is* a look."

I laughed. "No, I don't agree there's a look, but you seem determined to prove there is one."

"What is it?" she whispered.

I shrugged. "I don't know."

"You are such a bad liar. Your face gives you away every single time."

I put my snack bag and pulled her in toward me. "You're just treating this place like home. That's all."

Leah's eyes widened, her face dropping. "I didn't realize—"

"No, it's a good thing. I want you to feel like this is a comfortable place for you. I want you to want to come here," I said. "It's nice. It feels...familiar. It feels like you just came home."

Her face softened. "Yeah?"

"Yeah." I brushed her hair behind her ear and then inhaled. There were no secrets between Leah and me, but that didn't mean I wasn't still a little embarrassed to have to talk to her about my day. "I went to see the team therapist today."

"You scheduled an appointment? And went?" Leah did a terrible job of hiding how surprised she was to hear that, but I couldn't fault her for it. "How was it?"

"She was nice, actually. It was a good session. Obviously, still a lot of ground to cover, but it felt good to just...talk. Everyone was right that I should've gone to see her earlier in the season."

"At least you know for when you go pro," she responded. I appreciated that Leah didn't have a single *told you so* bone in her body—it balanced me out nicely. "And you'll have her for the tail end of the season. Lots of big games coming up. And hopefully March Madness again."

I smiled. "Yeah."

Leah stepped away and went over to my dresser to pull out some clothes, part of what was becoming our regular routine. It meant more laundry for me, but I let her wear whatever she wanted of my things. She could ask to wear twenty of my shirts over the course of one day, and I'd say yes; I loved seeing her in them.

"Should we order takeout tonight? I know we talked about saving money, but I kind of like the idea of something good that we don't have to cook ourselves. This week isn't ending quickly enough for my liking, and I am *so* ready for finals to be over," she said.

I watched as she maneuvered around the room, pulling her shirt over her head and then replacing it with mine, her bare skin glowing and soft. She pulled her hair out from the neckline and dropped her pants to change into a pair of my sweatpants that were just barely too long for her. My eyes wandered along the curve of her ass.

"Thoughts?" she asked as she turned around.

"Whatever you want to do."

She laughed. "You weren't listening to a single thing I said."

"In my defense, I was distracted." I smiled softly at her, my heart practically bursting. It was the most exciting, most intense emotion I'd ever felt. There wasn't a single person in the world whose company I enjoyed more. All of those things Theo said about Maya made sense to me; all of the love songs were clicking.

It wasn't anything in particular—it wasn't therapy or how good Leah looked in my clothes or the urge to lock her down now just in case I actually didn't get drafted. And it definitely wasn't to spite Mags, which had me very literally almost fall to the floor with laughter when Leah told me.

It was just *Leah*. It was how I felt around her and how I felt knowing she was in my life. I had just enough common sense to hold myself back—we weren't even official yet—but I was feeling just reckless enough and just certain enough to know it was a waste not to acknowledge it.

"I'm falling in love with you."

Leah stopped and looked over at me. "What?"

"I can feel it. I'm falling in love with you."

Leah's face lit up, her lips turning up in a tentative smile like she kept waiting for me to say that I was joking. She slowly started walking toward me. "Say it again."

I smiled—every single time I said it, I was even more certain I was making the right decision, saying it to her. "I'm falling in love with you," I repeated.

She squealed and took a running leap into my arms, pulling me toward her. She looked up at me with so much care in her eyes, nothing but absolute certainty between us. "I'm falling in love with you, too," she said and then smirked at me. "So *that* was the look you were giving me."

"Yeah, okay. Maybe. Yes."

She snorted. "I think there might be *one* little thing you're missing, though."

"I knew I should've asked for your parents' blessing—"

"*Stop*." Leah threw her head back with laughter, the sound that would forever and always be my favorite in the world.

I smiled, unable to pretend to be even a little bit cool. I was so *excited* to say the words; it was the best kind of high. "Can I be your girlfriend, Leah Moretti?"

Leah twisted her lips, pretending to think, and then giggled to herself, already proud of whatever joke was about to come out of her mouth. "Yeah, I think you'll do."

Chapter Twenty-Two
Leah

After what felt like an eternity, the Point Brook game had finally arrived. This was the biggest basketball event every season on the Lakeside Green campus, and the crowd didn't disappoint.

"I'm going to miss this," I yelled over the roar of the music and the sounds of the arena. We were in position at the edge of the court, pom poms waving as we waited for tip-off.

Soph bumped her shoulder against mine. "Look at you enjoying things."

I wanted to roll my eyes, but I couldn't. It was true—the less I had my parents in my ear, the easier it was for me to appreciate things for exactly what they were. Maybe cheerleading wasn't my professional pathway or my favorite thing in the world, but it had brought me some of my best friends and hopefully my post-graduation roommate. That meant something.

Speaking of my parents—I scanned the audience, looking to see if they'd already found their seats. They'd texted that they were going to be coming into town to see us and would like to take us to dinner. Thinking about seeing them made me feel legitimately nauseous, but I was pushing it to the back of my mind for now. No use in getting stressed about it; I was tired of letting them get under my skin and impact my mood.

And besides, I had a front row seat to my girlfriend's basketball game. I was busy.

The lights flashed, and the music blasted, telling us the teams were about to do their runout.

"Show time!" Soph giggled, her smile a mile wide.

In classic fashion, Point Brook ran out to a booing audience. Once their team was out of the tunnel, everyone began stomping their feet and cheering in preparation for Lakeside Green. The crowd was so loud that I could barely hear the announcer as he went through everyone's names.

We waved and cheered as each player ran out. When Mags was announced, fans unsurprisingly went nuts. Everyone loved a potential draftee and a local celebrity—except maybe me. But as annoyed as I still was with her, she was still my sister. There was a chance our personalities would clash forever; it didn't mean I didn't want her to succeed in the sport she clearly loved.

Once Mags was standing courtside, my heart started racing, already knowing what was going to come next.

"And our captain—*GJ Mitchell*," the announcer roared, drawing out her name. The crowd erupted, and I cheered as loud as I could. When she ran out, and her eyes found me, my heart soared. As much as I wanted to play it cool, my cheeks went hot. But in my defense, it was impossible *not* to swoon.

Soph grinned next to me, not needing to say a single word to express her approval.

I had to be the luckiest girl in the world.

Unsurprisingly, the game was intense. The only thing that had my stomach more in a knot than my parents being in town was watching GJ play, knowing how much this game meant to her. She'd been talking to Dr. Licht and working on staying off social media in preparation, so she wouldn't get so in her head; I just hoped it would be enough.

Scoring was tight the entire time, pretty much never more than a basket or two apart. The crowd yelled and cheered and argued with the refs. To my surprise, the players didn't seem that stressed—if anything, the Coyotes looked like they were having the time of their lives.

GJ had told me that she and Anna were developing what sounded like a friendship, and it was obvious in the way they were playing. It was also good to see Nia consistently back in the starting lineup after being out; she looked happy to be back, too, and was practically bursting with energy the entire time. GJ had mentioned she was considering not announcing for the draft, but I hoped she'd change her mind—she was too good not to at least try.

Fully aware I was on the baseline and visible to anyone in the audience, I fought to keep my face as neutrally happy as possible. We were encouraged to get into the game as cheerleaders, but it didn't seem fair to be very clearly biased in cheering extra hard for GJ.

As the game rounded to the last quarter, it was hard to keep my nerves in check. I was hopeful the Coyotes would win, but nothing about this game was a given—it was a complete toss-up who was actually going to bring it home.

I glanced over at the scoreboard. Point Brook was holding a very narrow lead, and the minutes were quickly going by.

"Come on," I mumbled, redirecting my attention back to the court. Everyone was playing hard, making me a little nervous that there might be another injury, but I was sure I'd assume that of every game GJ played moving forward.

When Anna sent the ball to GJ, I inhaled sharply. This was the opportunity to tie it.

GJ's shot was effortless, entirely cool under the pressure. The crowd erupted as the ball sank through the net.

"Oh my god!" Soph shouted and reached for me. The Coyotes' bench went to their feet, and the cheerleaders sitting near me screamed with excitement and offered me excited shoulder squeezes. On the court, GJ took a moment to celebrate, mean-mugging a nearby camera before celebrating with her teammates.

I giggled, already looking forward to the photos and videos of her that would inevitably be circulating tonight after the game. One major pro to dating someone who played a nationally televised sport was that there were a million clips online of her looking ridiculously hot.

That was the exact push in energy the Coyotes needed to take it to the finish. They gained the lead and then scored again, firmly closing it out by the final buzzer.

No one wasted a second when it came to celebrating. The fans immediately got on their feet, loudly singing the Lakeside Green fight song. I watched GJ make the rounds with her team-mates, even taking a moment to celebrate with Mags, before they got in line to shake hands with the Point Brook players.

After she was done, she directed her attention to me and immediately beelined. When she made it to me, she scooped me up in her arms and spun me around, making me laugh.

"That game was so stressful, I don't think I breathed the entire time," I admitted when she put me back down.

"You were more nervous than I was when I was actually play-ing—I think this means you're officially initiated as a WAG."

I snorted. "I can't believe I'm going to have to keep doing this over and over again. Might need to spend just, like, *so* much time at the nail salon and spa working all that stress off."

GJ pretended to nervously scratch at the back of her neck. "I gotta get on those brand deals."

"GJ!"

We turned to look and saw Theo and Maya. I bit back a smile. Theo had shown up a few times on the jumbotron throughout the game, so I had a feeling she'd make her way down here eventually. GJ mentioned previously that Theo snuck in for a game earlier in the season, but Theo's luck with laying low seemed to have run out.

"Dude!" GJ laughed and then jogged over to meet Theo for a hug.

When they broke apart, Theo turned to look at me. "This Leah?"

GJ looked over at me proudly, like he'd never been more excited to introduce anyone. "It is."

"This would've gotten so weird so fast if I wasn't," I joked, feeling weirdly nervous. Even though Theo was an alumnus and we'd bumped shoulders more than a few times at The 151, I was still a little starstruck to see her. She had a certain air to her now that she was playing pro. The difference of a year might as well have been a lifetime.

It was also the first time I was ever meeting a girlfriend's friends—or friends of the person I was seeing at all, label or not—which definitely didn't help my nerves.

Theo stuck her hand out to shake, making GJ and Maya almost start crying with laughter. "It's great to finally meet you, and outside of the context of being Mags's sister. GJ hasn't shut up once about you since you met—"

"Alright, that's enough. Cutting this conversation off right here, right now," GJ interrupted.

Maya reached for a hug. "It's good to see you again. I'm already looking forward to our double dates. We'll have to do a night out in Cedar Creek."

Despite the reluctance I felt toward Cedar Creek, the idea actually sounded really fun. I still would never want to live there, but having a double date offered to me so casually felt like checking off a bucket list item I never realized I had.

I smiled, genuinely touched by her warmth. "That sounds amazing."

"We'll see you guys out tonight, yeah?" Theo confirmed.

"Definitely." GJ and Theo slapped their hands together in goodbye. "I'll text you."

Theo and Maya walked off hand-in-hand, leaving me and GJ. I looked over at her, almost overwhelmed by how elated I was. But the feeling didn't last for long—across the court, I spotted my parents talking to Mags.

My stomach swooped. "Fuck," I mumbled, knowing I just needed to do it. I wasn't nervous about what I was going to say to them, but I was nervous about having to actually say it and facing whatever the fallout would be. GJ squeezed my hand supportively, and we finally walked over.

"Hey," I greeted my family. We exchanged our usual hugs, but it felt different this time—at least for me. I didn't actively pay attention to whether my mom hugged Mags for longer, or how I felt after the fact. Just because they were my parents didn't mean I had to like them as people, or like how they treated me.

"Hello." Mom offered a tight, practiced smile like she was greeting someone else's kid at the country club. She turned her attention toward GJ. "Your playing has gotten stronger throughout the season. Very impressive work today."

"Thank you," GJ said in a weirdly level voice, almost like she was using her customer service tone. I fought off an urge to laugh.

My parents looked between us, and I glanced at Mags, curious if word had spread yet. And then I realized I didn't actually care—maybe Mags was airing all of my shit out to my parents, and maybe they thought this was stupid of me, just like Mags did. But I was old enough to make this decision for myself.

"You already know her, but this is my girlfriend, GJ," I said, making sure there'd be no room for misinterpretation. My parents had a way of spinning things, and this was one of those times where I didn't want them downplaying what was going on in my life.

My parents mostly seemed unfazed, which was about what I'd expect of them. It stung for just a second that they were meeting my first girlfriend, and there still wasn't any kind of warm embrace or break in character. GJ's family had been nicer to me in the fifteen seconds I'd spent with them, and GJ and I weren't even serious at that point.

But maybe that was just how things were going to be—my family was always going to suck. At least I'd have GJ to go through it with me now.

"Girlfriend," Mags repeated. She squared her shoulders as she looked between us. I could see the urge to fight in her face. I braced myself for Mags to throw GJ under the bus to my parents and immediately set this up for failure. It was one way that was left for Mags to earnestly sabotage me. Navigating my parents' neutrality toward my relationship was one thing, but it was something else entirely for Mags to paint an ugly picture to make my parents hate me and GJ together.

"Girlfriend." I was just as direct, not backing down for even a second. There was no apology in my voice or willingness to discuss this. I'd made my choice, and Mags was just going to have to deal with it.

Mags took a long, deep breath. "Just don't hurt her or I'll have to go after you," Mags warned, and I nearly rolled my eyes. But it was progress—I had to give her that.

GJ put her hand up in a salute. I fought off a smile. "Heard," she said.

"Will you be joining us for dinner?" Dad asked, looking between the two of us. It seemed genuine enough, like he really did want us to go. But I wasn't going to subject GJ—or myself—to that tonight.

"No, we have plans already. But it was great to see you. Enjoy your evening."

GJ glanced in my direction, silently checking in. She didn't have to say anything for me to know that she was confirming that I really didn't want to go. I knew she could probably handle it, and we'd make the most of the situation, but I just didn't want to. Not right now. I'd much rather celebrate my girlfriend's big win with her, surrounded by the people who made us happiest.

I took GJ's hand and waved at my family with the other. As I walked away, I knew without a shadow of a doubt I was making the right decision. I wasn't going to ice them completely out of my life—or my relationship with GJ—but I was going to do things on my terms from now on. I didn't know exactly what that looked like yet, but I had my whole life to figure it out.

"God, they are intense. I can't tell if I'm still sweating from the game or if they were making me sweat that much," GJ whispered, and I threw my head back with laughter, wrapping my arms around her arm and leaning into her as we walked away.

Epilogue
Leah

"You're going to miss tip-off!" I shouted across the apartment, raising my voice over the music and the chatter of the people around me.

"I'm coming, I'm coming!" Soph rounded the corner with a freshly topped off drink in her hand. We knocked our glasses together. "We really killed it on the decorations."

I smirked. "We *definitely* did."

Life since graduation was a whirlwind. Soph received a job offer in Los Angeles, and I followed—entirely by my own choice for the first time in my life—and got my own job offer at a different company not long after. I wasn't getting paid well, and the only fun part about working for a corporate marketing firm was getting dressed up and gabbing with my coworkers. The job perks, like access to events across the city, didn't hurt either, even with the ridiculous hours and shitty managers. But I felt so incredibly lucky all the same.

Soph and I had been fortunate to find a cute apartment in West LA that was sun drenched and cozy. And between her and me, there was never a dull moment—there was always a coworker to meet up with, a birthday party for a neighbor, a girl we met in the bar bathroom to dance with. I loved being a tiny dot in a massive city with seemingly endless people to meet and endless possibilities.

There were some challenges that came with it, though—GJ had been drafted to a team in Louisiana, which was perfect for her and put her in much closer proximity to her family, but also put her far away from me. Fortunately, she wasn't *so* far that a quick trip was completely out of the question—or at least, it was possible with the help of ridiculous red-eye flights and melatonin gummies. I'd already taken a few trips out, and she'd done the same. And while it was too soon to plan properly, she'd casually mentioned a few times she was looking at getting a place closer to me to live in during the offseason.

I missed seeing her all the time—the transition was especially hard because she went from walking distance from me to a flight away in the blink of an eye. Basketball moved quickly, and getting drafted meant missing the last little bit of college. She wasn't able to be there for any of the graduation parties, finals week drinks, or the seniors' last party at The 151. But it was worth it knowing she was getting to do what she loved.

On the TV, the camera panned to different players on the court as they prepared for tip-off. GJ's teammates were quickly becoming familiar names and faces. I was also *obsessed* with the wives and girlfriends and the group chat we shared, so I was already looking forward to going out in New Orleans with them.

When the camera found GJ, everyone in the room—a mix of people from so many different areas of my new life, so many new people who loved me exactly as I was—cheered. GJ looked so beautiful, so handsome, so *mine*. She couldn't come home quickly enough.

Even though this wasn't GJ's first game—I'd been courtside for that; GJ's management had been all over social media trying to make us one of the hot new couples of the WNBA, and her team was playing off of the buzz—and we were deep into the season, the feeling of watching her play professionally hadn't gotten old. I had a feeling it never would.

As soon as the ball went into play, the Mitchell extended family group chat—the one with her sisters and their boyfriends and husbands and now me—immediately started firing off, my phone buzzing with a million messages all at once. My heart was so full it felt like it was going to burst out of my chest.

Reese texted, too, sending a sweet message just like she always did during a game.

Reese

Fingers crossed for GJ!!

Reese decided to stay in Colorado to be close to her family and figure out the next steps for work. I missed her and missed her dance classes, but I'd stuck with it and was trying out a new studio in the area. The classes were on an entirely different level out here, but I left every single one feeling amazing. It was like the last piece that had needed to come together for me.

I put my phone down and looped my arm nervously through Soph's.

"How do you think it's going to go?" I asked.

"I think Theo and GJ are going to kiss," Soph said, making me laugh so hard tears formed in the corners of my eyes.

"It's kind of crazy seeing them play against each other. I can't believe they're wearing different jersey colors right now. It feels wrong."

The main reason Soph and I went all out for this game day party was that it was the first professional game Theo and GJ were playing against each other. Based on team records, this wasn't technically one of the biggest or most important games of the season. Both GJ and Theo had been drafted in the early rounds of their years, meaning they were drafted onto teams with some of the worst records in the league. But even so, it still felt important. Anyone who watched college women's basketball knew Theo and GJ were a duo, but this was their opportunity to show off against each other. It'd caused a major ripple in the Lakeside Green fandom, and who was going to come out on top was hotly debated.

The one biggest thing on Theo's side was experience—playing professionally was different from playing at a college level, and GJ had an uneven start to her professional career. It was common for a lot of rookies, but I just worried it would be difficult for her to work through, considering how her senior year had gone. But she'd navigated it without issue and with the help of her new team's therapist, getting into the flow of things after just a few games. Her belief in her playing ability never came into question; if anything, she was the same GJ she'd been before her slump: cocky, certain, self-assured. It was sexy to see her like that.

Needless to say, it hadn't been a question for me; I knew exactly who I was rooting for.

GJ's games always flew by in the blink of an eye, but this one felt particularly fast. In a way, both GJ and Theo were assets to their teams during this one because they knew exactly how the other person played on the court. It made it extra exciting to watch—two people who were able to see what the other person was going to do before they'd even done it. Balls were turned over, and shots were blocked on both ends.

"My heart is beating so fast you'd think they just told me *I* was playing the second half," Soph joked. The game had been so good that we'd barely spoken to each other the entire time. It was funny to see some of our other friends who were just here to be supportive, having absolutely zero interest in what was going on on screen. It made it extra meaningful that they'd come as non-fans, braving the traffic just to come and be a good friend. It was the best kind of love.

"Do not ask me about the state of my armpits right now," I responded, and Soph laughed.

The game closed out with the Blizzards just barely winning. It'd been down to only a few baskets the entire last quarter of the game; the fans who were there live looked like they were about to pass out from stress.

At the end of the game, just barely outside of the frame of the on-court reporter, GJ and Theo ran over to each other to hug. Exactly as I'd expect, there was no bad blood or bitterness between them. They'd always be best friends first, if not basically siblings.

I wished there was a way I could take a screenshot on my TV; fortunately, I had a feeling about a million different angles of that exact moment would be shared all over social media in just a few minutes.

Soph took a deep breath. "I need a drink. Anyone want to play beer pong?"

As she walked away, I glanced at my phone to check the time, knowing exactly how long it would be until my phone rang. In the meantime, I started picking up stray cups and trash and fluffed up some of the pillows on the couch. A few of my friends headed out, ready to go to their next big thing, and a few more stuck around. Chances were high we'd all end up at a bar in approximately two hours.

When my phone rang—right on cue—I hurried off to my bedroom.

"Hi," I answered breathlessly.

"Hey, baby. I miss you."

"I miss you too," I said. "When are you coming home?"

"Not soon enough." Her voice was so gentle over the phone, so caring. Just hearing her voice made me safe and heard and appreciated and loved.

She sounded exactly like how home was meant to feel.

Coming Soon
Lakeside Green Coyotes Book 3

You might've noticed that details about characters and the story beyond GJ and Leah were left out of the epilogue. That was intentional (I'm sorry!!) because book three of the series takes place before the epilogue and features the last semester of senior year (for Mags, Gemma, Leah, GJ, Nia, and Anna, at least!). To avoid spoilers, they've been thoughtfully excluded. If you're curious about the drama of who else gets drafted and where everyone ends up, your answers will be in LSG3. See you there!

Acknowledgements

I always knew that the second book in the series would be about GJ, even before I started writing the first book. GJ was special from the very beginning, and it's been validating to see how many of you asked about when her book would be coming because she's always been my personal favorite.

There are a lot of things about *Bank Shot* I grew to love—after having a hell of a time trying to figure out how to tell GJ and Leah's story, it finally clicked. There's a lot of pressure that goes into writing a sophomore novel, especially when it's a series that's so personally meaningful. I felt a responsibility to make sure I was proud of it and that I was only giving you (and myself) the best version of the story that I could. In a lot of ways, my journey paralleled what GJ and Leah felt throughout *Bank Shot*—the uneasy pressure of following up on a really good year, the desire to want to impress the people around you. There's a lot of myself in this one because of it.

But outside of myself, I had an amazing team there for every step of the way: My editor, Emily Ladner, who I owe so much to and I hope to work with for a very long time; Margaux (Caravelle Creates), my cover designer who also worked on *Tip In* (and *With Spirit!*), and has such a way of turning my loose ideas into something so beautiful; Valentyna, who illustrated the beautiful chapter headers (I've never been so grateful for the Threads algorithm); Elena and Emily at Untold Stories for the social media support and for being there with me from the very beginning; Reggie for her extremely appreciated work as a sensitivity reader; and my PA, Carly, who is such a superstar in every sense in the word. *Bank Shot* would not be in your hands as a reader if it wasn't for her and the work she puts into promoting my books.

I'm also grateful to have so many wonderful people in my life who love and encourage my writing as much as I do. To my friends and family: you are the best thing to ever happen to me. Your constant support and belief in me has made this all feel way less scary. It's impossible to doubt myself because whenever I freak out, I always get a text that says *be so fucking serious right now*, and I appreciate that.

And of course to Baby Mae, my perfect furry son. There's no one else I'd rather have curled up on the couch with me. It means everything that we have so many books we'll get to write together. I love you forever.

About Josie Mae

Josie Mae (she/her) is a lesbian who writes sapphic romance. She's a sports romance girl through and through despite being generally unathletic, and she says y'all far too much for being a city girl. She has worked a million odd jobs, lived a million different lives, and wants to live for a million more years. Josie writes all of her books with her small but mighty chiweenie, Baby Mae, by her side.

By Josie Mae

Lakeside Green University:

Tip In

Bank Shot

Paranormal America:

With Spirit

www.ingramcontent.com/pod-product-compliance
Lightning Source LLC
Chambersburg PA
CBHW070847160726
48004CB00003B/964